Bereft

A NOVEL

Chris Womersley

SILVEROAK

New York / London

SILVEROAK

New York / London

An Imprint of Sterling Publishing Co., Inc. (New York)
and Quercus Publishing Plc (London)
387 Park Avenue South
New York, NY 10016

SILVEROAK BOOKS is a trademark of Sterling Publishing Co., Inc.

© 2012 by Chris Womersley

ISBN 978-1-4027-9813-9 (hardcover)
ISBN 978-1-4027-9839-9 (ebook)

This book was originally published in 2010 in Australia.

Distributed in Canada by Sterling Publishing
c/o Canadian Manda Group, 165 Dufferin Street
Toronto, Ontario, Canada M6K 3H6

For information about custom editions, special sales, and premium and corporate
purchases, please contact Sterling Special Sales at 800-805-5489 or
specialsales@sterlingpublishing.com.

Manufactured in the United States of America

2 4 6 8 10 9 7 5 3 1

www.sterlingpublishing.com

For Roslyn, who always believed

"Every angel is terrible"
Rainer Maria Rilke, *The Duino Elegies*

PROLOGUE

✼

On the day twelve-year-old Sarah Walker was murdered in 1909, a storm bullied its way across the western plains of New South Wales and unleashed itself on the fly-speck town of Flint. Sarah's murder became the warm, still heart of several days of frantic activity in which almost every one of the town's two hundred or so residents had a tale of chaos or loss. Trees cowered and snapped in the winds; horses bolted. Desperate to escape the river's rising waters, snakes invaded the Porteous house, forcing Mrs. Porteous and her two infant daughters to spend several hours perched atop the kitchen table with dresses hoisted about their knees until husband Reginald returned from work to save them. Jack Sully the blacksmith broke his arm trying to secure his roof, although there were well-founded rumours he was actually drunk at the time. Dead cows, swollen tight, bobbled about in the floodwaters for days. And old Mrs. Mabel Crink lost her sight, which partly accounted for the name by which the maelstrom became known: the Blinder.

Sarah's father, Nathaniel Walker, said he scoured the entire area for Sarah and her older brother Quinn, neither of whom had been seen for most of the afternoon. He searched their usual hideaways: behind the chook shed; under the house; in the hollowed-out gum by the eastern fence of their property. Nothing. Eventually, he stumbled upon them in the abandoned shed by the lake at Wilson's Point, two miles from home. By then it was too late, of course. Nathaniel was speechless. The boy appealed to his father, but his words were drowned out by a rumble of thunder. Nathaniel's brother-in-law, Robert Dalton, appeared huffing that very moment at Nathaniel's shoulder, saying, "Good God, what happened here?" even though—what with the blood on Sarah's thigh, the disarranged clothing, the knife in Quinn's fist and the blue of his sister's lips—Blind Freddy could have seen what had taken place. Young Quinn flung down the knife, clambered through a hole in the shed wall and vanished into the storming darkness. It all happened so quickly, Nathaniel and Robert were too stunned to give chase. The boy was able to slip away unhindered.

Sarah and Quinn's mother, Mary, was home reading at the bedside of her eldest son, William, who was that week stricken with a fever. Rainwater spooled heavily over the eaves, and the air rattled with thunder. Their house was solid, well built, but she feared for them all and for many years afterwards she recalled stopping mid-page and looking up with a prick of dread. It was the feeling she recognised from when she lost another child back in 1890, the half-formed one that slithered from between her legs three months too soon. *Come in, Huck, but doan look at his face—it's too gashly.* Mary closed the book softly so as not to disturb the drowsing William.

She was a woman of faith, mildly superstitious, and for the remainder of the dark afternoon was unable to shake off a sensation of doom so acute that when Nathaniel arrived home in the evening, bedraggled, weeping, it was with a certain resigned stoicism that she listened to the appalling news. Of the precise details she refused to hear anything, saying that it was enough it had happened, it was enough such a thing had happened at all.

Naturally, the town was aghast and the particulars of the horrific crime—such as they were known or deduced—were speculated upon wherever people gathered: at the bar of The Mail Hotel; in clattering kitchens; on verandas; round the back of Sully's place where men huddled to smoke; on blustery, wintry street corners. A reporter from the Sydney *Sun* with the unlikely name of Mr. Philby Rochester arrived in Flint and proceeded directly to The Mail, where he gathered information for the wide-eyed delectation of his city readers. The town had not seen such drama for many years, certainly not since the gold rush had faltered, and there hovered about its public places a guilty air of ill-gotten excitement.

With the Walker family in mourning, Robert Dalton took on the role of unofficial chronicler of the event. He told the reporter and anyone else at The Mail who would listen that he had always known something sinister was brewing between the two siblings and that he could have prevented the terrible crime had he or the boy's father arrived on the scene earlier. "Just a *few* minutes," he would say, emphasising the tragic smallness of the moment with thumb and forefinger almost pincered. "If that boy so much as shows his face around here again, I'll hang him from a tree."

He claimed there had always been something unusual about Quinn, a feeling the boy's father, Nathaniel, also professed to have shared, much to his eternal regret now that it was too late to do anything about it. He had tried to keep them apart but they clung to each other like bloody burrs to a sock.

The town's notoriety was brief. On the third day after the murder, the reporter Mr. Rochester was found passed out drunk in an area by the river known as the Flats and unceremoniously bundled aboard a coach bound for Bathurst, some thirty miles away. Despite their best efforts, police and the local tracker Jim Gracie were unable to locate Quinn Walker, as the heavy rain had washed away all traces of the murderer. Sarah was buried several days later in soil still sodden from the storms.

Although police forces in Victoria and Queensland were notified, and a reward of £200 posted, Quinn was never found. It was generally assumed the sixteen-year-old fugitive had met a fate satisfying to the world's innate sense of justice. Theories popular for a time held that he had been eaten by wild dogs that roamed the nearby ranges; had fallen into a disused mine shaft; had been speared by blacks.

Flint residents continued to tell stories of the dreadful crime, particularly on stormy afternoons that prompted men to remark to their wives something along the lines of: "Terrible day. Always reminds me of the Walker girl murder." Whereupon the fellow's wife would stop rolling out pastry or plucking a chicken, stare wistfully into the middle distance and shake her head. "That poor, poor woman. To have a son like that."

Years later, in 1916, Mary Walker received a telegram from an officer serving in the Australian Imperial Force in France regretting to inform her that her son Quinn was missing in action, presumed killed, but that he had been a wonderfully brave man etc. etc. It seemed the boy had escaped all those years earlier after all, only to die somewhere far from home. When he heard the news, Nathaniel sniffed his good riddance and went about his business. Mary wept all over again.

Over the years, the townsfolk indulged their human propensity to make something from tattered scraps. They embroidered a tale as one might a blanket or quilt—a rumour here, a supposition there—until the story of Sarah Walker's rape and murder became historical, complete with a beginning, a middle and an end.

Part One

THE LURE OF
THE OCEAN

1

~~~~

The troopship *Argyllshire* carved through the ocean. Sergeant Quinn Walker leaned against one of the worn rails along its deck. He listened to the endless hiss of the waves and watched the glitter and trick of sunlight upon the water. A cigarette burned down to its soggy nub between his fingers, the tips of which were as yellow as ivory piano keys. Not only was his hair now flecked with grey, but also his eyes, as if the ash of the passing years were silting down through his innards, turning perhaps even his liver and heart to soot. Although only twenty-six years old, he had grown up in unexpected ways. No longer did he resemble the boy he had once been. He had become furtive, alert to the turning of the world, a man perpetually on the verge of departure.

A pod of dolphins threaded out and back beneath the water, spinning and hanging suspended for a second before vanishing again under the waves. Birds bathed in the rainbows that materialised in the spray. Quinn found it impossible to watch the ocean's surface without imagining what might be swimming in the dark universe below: whales and sharks; fish that barked; lizards that prowled the coral beds; the mighty leviathan. All the creatures known and unknown.

From a tunic pocket he withdrew his Military Medal, a bravery medal awarded for actions undertaken on a night he now could not even recall, even though it was little more than two years ago. Perhaps the spit of gunfire, the wailing of men, the taste of dirt in his mouth, but these sensations could be from any night of the war. Of all the things in his life of which he had reason to be ashamed, he was perhaps most ashamed of this medal. *Conspicuous gallantry*, the citation had read, *and devotion to duty. He has shown great courage in rescuing men buried in galleries and has performed consistent good work throughout.* The coin and attached ribbon fit snugly in his palm. What a bloody joke. He cared not a jot for his own safety: that was not the same as bravery.

When he was certain no one was watching, he drew back his arm and flung the medal out over the waves. He was disappointed to lose sight of the medal immediately; he had hoped for the cruel satisfaction of seeing it trace a shining arc, glimmer in the sunlight and vanish with a minuscule plop into the vast ocean. No matter. The thing was gone.

All around him men drew on their English cigarettes, forming wraiths of smoke that were whisked away by the wind. A line of soldiers rested on the rails and stared at the horizon. Those soldiers who had become afraid of open spaces stayed below deck with the sick and the lame, snug within their hammocks, more secure in the warm, smoky brotherhood of men.

Quinn kept to himself, always shy in the company of others. At the start of the war they had nicknamed him Meek—Meek Walker—but as the war dragged on, and more and more men had become remote and wary, such shyness as his was no longer deemed worthy of comment, was barely even noticed.

Sometimes blokes clambered onto the railing and launched themselves into the air, arms flailing as they fell to the water, perhaps a glistening head before it went under for the final time, never to be seen again. A dark, wide mouth inhaling a last breath, lured by the enchantress Morgan le Fay into her palace beneath the waves. Quinn imagined these men descending into her dim and peaceful realm with seaweed about their necks, garlanded with bubbles, free of the earth and its mortal woes.

Those on deck shook their heads at the waste and reminded each other they had been warned before they set sail that the ship would not turn around to rescue anyone who fell overboard. There was no point in even mentioning it. *Imagine surviving all that we survived and then going like that? When so many men were lost? Bloody crazy.*

Quinn understood it, however, this lure of the ocean. To be so engulfed. Absolutely. Yes.

ﷺ

At North Head quarantine station, he stood with the rest to be hosed down. After everything, the sight of naked men still shocked him. Their unguarded selves were delicate, unwieldy creatures beneath their uniforms. Skin so thin and pale. Hidden away. Armless, many of them; legless; boys and men spattered with burn marks and coin-shaped scars. No wonder so many millions of them died: men are nothing when thrown into the machine of history.

Their luggage was fumigated and afterwards they were forced to inhale a solution of zinc sulphate to clear their lungs and prevent the influenza from taking hold.

The accommodations at North Head were lousy and there were angry grumblings among the men. It was much less than returning soldiers deserved, they said. No way to treat war heroes. After all they had done for their country, for the Empire. Some whispered of escape, of setting out into the scrub. The mood turned mutinous, and it wasn't long before the men, all one thousand of them, marched through the gate down to the wharf at Manly where they took the steamer to Fort Macquarie. Quinn had imagined a cat's cradle of streamers; mothers and sisters and wives, a doughy press of women welcoming home their men, or what was left of them.

But there was no such fanfare. The soldiers were a rabble, ill-shod and half-broken, tubercular, mutilated and blind. Many hobbled with crutches, on bandaged legs. They all wore the gauze masks issued to prevent the spread of the epidemic. They marched as best they could from the quay through Sydney towards the cricket ground where they had been promised better accommodation. A crowd gathered about George Street and Oxford Street to have a gander. Trams were held up in the crush. Boys dashed out to touch the soldiers' legs or shake their hands. Young women smiled nervously and twittered to each other. Quinn shrugged past them all with his kitbag, acutely aware of the disappointment on the faces of those older women who hoped he might be someone else, a husband or brother or son—or a man at least known to them. He was glad of the mask that covered his ruined jaw; unlikely as it was, he had no wish to be recognised.

Quinn concentrated on the ground immediately ahead of him until he could bear it no more. He recalled some of the stories his mother had read to him and decided the Greeks should have been grateful the gods prevented their homecoming after the sack of Troy; the return from war was surely worse than the leaving.

In the excitement it was easy to peel out of formation, slip between the crowds and disappear into the city's quiet and muggy streets. His heart shivered in his chest. His stomach cramped. In a dank Darlinghurst alley, he coughed and doubled over, hands on knees. Sweat jewelled on his forehead. A frightful sensation, tearing at his innards. He had been gassed during the war, and the residual malevolent fogs still hovered about the hollow parts of his body, settling here and there when he slept or was otherwise still. Although not as badly injured as many, there was no doubt the gas had damaged him, particularly his throat, which sometimes felt like, say, a violin with a frayed string that fluttered useless and annoying, tangling in those strings still tuned tight and in working order.

A marmalade cat eyed him dispassionately before setting about licking its paw. Quinn thought of oranges. All through the war in France he had craved one. Sometimes he woke at night with his lips dry as carpet, having dreamed of cramming a sliced quarter into his mouth, as he had done when he was a boy. On occasion he became obsessed and was unable to pass a farmer's cart or street stall without trying to locate one. The fruit assumed mythical, magical dimensions, as if it might cure him of not only his thirst, but of all that ailed him: his homesickness, his guilt, his sorrow.

Some months ago, in France, he glimpsed one in a girl's basket as she passed a truck in which he was sitting. She was only about ten, but she possessed the manner of someone much older, the way all children did in those long years. She had the basket wedged on her hip and paused to talk with a shawl-draped crone before hoisting her load and entering a tabac. In the truck's cold and smoky cabin, Quinn watched her and prepared to follow—had even tensed his body to do so—when the burly sergeant returned with the orders and rumbled the engine into life. *Righto, let's go get some of them Germans, eh?*

⊰§⊱

A thin, harried doctor working at a special table at Central Station examined Quinn and issued him with a certificate declaring him free of influenza. A nurse from the Red Cross pressed a paper bag full of cheese sandwiches on him and warned him the state borders were closed because of the epidemic. He boarded a train and travelled across the Blue Mountains, dozing in the heat, then down onto the brown pelt of the western plains beyond.

The train was packed with returning soldiers—a few silent and withdrawn, most of them smoking and carousing—but civilians as well. There was an elegant woman with her arm around her young son's shoulders, a hare-lipped farmer who reeked of beer, a boy with milky eyes, and a pair of girls who each wore red ribbons cinched tightly about their left wrists—one of the latest superstitious protections against the epidemic. The carriages were warm, the air thick with cigarette smoke. Quinn stood in the narrow passageway and stared out the window. He had removed his influenza mask to better enjoy the breeze upon his face. The countryside was dun-coloured and exhausted. A cluster of men at the far end of the passageway gossiped about the Wynne murder, in which a well-known Bathurst doctor had shot his philandering wife and fled the previous week. A sickly baby whimpered.

Like a bizarre spider unaccustomed to its surfeit of appendages, four drunken soldiers lurched arm in arm down the passage. Each was singing a different song with ramshackle gusto, and one of them appealed for the others to start again so they might sing in time, but they paid him no heed. One tripped and cut himself on a metal window lock. The soldier held up his bleeding hand. "I'm wounded," he wailed in mock despair as his friends laughed and clapped him on the back, grins splashed across their foolish faces. "Send me home, Captain. Oh, please send me home."

It was held that those who had seen death—been in accidents or war or the like—were sometimes filled with an unnatural exuberance and verve for life in the wake of their survival. If anyone were acquainted with death, it was these soldiers returning from war in Europe; Quinn recalled the atmosphere in London among those yet to be demobbed as one of barely restrained mayhem. Disbelief and guilt were a hazardous concoction. Men took risks riding on the backs of carriages or diving into the Thames on frost-bitten mornings, all whoops and crazed laughter, teeth flashing, a bottle in one hand and a slouch hat in the other. Quinn experienced none of their elation; he feared that, for him, the worst was yet to come.

He found himself stealing glimpses of the hare-lipped farmer for most of the journey, incredulous that this man had been going about his business at the same time that Quinn was thousands of miles away up to his chest in mud and blood and wreckage. The farmer smiled back ruefully, as if he imagined they shared something on account of their misshapen faces.

A young man in a smart suit and a boater approached Quinn, offered him a cigarette—a Havelock, gladly accepted—and struck up a lazy conversation. The stranger smelled of menthol and cloves, and carried a white handkerchief with which he periodically dabbed his shining upper lip. He introduced himself as Mark Westbury. The chap was unsmiling but cordial, and attentive to the little Quinn told him of his time at war. Quinn was not inclined to idle conversation at the best of times, and found it difficult to hear over the clatter of the train and the general hubbub.

"And where did you serve, Sergeant . . . *Walker*, is it?"

Quinn started. "How did you know my name?"

Mr. Westbury indicated the name tag on Quinn's tunic. Of course.

The train rounded a bend. In the adjacent compartment a package wrapped in brown paper fell from the luggage rack. "France, mainly," Quinn said when he had steadied himself. "Turkey as well."

Mr. Westbury studied Quinn. Now they had introduced themselves, he felt comfortable enough to stare at Quinn's scar. "You're lucky," he said.

Quinn had heard this a dozen times already. At the field hospital in France, again at Harefield Hospital when a wimpled nurse was making the bed next to his after taking away some poor bastard who had died in the night. *You might not fink it now, but you're one of the lucky ones.*

Again on the troopship home. People said it to him all the time and were disappointed if he failed to invest his accord with commensurate enthusiasm.

"You're lucky to survive, I mean," Mr. Westbury added. "Even with the . . . that scar and everything."

"Yes," he said at last. "I'm lucky."

Mr. Westbury said something Quinn was unable to make out over the noise of the carriage.

"What?"

"I said: You were *spared*."

"Yes."

After an awkward silence, the young man asked where he was going.

"Flint," Quinn replied.

Mr. Westbury nodded, although it was clear he had never heard of the place. Few people had. There was little reason to visit, now that the gold had been mined. Hardly anyone lived there. Not even cartographers bothered with it anymore.

"That's your home, I take it?"

Quinn observed this starched fellow, who had told him he was ineligible for military service on account of an impairment with his vision. He shrugged and drew on his cigarette, which caused a mild coughing fit.

"I suppose it is," he said when he'd recovered. "It is where I was born. There is something I need to set right."

Mr. Westbury dabbed impatiently at his forehead with his handkerchief. "Well, lots of places have gone to wrack and ruin, you know. Lots of places." It seemed he had lost interest.

Quinn threw down his cigarette and ground it out under his boot heel. A woman and her young daughter indicated they wished to pass, prompting Quinn and his new companion to stand back as far as the cramped space would allow.

They remained silent until the man, who had again been staring at the muddled scar along his jaw, motioned for him to lean in and said, in a tiptoeing voice, "You should do something about your face. Cover it up, perhaps? Do you have a flu mask? You are frightening the children, you know."

And Quinn, usually so reserved but seized by the devil, replied, also in a whisper, "Well, the children have good reason to be frightened."

⁓⁑⁓

At Bathurst he slunk from the station and began walking north-west. He left the town and kept going, at times along the road, at others clambering across plains or ragged outcrops of rocks. The earth was dry and hard under his feet, and the sky—blue and cloudless—yawned overhead, higher and more vast than any skies he had seen elsewhere in the world, a continent unto itself. Hawks circled like dark, watchful stars disentangled from their orbits.

He unpicked his name tag from his tunic and avoided places he might encounter people who could recognise him. The few farmers he saw nodded or waved their hats, glad to welcome home a soldier from the Great War. A family lumbered past with their possessions and five children piled atop a horse-drawn cart. The mouth and nose of each was covered by a gauze mask and they stared away and offered no greeting, obviously terrified of contagion. By and large, people paid him no heed. The sight of people walking alone was not so unusual after a war; there must be entire armies of men returning home, each in a ragged uniform, wandering tiny across the face of the earth. He had a nap beneath cypress trees in the middle of the day and pressed on until it was too dark to continue.

The countryside teemed with animals. Lizards and snakes, rosellas and magpies. At dusk, grey kangaroos bobbed in grassy fields and stood on their hind legs to watch him pass. Rabbits darted at the edges of his vision, and pairs of orange butterflies flitted about him wherever he walked. And the hum, always the hum, heard even through his murky hearing, of flies and bees.

He was accustomed to walking long distances and made good progress. It was pleasant to feel so free, despite the trappings of war he carried still—his kitbag, the satchel with his gas mask, and his revolver jammed beneath his unbuttoned tunic. He took no bearings but just walked as if his forward motion might unravel the stink of war and all that had happened in the years he'd been away. Mirages trembled along the horizon. He saw massive vessels, a line of elephants, once an entire city with buildings and steeples, some vast metropolis that receded, then receded, then receded every time he drew near.

At the close of each day the sun sank from sight and set the horizon aglow for ten minutes. He camped away from the road and stared into the flames of his fire, his human replacement for the vanished sun. He rationed his sandwiches carefully. He prayed in his strange way, which was more like a sort of querying. At least now, after all these years, he had a sense of why he'd been spared. It was some consolation.

He fell asleep thinking of his sister, Sarah. Even with his eyes closed he knew where he was on the earth, could imagine his exact position as his internal compass swung about to orient him home.

2

After several days, the country became more familiar. Quinn began to recognise features in the landscape: a cluster of rocks that resembled a family of pigs snuffling in the scrub; the tree where Bill Clayton hanged himself in '05 after his wife ran off with the Salvation Army drummer; the mullock heaps of abandoned gold mines. He came across gullies carved out by mining, abandoned shafts, the rusted remains of machinery half sunk in the red soil.

Fifty years earlier these hills were full of gold and the town of Flint had swarmed with hungry men and their hungrier families, but the boom was fleeting and left in its wake a landscape riven and tortured, littered with the ruins of rock stampers and wooden scaffolds that had been erected over shafts. All that remained was the large Sparrowhawk Mine, but the mountains and gullies throughout the area were encrusted with the wrecks of small settlements where families had gathered according to their countries of origin: the Welsh Village, Irish Town, Chinese Flat. The ground was hard and rocky. Scottish thistle bloomed everywhere. Even the native trees looked to have grown not from this country but, rather, to have been thrust—unwilling, straining skyward—into the soil from which they now attempted to writhe free.

Quinn had wandered these hills as a boy, shooting birds and rabbits, often with Sarah tramping behind him, rebuking him for wayward shots. They had found nuggets of gold, which they'd hoarded and planned to sell when they were older so they might travel to strange countries and purchase exotic animals and jewels. *Treasure*, Sarah called the nuggets as she solemnly placed each of them in a cigar box, alongside several buttons she deemed precious, a brooch, rare feathers and a postage stamp she had found one day in Orchard Street. Sarah often carried one of these tokens as a kind of lucky charm and would take it out to inspect during the day. Not that it helped; Quinn knew for a fact she had a lucky red button sewn to her dress on the day she died.

Now, for minutes at a time, pausing in a gully or beneath a tree, Quinn was suspended in the cooling amber of memory. It was a queasy brew of longing and regret. He was amazed at how little things had changed in the ten years he had been away. The world looked the same, but it had been thrown off course forever by Sarah's murder. He steadied himself against a tree and was afraid. Like a different sort of Eden, the air here quivered and shimmered as if struggling to contain the variety of life it was obliged to sustain. It was easy to imagine the beginning of time here, but also, perhaps, its end.

He sat on a stump in the shade and unbuttoned his tunic. The ground was hard and hot, but it made a pleasant change from the mud of France where a man struggled sometimes to take a single step. He picked burrs of thistle from his socks and the hems of his trousers. He thumped the side of his head in an attempt to dislodge the thickness that had accumulated there and which rendered the world remote, less decipherable than ever. He drank from his water flask and glanced up, startled to see a man standing ten feet away carrying a rifle. Quinn thought of his revolver but realised it was impossible to retrieve quickly.

The man grinned, raised a hand in greeting and crunched through the leaf litter towards him. Hanging about his waist was a gruesome belt of bloodied, ragged dead rabbits.

"G'day," he said.

Quinn was too startled to speak. Water drooled from his chin. He thought about fleeing. Standing, he recognised the chap as the good-natured idiot Edward Fitch, infamous in these parts for asking endless questions, and for his precise recall of the date of everything that happened in Flint and the weather that accompanied it. Quinn swore under his breath.

Edward approached. He was stocky, eager, a famished boar of a man. He looked Quinn up and down, licked his lips and muttered something. Quinn cupped a hand to his ear to indicate he hadn't heard properly.

His partial deafness required him to recalibrate his limited hearing to each new person—according to the individual's manner and volume of speech—in order to understand them.

"I said: 'You been at the war?'"

"Yes."

"Looks like you really copped it," Edward said, indicating on his own grubby jaw the scarred portion of Quinn's face.

Quinn blushed. He knew the scar was hard to ignore. It resembled a slur of porridge. "Yes."

Edward shook his head. "Not as bad as some I seen, though. Some of them are bloody awful. Jack Williams got it real bad. Nice uniform you got on. How's it going? Kill some Boche?"

"The war is over."

Edward tucked his chin into his chest to ponder this information. It occurred to Quinn the dolt had not recognised him. He jammed his hat on his head and bent to gather his things. He might still be able to get away.

"Where are you going?"

Quinn straightened. "I'm . . . looking for work."

"You escaping the plague?"

"The plague?"

"The Black Death."

Quinn had heard this rumour before. He shook his head. "It's not the bubonic plague. It's influenza. Pneumonic influenza, they call it."

Edward wiped a hand across his mouth, then held up two fingers. "Ginny Reynolds died in two days. Up and died. And she was healthy as a horse. They call it the flu but everyone knows it's something else. Something worse. Mr. McMahon, too. Blood came out his eyes. Flu don't do that, mate." Edward hitched his belt and the mass of flies ballooned into the air before resettling over the rabbit carcasses. With a crucifix aglitter around his neck, sweat-stained hat, filthy vest and knife wedged into his belt, he resembled a medieval anchorite.

Quinn took up his kitbag. "Have faith," he said in an unconvincing voice. "God will take care of us."

"God?" Fitch mocked. "Not sure about *him*."

Quinn scowled. He recalled what some townsfolk had said about Edward Fitch when he was a boy: that his mother was an unbeliever, that she had brought Edward's malformed nature on her own head by attempting to rid herself of him before he was even born.

"You shouldn't say such a thing," Quinn warned.

"They reckon down at Sully's that God don't exist. That he's dead, believe it or not, what with the war and everything."

"And what would they know?"

Edward Fitch smirked. Obviously, he had gotten the reaction he desired all along.

"What about that cross around your neck?" Quinn asked.

"That's nothing. Found it."

"Then why do you wear it?"

Edward gave him a look of sullen reproach. "I like it."

"Anyway," Quinn said shaking his head, hoping to make clear his disapproval, "I have to keep moving. Goodbye. Good luck to you."

"You want to buy a rabbit before you go on?"

"I have no money."

Edward untied one of the bloody creatures and held it out to him. In addition to the smell of freshly killed rabbits, he reeked of souring milk. "Don't matter. Take it. A present."

Quinn hesitated. His sandwiches had almost run out; some meat would indeed be wonderful. His mouth actually watered at the thought of it. "Thanks." He took the limp creature.

"That's alright, mate." Edward licked his lips, inspected him. "I didn't recognise you at first. You changed a lot. And not only cos of that thing on your mouth."

Quinn's tongue turned to wadding. He should never have engaged in conversation with this fool. He should have taken his leave immediately. And now it was too late. He thought again of his revolver.

"Didn't think you'd show your face around here again, Quinn Walker," Edward went on without apparent malice, nodding sagely as he riffled through the facts stored away in his head. "Not after what happened." A pause. "July 5th, 1909. Raining real hard. A Saturday—no wait —Sunday. A Sunday it was."

Quinn remembered the driving rain of that terrible day, a flicker of lightning, a red shoe in the dirt. He winced at the unbidden images. He ran a hand over his sweating face, disbelieving, cursing his luck for having walked all this way to avoid encountering anyone who might recognise him, only to meet this idiot Fitch on an otherwise unused dirt track.

Edward retied his bundle of rabbit carcasses. "I'm not afraid of you, though."

Quinn shoved the rabbit Edward had given him into his kitbag and wiped his hands on his tunic. He turned to leave.

"You must be confused, sir. I don't know you. I'm just passing through—"

"They were talking about you the other day. Last Wednesday, I think. Bloody hot it was. Down back of Sully's place, saying what a life your poor mother has had, what with one thing and another . . ."

"Who was saying that?"

"People. You was reported as dead ages ago. That's what your mum said. In the war. Killed in the war, you know."

Quinn had heard of countless instances in which the Army registered men as dead or missing when they were, in fact, hale and hearty. These kinds of mistakes were common in the chaos of war; men considered dead often reappeared in the ranks, having been in English hospitals where they had been patched up. There was even the story of a bloke showing up at his own wake in Brisbane, asking, *Who died?*

"But they all say how they'd love to string you up if they saw you again," Edward Fitch continued. "Even your father says it. And your uncle, too. Kill ya all over again."

He tugged at the excess skin at his neck, rolled his eyes back and lolled his tongue to clarify his meaning.

"My uncle still lives in Flint?"

"Yeah. Of course."

Quinn paused. "And is my mother alright?"

Edward made a face. "She's sick with the plague, you know. There's lots of them around here with it. Lots of people dying because of it, too. Ginny Reynolds, Solomon Quail. . . ."

Quinn wiped his forearm across his brow. He had become aware, in the past few minutes, of the *thunkity-thunk* of his heart and the crackle of sweat as it seeped from every pore. He felt faint.

"What about the rest of my family? My father?"

"Well, your father is alright, I suppose. Still at Sparrowhawk. Your brother went to Queensland a long time back. I don't know why."

Quinn placed a hand on Fitch's shoulder. "Listen. You don't need to tell anyone you saw me."

Edward was crestfallen. "Oh. What will I say then?"

"Don't say anything. Nothing. You don't need to say a word."

Edward straightened his belt of carcasses and waved a clutch of flies from his face. His Adam's apple somersaulted against his furry throat, and Quinn sensed what he'd said making itself understood in the fool's muddy intellect, like the delayed splash of a rock dropped into a well.

Taking advantage of his momentary confusion, Quinn snatched Edward's rifle from him, made sure it wasn't loaded, then handed it back.

"Is your mother still alive, Edward?"

"My old mum? Course."

"Still living alone down the end of Main Street there? In the little green house?"

"Yes."

"Good. If you tell anyone you saw me up here today, I'll go down and kill her. Do you understand me?"

"Why would you—"

"Do you understand me?"

Edward's bottom lip trembled. "Yes."

⁂

Quinn lingered in the cathedral shade of the hillside pines, where the air was soft and scented. The war had taught him to mistrust open spaces and it was only among such trees that he felt suitably inconspicuous. He felt ashamed for having threatened Edward Fitch in such a manner, but it was crucial no one knew he had returned to the district. The fool was certainly right when he said they would hang him if they found him.

The town of Flint was arranged a mile below in a shallow valley. It comprised little more than half-a-dozen proper streets spread over an area of about three miles, criss-crossed with numerous cart tracks and alleys furrowed between properties by the scampering traffic of children and animals. The business district, such as it was, slumbered on a slight rise leading up from the flatter environs of the Flint River, beside which hunched a number of willow trees. The more prosperous citizens lived in the elevated section around Orchard and Alexander streets, a leafy area bordered by lush apple and nectarine orchards on one side and the grounds of the Anglican church on the other. Dotted along Gully Road were the wrecks of long-closed businesses—a tailor, Kilby's photographic studio, a fancy gift shop—that had flourished during the rush but struggled to remain viable once the big-spenders had decamped.

During the gold boom, the population had seeped into the surrounding bushland. The Flats, which sprawled along the north-west shoulder of Flint, had once sustained almost one hundred shabby miners' tents and dwellings, but was now little more than a few haunted acres of blackened stumps, treacherous ditches, broken glass, shards of crockery, rusted cooking equipment and rotted clumps of clothes. When the miners left the Flats for goldfields further away or for more salubrious accommodation, the more forward-thinking citizens of Flint were eager to clear the land and make use of its proximity to the river, but nothing was ever done and the Flats remained squalid, prone to flooding in winter and restless with snakes in summer. Even the children of Flint, who were generally an adventurous and fearless bunch, avoided the area and preferred to take the long way to the river rather than risk being grabbed about the ankles by the bunyips and yowies that lurked in its waterlogged gullies.

Quinn recalled his father once telling his children how he'd witnessed an Irish woman giving birth unassisted on a patch of muddy grass near the river amid the chaos; and how, afterwards, when the woman had staggered away with her mewling baby, a dog sloped from the shadows, snatched up the many-veined, bruise-dark afterbirth and fled with it twitching in its jaws. *That's the bloody Irish for you*, would be his father's laughing postscript, a comment guaranteed to prompt a fierce *Hush, Nathaniel* from Mary Walker.

From his eyrie, Quinn could see his family's farm on a low rise at the town's fringes. It consisted of a stone house built by his father, a stable, a chook pen, and a paddock for a few sheep and goats. The tin roof of the house gleamed in the midday sun. A glimpse of dirt road lay like a fuse through the elms.

Around him in the trees near and far, in the bracken that littered the bush floor, animals and insects whispered and thrilled, atwitter at his return after all these years. After a while, he lay down and dozed on the ground. He thought of what Edward Fitch had said: *They all say how they'd love to string you up. Kill ya all over again.* He checked his revolver and tested its weight in his palm, prepared for anything. Shapes stirred on the outskirts of his memory, yawning and stretching, casting about for him. It was not a comforting thought.

❧

Quinn watched over his father's property for most of the following day, but saw no one arrive or leave. The apparent abandonment disturbed him. Had everyone fled the influenza? He gnawed at a thumbnail. He rolled and smoked cigarettes. From habit, he checked the linings of his coat and trousers for lice. *Reading your clothes*, they had called it in France, as if they might ennoble the practice by imagining themselves scholars seeking meaning in tattered manuscripts.

A crow on a nearby branch harked and shrugged its neck feathers before turning its gleaming gaze on him. Again the bird cried out in its language. Was it a greeting? A warning? They watched each other for some minutes, two creatures of God's earth, before the crow shuddered as if displeased and launched itself into the air. It landed on the next gum tree and set about preening itself jerkily while keeping a beady eye out for food or danger. He wondered if it could see the ocean from its vantage point, other countries, the desert? The future, the past? This was the bird that Noah dispatched from his Ark to check if the waters of the great Flood had receded from the lowlands: surely it knew everything.

Every now and again, Quinn's stomach and chest were racked by burning, and he was forced to stop whatever he was doing and double over until it passed. His eyes watered and unstrung hammocks of saliva hung from his lips. The gas. The bloody gas was what did it. It was in him like a disease. There was no doubt it would infect him forever.

Holding up a shaving mirror to his face, he practised speaking from the right corner of his mouth, the undamaged side, making a flattened circle of his lips as they had instructed him at the hospital all those months ago. *My name is Quinn Walker. Ring a ring a rosie. Fee fi fo fum . . .*

Sometimes he wept, just wept, would wake from drowsing with a damp face and a leaf or twig pressed into his cheek.

Towards the end of the day, smoke began to unfurl from the chimney of his parents' house. Twenty minutes later, borne on a rising wind, Quinn detected its scent. He saw no other sign of life until a lamp was lit inside the house and set the kitchen window aglow. Although unable to hear any of it, he knew dogs were barking down there in the twilight, screen doors were slamming shut, and mothers were calling in their children from the streets and orchards. Soon the house was swallowed by the creeping darkness.

He scooped out a hole in the ground, made a modest fire and sat hunched with his hands clasped around his knees, a blanket over his shoulders, shaking. A fire was a greedy luxury. Back there, during the war, there was rarely a chance to light a fire, even in the coldest months when snow dusted them.

He cooked the rabbit Edward Fitch had given him. The lean creature, skinned and rammed through on a stick from mouth to arsehole, dripped its juices into the fire. After devouring it with his bare hands, cracking open each sinewy piece and placing it morsel by morsel into his mouth, he balled his trench coat into a pillow and lay down to watch the flames. The coat smelled of foreign places, of mud and, faintly, of chlorine. The darkness beyond was made deeper by its proximity to the flames, and the trunks of nearby trees twitched in the flickering light. He tried to calculate how many days since his arrival back in Australia. Four? Five? Beneath him was the dense meat of the turning earth, going on and on for thousands of miles. He imagined fires down there, the screech of metal, those goblins and devils with their peculiar industry.

Something shouldered through the nearby undergrowth. He sat up brandishing his revolver and waited for the snuffle of a wombat or the hoarse cry of a possum, but nothing was forthcoming. Then, dimly, moored in the fog of his partial deafness, the snap of a twig. He raised his weapon and waited for several minutes. Surely that idiot Fitch would not have followed him? Had he told someone of their meeting? He tilted his head to favour each ear in turn but heard nothing more. Probably a kangaroo.

After half an hour he relaxed and went to sleep. But in the middle of the night, when the fire was embers and the world was otherwise silent, he heard the distant lull of artillery, almost a heartbeat, as he knew he would. Then the sound of the gong from deep within his dreams.

He woke immediately and scrambled for his cotton satchel, usually right beside him but not tonight for some reason. Damn. Damn. He was getting lazy, and lazy soldiers die. It was hard to see in the meagre moonlight. The night was unusually warm. He tried to stay calm, remain low to the ground, to keep movement and breathing to a minimum, the way he had learned. He glimpsed the satchel, partially hidden beneath his coat. *Gas, gas, gas, gas, gas.* If you taste it, it's too late. His fluttering fingers pale as moths. The fabric strap snagged on something. Christ. He tugged, to no avail. A rock dug into his knee. He tore his way into the satchel and fitted the mask over his face—straps across the back of his head, clamp tight on his nostrils, then the rubber mouthpiece. Breathe through your mouth only. Always worried the mask wasn't the correct size, or that he had in his haste picked up the wrong one, that he would wind up dead and swollen like that poor bloke from Melbourne, face down in the mud. The goggles rendered the world glaucous and vague. *Move it, move it, move it.* The interior of the mask reeked of rubbery sweat, of his fraying lungs. God help me, he thought. God help me.

On his haunches, keeping as low as possible to the ground, he ran his trembling hands around the edges of the mask. He pressed it down into the collar of his tunic, against the tender skin at his throat, his head now a vessel atop his thin frame, sealed off from the world, soundless, in a climate of its very own. Only then did he realise. Bloody hell.

3

The next day, Quinn left the cool shade of the pines. He scrambled through bracken and along dry gullies, beating his way with a stick, gathering about the exposed parts of his body scratches and cuts from passing branches. It was familiar countryside and yet it felt strange, as if he were travelling across a landscape from a much-read book.

Careful to stay hidden, he squatted in the scrub beyond the perimeter of his father's property. He knew he would be camouflaged perfectly well if he remained stationary. It was hotter down here out of any cooling breezes. Unseen insects bit his ankles and forearms. The house appeared unchanged, built from stone and wood, the very materials of the land on which it sat. A veranda edged by bushes and flowers ran around three sides. Torch lilies and lavender. A limp, yellow flag hung from a makeshift pole jammed into a porch railing. Quarantine. Edward Fitch was right. Someone in the house was infected.

After about twenty minutes, a man appeared from the stable and pulled open its wide doors. He was familiar, but just barely. He moved with awkward-legged steps, as if his feet were made of glass or clay. It was his father, Nathaniel Walker, older, lank hair gone grey, even rangier than Quinn remembered. He shrank deeper into the bushes, and presently his father led a horse from the stable, heaved himself into the saddle and rode away through the guard of cypress trees that lined the short driveway, leaving plumes of dust that took several minutes to settle in his wake.

Quinn remained amid the crackle and hum of the bush. If nothing else, his time at war had taught him to keep still for long periods of

time. Flies buzzed about his sweating face. Mesmerised, as if it were
constructed from the detritus of an hallucination, he stared at the house,
two hundred feet away. It was smaller than he remembered, but things
always were. That, or larger. Memory was imprecise, after all, not to
be trusted.

When it seemed his father was not returning and there was no
one else at home, he crept from the undergrowth and approached the
house, scuffing up dust as he went. He paused at the bottom of the
steps to run his hand over the bobbing heads of lavender flowers. He
broke off a handful of flowers, rolled them between his fingers and
held them to his nose. It was one of the few plants, he thought, whose
perfume matched its appearance. Musty air wafted from the space
beneath the house, bringing with it a flood of memory, the shout
of a child at play. In summer he used to crouch with his siblings in
the shade there to play hide-and-seek or knuckles. Even now, there
was probably hidden somewhere in the dirt a rotted linen bag of
sheep bones, along with the names he and William had carved with
a knife into the stumps, and the fantastic winged animals Sarah had
drawn with her nub of chalk. William had always been pleased that
his initials were WW and never hesitated to scratch them into trees
or posts whenever the opportunity arose.

Still mindful of what Fitch had told him of those eager to do
him harm, Quinn drew his revolver and stopped at the screen door. A
sepulchral draught flowed from within. He wondered if he should leave
now, before it was too late, then realised it already was too late and had
been for many years. No. He had to carry on. After coming all this way.
After all these years. He stepped inside.

In the kitchen he inhaled and detected a smell of—what?—
something sharp, medicinal, at once homely and strange. Everything
here was dry and exhausted, rinsed of colour. Melancholy suffused him,
like wine moving darkly through water. Ahead, the scarred, wooden
table at which he had eaten hundreds of meals with his family. Where
William would leer at him with lips smeared with jam, where Sarah, dear
Sarah, would lean across and whisper into his ear her latest idea for their
next adventure. Where their father would relate the latest notion he had

heard from a bloke down The Mail as their mother urged them to please be quiet and *eat*.

The table's accompanying chairs faced this way and that, as if those who had been sitting here had fled, which perhaps they had. Crumbs of bread on a cutting board, a tin of honey. There was a basket filled with plates and jars on the floor by the door. A pearl of sunlight on a teaspoon, a pink daisy broken-necked in a disused medicine bottle. Quinn's heart ballooned in his chest. He heard a low groan, something creaking, and paused to listen. He jammed a finger into his ear. Again he heard it, the mere ghost of a sound. Then nothing. The house around him, above and below, was quiet. Then again, a soft moan emanating from his parents' room. He forced himself to creep along the dim hall.

He paused at the threshold. He could discern little but darkness, a thread of light in the join of the curtain. After several seconds, through the ship-sunk dark, the glint of a mirror and a hairbrush atop a dresser. Motes of dust glimmering and vanishing. A wooden chair. Teetering piles of books on the floor. The rest of the house, indeed the entire world, felt a long way from here. And high on a wall, in a wooden frame, an image of the suffering Christ melting from his cross—shoulders collapsed, blood weeping from the gash at his side, the thin and ruined hull of his ribs. Then, gaining shape, a bed hard up against a curtained window, hotly rumpled, its bedding a miniature mountain range. A hand on the coverlet. Long, thin fingers. Someone asleep. A woman.

The curious smell he had noted earlier was stronger here, almost overpowering. He held the sprigs of lavender to his nose and suppressed a cough. He stood there for several minutes, until he succumbed to the gravitational pull of history, of family, of love, and crept to his mother's bedside.

She did not look well. She lay in the middle of a large bed beneath a mess of blankets. Her face, which he remembered as round and smiling, was now thin and elongated. Her breathing was thick, bubbly, as if she were half buried in mud. And around her neck, hanging against her sweaty throat, was the source of the unusual smell: a clumsy necklace of camphor balls threaded on twine.

Quinn watched his mother for some time, transfixed. Her long, dark hair sprawled on the pillow. One of the camphor balls nestled in the damp and trembling notch of her throat. The clock ticked. She looked awful, but at least she was alive. The flood of Quinn's relief swept all before it.

She shifted beneath the pile of bedding and opened her eyes. She focused on him at once, as if she had known all along where he would stand upon his return, no matter how many years later. But still she cowered. "Who are you?" she croaked.

Quinn removed the handful of lavender from his face.

"My God," his mother said. "My God." Her eyes dropped to the revolver in his other hand. "Have you come for me, now? I am not ready. Not yet, please."

Quinn was speechless. He stared into his poor mother's terrified eyes and fled.

4

A nother day passed. Shocked by the condition of his mother in that gloomy bedroom, Quinn stayed close by his campsite, loose-limbed and agitated, venturing now and again into the surrounding bushland, falling in and out of sleep the rest of the time. From behind his eyelids, the face of his mother reared up at him, gaunt and afraid.

In the late afternoon, when the sear of the sun had lessened, he stumbled on a circular grass clearing. He hovered for a minute in the comforting shade of the trees around the clearing, but then crept into the sunlight. After all, it was not France; there were no snipers here. Even so, he dug a hand into his tunic to touch his revolver as if it were a crucifix that, through his caresses, might alert God to his anxieties. The grass was as high as his knees and long sheaves of it bent and hissed in the wind. He stared up at the blue sky. Crows and other birds, those fortunate creatures unburdened by gravity, drifted high overhead, specks against the blue wash of sky.

He closed his eyes to better enjoy the sun's warmth. Soon he was startled by a sharp cry. He looked around blinking and saw, at the edge of the clearing, a small, trembling lamb. A farmer must have brought his flock up here to graze and this poor creature had become separated from its mother. Only its head was visible as it stumbled about in the high grass. The lamb saw Quinn, cocked its head and trotted over to him, bleating. Quinn remained motionless, surprised it approached so eagerly. The lamb stared up at him with its doltish eyes and twitched flies from its ears and face. It bleated again and butted his leg. Quinn kneeled to stroke its bony head. He brushed away grass seeds that peppered its frail, white body, its legs so thin. The animal made a sound like a giggle. It gambolled about the long grass for several minutes before returning to where he crouched. He could smell its moist and grassy breath and the scent of it—so warm and trusting, so alive—prompted him, inexplicably, to sob. The lamb nuzzled his shoulder. Quinn found himself consoling the creature in a whisper, saying to it the things one might say to an ailing infant or one who has woken crying from a nightmare.

They stayed unmoving for a long time. It was the most peaceful moment he had experienced for many years. He felt secure. Shadows stretched over them as heat drained from the afternoon, and Quinn wondered what God would make of them, man and beast, as he cast his all-seeing eyes over the land.

❦

Crouching in the bush, Quinn continued to study his father's house over subsequent days. Nathaniel often lingered uneasily on the veranda, apparently talking to himself. He realised his father—fearful of infection—was speaking with Quinn's mother through the open window to her room. Before he departed on horseback, his father would stand in the dusty yard for minutes at a time and stare into the distance, as if waiting for everything to make sense. It was an attitude Quinn recognised, and he recalled his father gazing into the air as he considered the possibilities of the latest rumours he had heard at Sully's or in the bar of The Mail.

Nathaniel was an enthusiast. He considered himself at the forefront of modern thought and was at his happiest when seated with a stranger newly arrived from Sydney, brow knitted, chin in one hand, mulling over the latest outlandish idea shipped in from London. There were few notions Nathaniel Walker didn't countenance, at least briefly. After all, he would say to those (namely Quinn's mother) who sought to pull him up, hadn't he taken a chance in bringing his young family to Flint in the first place? What of the money they had made, how they had prospered! If he had listened to the bloody naysayers he would still be digging ditches for some farmer out west. Quinn's father had in his time flirted with growing rice, been a Fabian Socialist and invested in an oil called

Gingerman's Lotion, which was guaranteed to cure baldness but left the sufferer smelling like a sodden wombat. He was excited by electricity, by aeroplanes, at the myriad possibilities of alchemy. He was, in short, a man enamoured of possibility. *Can you imagine?* he would say, shaking his head in wonder. *Can you just imagine it?*

There were other beliefs that lodged in his father's imagination permanently and from which he refused to be swayed. He thought Chinamen lived in holes in the ground; he swore he had spoken with a yowie one night out near Sparrowhawk Mine; and he couldn't shake the suspicion that Quinn and Sarah's relationship was unhealthy and couldn't his wife *do* something about it, look at the pair of them, people are starting to talk? So convinced was he that—when Quinn was twelve and Sarah eight—he forbade them from playing together, an edict that lasted two days before it was ignored.

As Quinn watched from his hiding place, women arrived on bicycles carrying plates of food and baskets with other items they deposited on the doorstep before hurrying away. If he were present at the time, Nathaniel would exchange solemn greetings with these envoys from the Women's Auxiliary, and they would chat uncomfortably for a minute or two before the ladies remounted their contraptions and wobbled away down the road.

One such afternoon, Quinn waited until his father had left and stole again into the house, along the dark hall to his parents' bedroom. This time his mother was awake. She regarded him with chilly hauteur.

"You resemble my son," she said after some time, "but I am reasonably sure he would not return to this place."

He stayed at the threshold.

There followed a watchful silence until his mother drew herself up with obvious effort. "Come here, then. Let me touch you, boy."

He shuffled to her bedside and held out one hand.

His mother prodded his palm with a finger. She cowered, as if scorched. "You are no ghost, then? My God. But are you able to speak?"

Quinn touched the scarred side of his mouth. "Yes," he said, aware of the watery lisp of the word snagging on his barbed-wire mouth.

"Quinn? Is it really you?"

"Yes, Mother."

"My . . . *son?*"

He paused. "Yes."

"But they told me you were dead. I even have a letter."

"They were wrong."

She considered this for several seconds. "What could you want here?"

"I came to tell you something."

"Tell me what?"

"I came to tell you I didn't do it."

She glanced away and whispered words he couldn't hear.

"It wasn't me," Quinn went on, desperate now. "I swear to you. I didn't do it."

She coughed, then faced him, eyes laced with fury. "You came to tell me this now, after ten years? Ten *years*, Quinn. Where have you been all this time? All these years I have wondered about that day. Did you not think of us—of me?"

"Yes, Mother. Of course I did." It was true. Rarely had a day gone by that he hadn't pondered his mother and father or imagined his own return, but with each passing year, less was he able to envisage himself back in Flint. Even now, it was a quirk of history that he should find himself standing here. His new-found courage was purely accidental. He thought of the Military Medal he had flung into the ocean. "I'll go to the police, I'll tell them it wasn't me."

"But what happened that day, Quinn? Tell me now."

He shook his head. It was almost too much to bear. "I don't really know," he lied. "I just found her there."

She searched his face for signs of deceit. Then she turned away and coughed into a handkerchief she had balled in one sweaty fist. "Of course I never thought you did it. Never. My God, such a thing. You were a lovely boy. But I should warn you— I am alone in thinking that."

Only then did Quinn realise he had been holding his breath waiting for this response.

Neither of them said anything for several minutes.

She faced him again. "They sent your description to police everywhere, you know. There was even a reward. They got a tracker out, but the storms had washed away any trace of you. Your disappearance was so"—she searched for a word—"complete. I have mourned for you, Quinn. Robert and your father told everyone what they saw—"

He lurched forward, interrupting. "What they think they saw. What did they tell you exactly?"

His mother closed her eyes. He thought she had fallen asleep, but presently her eyes flicked open. "I didn't want to hear too much of it . . . My brother told me you were crying and that you were covered in blood. He said you had a knife in your hand, Quinn, and that you looked guilty. You ran away. I saw the way people stared at us with pity. There are things a mother doesn't need to know, but the story is now carved, as if into stone. It was in the Sydney newspaper. Stories are difficult to rewrite, especially after so long."

"And they prefer to think I murdered my own sister?"

"It is terrible to admit, but I was glad when they told me you had been killed in the war. It meant the dreadful story was over." She studied him as if fearing he might leave at any second, then pushed aside a sheet and attempted to sit up. "My God, but you shouldn't be here at all. Did you not see the flag? The house is quarantined. The yellow flag?"

"I saw it, but I had to come in. I had to see you. The place looks abandoned."

Again she coughed. "It might as well be. Are you infected?"

"No."

"Not yet. Even your father . . ."

"What?"

"He sleeps in the stable. Stays out of the house so he can keep working at Sparrowhawk. Until the quarantine is lifted. Only the doctor comes in. You should at least wear one of those masks." She stared at the wall over his shoulder, as if the killer might be there in the shadows. "God will have his way with him, whoever it is. Whoever did that thing. God will see to it. One cannot escape such a crime. Remember Isaiah, Quinn. *Be strong, fear not: behold, your God will come with vengeance.*"

Quinn nodded. It was a thought with which he had attempted to console himself when troubled by thoughts of the man who had killed his sister.

After a short silence, he said, "I will try and make things right, Mother."

"To make a crooked thing straight?"

"If I can. I'll tell Father it wasn't me. It's not too late for some sort of justice for our Sarah."

"No, Quinn. Your father will kill you. There are things he *refuses* to believe, you know how he is. He is not the same man. It ruined him. It ruined all of us. Thank goodness for my brother. Robert has been my saviour in all of this. He was as devastated as anyone by what happened. He loved her, you know. He curses himself for not catching her murderer. He is as sure as anyone it was you. There is nothing to be gained. It is all too late now." She coughed. "Quinn? Why did you stay away so long?"

"I was afraid. I heard what people thought of me."

Again she inspected him, allowing her languid gaze to drop as if following the progress of a feather visible to her alone—from the scar at his mouth, to his throat, to the dull buttons of his tunic, until she stared at his hands now dangling at his sides. "You have been at the war? That at least is true?"

Quinn nodded.

She mouthed something and, when he indicated by a frown and shake of his head that he hadn't understood, she repeated. "Was it terrible?"

A rupture of the earth, a soldier sodomising a corpse at dusk, a tank marooned in the mire, the silence after the barrages as nations tallied their dead. He could tell her nothing of this. He could tell no one, for they would think him a liar; no one truly wished to know what humans were capable of.

He had been laying rail tracks south of Grafton when he joined up and had foolishly thought war an elegant affair with clear results. He recalled the colour poster on the side of a cart with the slogan *TAKE UP THE SWORD OF JUSTICE*, the words accompanied by a painting of a handsome woman charging forth with one such weapon in her upraised fist. At the time it was exciting, and he had felt part of something—a sense that had been missing from his life for so many years. They told him there would be glory, that they would partake in something marvellous, but it was nothing but ruin and din.

Mary ran a hand again across her damp hair. She licked her lips. "It has already been a dark century. Who knows what is still to come? At least God spared you, my son. At least he spared you."

At the auxiliary hospital at Harefield, a nurse had told him the same thing. The sudden waft of carbolic and boiled brussel-sprouts gone cold, the moist scrunch of rubber-soled shoes. *God spared you, alright. You should see some of them. Make your bleedin' hair curl. You been saved for somethin'.*

"What happened to your face?" his mother asked.

"Shrapnel. From artillery in France."

"Are you in pain?"

"Not anymore. They fixed me up quite well. There are much worse. I was . . . lucky."

She coughed and drank from her water glass. "They say those Germans crucified a man against a shed. That they did . . . unspeakable things to girls."

Quinn recalled the dull winter afternoon the crucifixion rumour fevered through the trenches.

His mother slumped back down. "We adapt to our sorrows, I suppose, as unpleasant as they might be. One cannot weep forever. One simply runs dry of tears. I would do anything to have Sarah back again. Anything."

Neither of them spoke for several minutes. His mother turned to peer through the curtain. Tears jewelled again on her lashes. Her grief was not exhausted, it seemed.

At last she turned to him, and her mouth creased into a thin smile as if she were only now, after these twenty minutes in his presence, willing to truly believe he was here with her. "Ah, Quinn. You have returned. Against all hope. As I have prayed."

"And do you believe me?"

She considered before answering. "I never really thought you would do something so terrible. Mothers always assume the best of their children. But it's hard to believe *anyone* would do something like that." And her eyes clamped shut, indeed her whole face closed over, excepting the few dry sobs that escaped her cracked mouth.

After a few minutes she regained her composure. "My beautiful boy. My beautiful girl. You were like twins. The way she ordered you around. You, her older brother. You were so *devoted*. A lovely brother to her. She could make you do anything. You remember the running race, the time she made you and William dress up like fairies or something? Drove your father mad, of course."

He smiled, relieved. It seemed a border had been crossed. He waited while his mother appraised him again, and felt as if he'd been rendered an infant, awaiting punishment or love. She coughed, and grimaced with the effort of it.

When the episode had subsided, she turned to him and said in her damp-gravel voice, "Come closer. Let me see you. It's so dark in here."

He leaned in even further until he could sense the hot machinery of fever grinding away in her body. She rummaged among the bedclothes for her handkerchief, into which she coughed again, this time for some minutes. The attack exhausted her and, when she turned away, Quinn saw that her neck was patterned with purple spots. She closed her eyes and fell asleep.

Emotions burrowed through him like mice. He should never have returned. He should have come sooner. He should not have left. His mother was feverish, so if she were to mention seeing him to anyone they would assume it an hallucination brought on by her illness. He wiped his mother's brow with a damp cloth. Then he slunk away.

5

L eaving his father's house, Quinn tramped through the bush, pausing here and there to reassess his direction or navigate past a rocky outcrop or fallen tree. He felt dazed by the conversation with his mother, but his despair at her condition was at least tempered by her belief in his innocence. For that alone it had been worth returning. The back of his neck grew tender under the afternoon sun.

It came as a shock to find himself at the town's cemetery, situated on a low hill about two miles from Flint. At the rusted gate, he turned to look down at the town. In the distance, he could see the tip of the church spire and, beyond that, the mountains blue and simmering in the haze. Heat pulsed from the ground and cicadas blazed in the surrounding trees.

Alongside the older, ramshackle graves with their carious, half-sunken headstones were fresh mounds of earth, each decorated with recently cut flowers and clean headstones. *Ginny Reynolds, Les McMahon.* Flu victims, all of them.

He had not intended to visit the cemetery but found it curiously calming, and he stayed for some time, drifting among the dead, daydreaming. There were worse places to spend eternity, he supposed, and thought of those millions interred beneath the icy soils of France, in butcher-shop pieces.

It was inevitable to ponder death in times of war and illness, but he could never imagine an afterlife. He had endured nights in France in close proximity to dead soldiers and always found their presence claustrophobic, as if their silence were an impossible demand. He remembered a man slumped over a roll of barbed wire, teeth bared, the dull gleam of his smile. To feel nothing, to know nothing, to be nothing, to have nothing. No wonder man invented heaven.

Sarah's grave was beneath a towering gum tree. A fly buzzed about Quinn's face. He paused, panting in the drowsy afternoon. He stared at the headstone and felt a long way from anywhere, as if the rest of the world had drifted off, or he from it. He grabbed at a tree branch as one might the railing on a pitching ship until the sensation subsided. He waved away the damn fly, but it was replaced by another. His immense grief was precisely why he had not visited until now. He knew it would be like this. His sister. His poor, murdered sister. Would that he were able to exchange places with her—even for alternate days, as the twins of legend, Pollux and Castor, had been permitted to do.

The inscription on the headstone was weathered but perfectly legible.

Sarah Louise Walker
1897–1909
Taken too soon
Blessed are the pure in heart

He squatted by the grave and squinted out over the countryside. It was almost beautiful here. He pondered what his mother had said, over and over, until the words tolled like an incantation. A distant flock of birds caught his eye, and for a second, as they banked, they appeared not to be flying at all but rather hanging in the blue sky. Indeed, the entire world seemed stilled. *I would do anything to have Sarah back again. I would do anything to have Sarah back again. I would do anything to have Sarah back again.* A light breeze ruffled his hair. The world continued its revolution. The illusion gave way.

He plucked a length of dry grass and chewed on it. It was tender and sweet—grass that had perhaps been nourished by the remains of his sister, its threadling roots having sprung from her hollowed-out ribcage, the place where her heart had once thrived. He rested a palm on the baking earth, as if to reassure Sarah of his determination to help. He would do whatever she required of him, as soon as it was clear.

Last year, Quinn had met people in London who believed the dead could communicate with the living, but he reasoned it had little purpose unless the living were also able to offer something to those who had departed. Not that he knew what he might say to Sarah, should he ever have the opportunity. *I'm sorry* was inadequate now. *I'm sorry I was so late.*

Ever since Sarah's birth, Quinn had been amazed by his sister. Like their mother, Sarah was renowned for her beauty, her wit and her exuberance. Her presence altered any room she entered, as if she possessed a current that charged the very air. She convinced William for a time she could fly but chose to walk so people wouldn't know of her powers. She tried to hypnotise their father with his own fob watch. She could draw forth cicadas by means of a curious song she warbled in her throat. His mother was right: Sarah used to order him around, could make him do almost anything. Once she demanded he wheel her about in a red wooden trolley for an entire day after he lost a wager over some minor matter that he couldn't even recall. Any other older brother would have refused—there was no way William would have ever agreed to such a demand, assuming he had been of the temperament to make such a foolish bargain in the first place—but Quinn acquiesced and endured the opprobrium of his brother and father, who suspended work on the fence they were repairing to watch. *Look at that*, they'd muttered. *Bloody hell.*

⁂

When Quinn returned to his campsite beneath the pines, he felt sure someone had rummaged through his bag. The black, tubular entrails of his gas mask spilled from its haversack and his trench coat, which he had hung securely from a branch, was slumped in the dirt. Nothing was taken, however. His demob papers, his pay book, his few clothes were all there. A chill clambered through him. He stood still, expecting to hear or otherwise detect something in the breeze, a whisper or shift that might alert him to an unwelcome presence. He drew his revolver and patrolled the immediate vicinity, pausing here and there to examine a broken twig or possible footprint. But he found nothing and returned to his camp to make a fire.

During the war he had heard of soldiers being driven mad by the certainty they had been selected—through what process no one could say—by an enemy sniper, and these crazed men would expend valuable energy dodging and weaving through the trenches and across duckboards in the hope of escaping the bullet they were convinced was intended for them. It was a sensation Quinn now understood. Every so often he swivelled in the expectation of spying the looming shadow of the idiot Edward Fitch or, worse, his own uncle and father, come to hang him. It was well known that the bush in these parts sustained creatures undiscovered by natural science, and as a boy he had seen unfamiliar smears and paw prints in the mud by the river, perhaps those of water babies, or frog people, or hairy giants; those beasts created far from the sight of God. The blackfellas said there lived nearby a being who possessed the shape of a man but was red all over, with suckers at the ends of his fingers and toes to drain the blood from his victims.

Quinn strained his hearing. He jammed a finger into his ears. Nothing. Still nothing.

The doctors had told him the loss of hearing was a result of the booming sixty-pounders and there was little they could do for him. They said it would be temporary, but sometimes it felt as if the mud from those damn French battlefields would clog his ears forever. At times he heard the roar of a bushfire, at others a high-pitched keening. Over the past few months he had become accustomed to the noise, but the relative silence of the Australian countryside only made him more conscious of it, as if the war were still going on inside his skull. Indeed, his limited hearing now made him acutely aware of the sounds of his own body working away beneath the skin—of the creak of neck joints when he turned his head, his plodding heart, the gurgle and sing of his blood. Still, he was lucky. He had been told of one fellow who suffered a similar complaint, but for whom the sound in his ears was of a cat purring at his shoulder all day. There were, however, compensations for his diminished hearing; he felt sure his eyesight had improved in order to balance his damaged senses and believed he could now see things others could not. In London, for example, he had been able to spot acquaintances in milling crowds that remained unseen to those with him.

He sat on a log and stared into his fire. A spark corkscrewed skywards, like an angel being dragged back to heaven. It was odd to be alone. During the war he grew used to the press of many bodies, to the whiff of other men and their whispering hearts of fear. They were a brotherhood of terror huddled in the trenches with their foreheads pressed to earthen walls, from which they would pick scabs of dirt while awaiting bombardment or rifle crack. He didn't fear death. He imagined there were few miseries he hadn't experienced, and while those around him prayed for their lives, his prayers were far more simple—for release from all this.

Again he circled the immediate area surrounding his camp but could find nothing further and, when he was sure there was no man or creature observing him, he collapsed to the ground and fell into a fitful sleep.

6

The next day Quinn again made his way to his father's property. As before, he waited behind the low shrubs until certain there was no one else around, then trotted across the yard and crept into the house.

His attention was drawn to the short, horizontal pencil marks on the doorjamb between the kitchen and hallway. They recorded the heights of all three children. Each birthday, his father would brandish a ruler and pencil with ceremony (*No standing on toes! No slouching!*) to measure how much each of them had grown in the past year. Nathaniel, whose tongue always protruded from his lips when he concentrated, saying, *Hmmm, not so good this year. Must eat more carrots.* Mary laughing and gathering the other two squealing children to her, patting their hair in place with a wetted palm.

His father's crooked scrawl was now almost illegible. Quinn bent down and ran his fingertips across the words. Within the simple *William 1900 12yrs or Sarah 1905 8yrs* there nestled entire sagas of bruised knees and the time William nearly cut off his hand while chopping wood. How Sarah was always short for her age on account of having to spend a winter in bed with fever. She also missed a year when she decided she was too old for that sort of thing. Of William, who spent a night beside Sutton Creek to wait for the bunyip Sarah said she had spied there one day, describing the awful creature in such detail that Quinn—who knew the tale to be fabricated—found himself avoiding the area for some weeks. And his sister, poor Sarah, whose measurement for her twelfth birthday was the final entry for any of them.

When Quinn entered his mother's room, she was asleep but woke with a start after several minutes. Her bony hand wandered out to him. Her tongue clacked in her dry mouth.

"Quinn?"

"Yes."

"Is that really you? Here in this room? I thought I dreamed you before—I mean I *have* dreamed of you. Many times. What are you doing here?" Her disbelief was heartbreaking. "I told people all sorts of things. Stories. We thought you were dead. I assumed you were dead. Everything so sudden and fast. I have mourned you, Quinn. For you and your sister both." She fumbled at a sheaf of papers by her side until she located what she sought, and pressed on him a crumpled piece of paper.

"What's this?"

"It's the telegram they sent. From the Army."

Quinn handled the telegram with distaste. Her eagerness to show him news of his own death was disconcerting. He hesitated before opening it. The words were faded. He skimmed and made out *Regret*, then *Sergeant Walker. Died painlessly. Pozières. Gallant. His country.* He refolded the telegram and handed it back to her.

Again she stared at him until, with a vague wave, she indicated her own face. "Your injury. You have changed so much. Surely only I would recognise you."

"You have changed, too."

She nodded as she drank from a glass of water, handed the glass back to him. "Well, a lot has happened. Besides, I suspect I am dying. The doctor refuses to say a word about it and your father thinks there will be a miracle cure any day now, you know how he is. He pores over journals and talks to anyone he thinks might know something." She paused to catch her breath. "I have lost almost everyone, you know. All my children. Sarah, of course. You. Your brother moved to Queensland. My parents. Dear Robert comes by sometimes, but he is busy with his job. So many good people died in the war. Your father has gone wild.

He took up drink and gets into fights at Sully's. He *will* kill you if he finds you. He has told me a hundred times. Robert, too. They will not be swayed. Your father became someone different from the man I married—I mean, he was always of his own mind but he never goes to church since it happened, and I am here lying in bed, dying. They call it a flu, but it is surely something more serious than that. There is talk of other, worse things. Some say it is the plague. Here, in the twentieth century, can you imagine, Quinn?"

The heat of the room was mammalian, oppressive. Quinn stepped over to the curtain and parted it a fraction to peer outside. A slice of daylight keened into the dim room.

"Do you remember how Apollo inflicted a plague on the Greeks for kidnapping Chryseis? Do you remember how I read that to you, Quinn? *The Iliad*? When you were a boy? Those stories I read to you and . . . the others?"

She licked her lips. "When my parents died I inherited my father's library, as you know. He had been a voracious reader, had books sent out from London, journals and the like. This is right after I was married, and Robert had left for England. Your father and I had moved to Bathurst, and I was dreadfully lonely. And I recall picking a book at random from one of the crates and starting to read, and before I knew it the afternoon had darkened and my weeping had been kept at bay for several hours."

Mary took another sip of water. "*A Thousand and One Nights*," she said with relish. "Even now I think of the City of Brass, the dead queen with quicksilver eyes. Magic carpets. I read them to you. An old book it was, with purple and gold pictures. My goodness. Full of genies and bearded men and giant eagles, a magnetic mountain that sucked the nails from the hull of a ship. Those stories were better than dreams. They transported me, Quinn. Not even the Bible had managed that. Your father was quite alarmed, not helped by the foolish legend going around that anyone who finished all the stories would die. He thought it unnatural for a woman to read so much. I credit those crates of books for—well, not quite saving my life, of course, but something close to it. A good story is like medicine, in my opinion."

His mother had become more animated, but now she closed her eyes, as if the effort of speech had exhausted her. Quinn traced the lumpy scar at his mouth. The bed squeaked under him when he shifted his weight.

"And do you remember all those other stories I told you?" she asked.

Of course he remembered. His mother's storytelling abilities were renowned. On winter nights all five of them would assemble in front of the fire—Nathaniel sucking on his pipe, William huddled with arms folded about his knees, Sarah resting against Quinn's shoulder—as their mother's voice, pitching and growling, altering with each character, swirled around the darkness. She told them of Tom the chimney sweep and his encounter with the water babies, of Peter Rabbit, of Gulliver's travels to the land of the savage and frightening Yahoos. She didn't even need a book. If called upon to manufacture something from thin air, she could stitch together a tale from all she had heard over the years, even adding a few creations of her own: a race of tiny folk who lived in the garden on old tea leaves, an insect with the face of a dog. She could make even the moral verses from the *Boy's Own Paper* exciting.

"How I have missed my children," she continued. "A cavern inside me. And I have ventured there often searching for you, but it is always empty. I want to ask you more but I am unsure if I even want to know. I have resisted hearing too much about that day. It is enough that it happened. More than enough. I would often sit in your old room, the room you all shared, and an entire day would pass. Your brother was unable to sleep in there after what happened and left soon afterwards, in any case. He slept in the hallway or on the veranda until he went north. You all left, but the room is the same.

"You remember Sarah's little cigar box of things she collected? Her lucky things? She had a feather in there and I went through a period when I would clutch it—you will think me mad on this—in my right hand and hold it to my forehead and pray. Later I developed a peculiar certainty that by doing so and saying a part of some Byron poem she might return to me, or perhaps I to her. That you all would, because it was only after that day that so much went wrong. Her . . . her death was at the heart of everything."

Mary paused again. "I did the same sort of thing with your cigarette cards, William's soldiers. Incantations they were, I suppose. Blasphemous, probably. Your father hates that I go in there. Says I'm being maudlin. Perhaps he is right but now he leaves me to my own devices. He almost never spoke of her death. Said he didn't want to infect people with our grief. In*fect* them, what a word! It is one thing to die but another thing entirely to do so in such a manner. Murder. No one knew what to say to me. Even the minister. And now the war, the plague. No one knows what to say to anyone anymore . . ." Her voice trailed away.

Soon she fell asleep. He watched her for a long time. She gasped for breath, twitched, whispered words he was unable to decipher. As he cooled her face and neck with a damp cloth, an idea took hold in him until it had assumed the status of a conviction. To care for his mother, to allow her some peace, at least, to ensure she knew no child of hers was guilty of murder: perhaps this was why he had been summoned? Somewhat heartened, he kissed her burning cheek, and returned to his campsite.

7

That night, Quinn lay back, snugged into the curve his shoulders had made in the pine needles and stared up at the darkness. The moon hove into view. The forest spoke in its secret tongue, and if he turned his head and pressed his ear to the ground he fancied he might hear the millions of dead rustling in their mass, unmarked graves on the far side of the world. Sarah had always claimed to understand the language of animals and trees, the growls of possums and wallabies. But what of the dead?

The previous year, while on leave in London, he had visited a celebrated spiritualist with his friend Fletcher Wakefield, whose fiancée in Adelaide had died of tuberculosis. Fletcher grinned a lot, one of those fellows invariably described as *irrepressible*. In their dormitory at Abbey Wood, he talked to Quinn about his late sweetheart and of the wedding they had planned. Although this conversation took many diversions, it always ended with Fletcher regretting how he had missed his chance to tell Doris how much he loved her and how she was without a doubt—without *any doubt* in the world—the most beautiful woman he had ever seen. *Far too good for me*, would generally be the self-mocking postscript. *Far too good.*

Quinn was reluctant to attend, but Fletcher, who had gone to numerous séances before, assured him the spirits only spoke to those with an open heart and who asked the medium a specific question. The spirits, by their nature, were only concerned with those interested in them. This was perhaps some consolation.

London was teeming with such places at the time and there was no shortage of people wishing to communicate with dear ones who had crossed over. There were women who conjured spirits that rapped on the undersides of tables, men who photographed ghostly faces hovering about one's shoulders in velvet-dark rooms, a medium who spoke in the voice of a long-dead Indian chief. Quinn had even heard of a young lady who, from her ears, could draw forth the gelatinous substance of which ghosts were made. To Quinn it seemed the world was suddenly so full of grieving people that to wander London's streets was to feel the press not only of those present and alive, but also to be aware of their collective longing for loved ones killed in the Great War.

Along with eight others, Quinn and Fletcher filed into the wood-panelled parlour of the Marylebone house of a Mrs. Alice Cranshaw whose triplet daughters, it was said, possessed the ability to hear the voices of those who had departed this world, and to relay their messages to those still living.

Mrs. Cranshaw's parlour was warm and dark. The lady herself was stout and middle-aged and smoked a cigarette in a holder while casting an imperious gaze over the throng. Fletcher greeted an acquaintance, leaving Quinn unaccompanied. He felt conspicuous in his uniform and endeavoured to remain unnoticed, but Mrs. Cranshaw beckoned to him and drew him so close he could feel her breath's wet bluster on his cheek.

"And who are you here for, my dear?"

"Pardon?"

The woman made an odd movement with her mouth, as if chewing her own tongue, before sliding the glistening holder between her lips. Her hair was like so much wire arranged atop her head. Quinn cast about for Fletcher, but he was still engaged in conversation. Mrs. Cranshaw gripped his arm. There were flecks of spittle on the corners of her mouth. "Don't worry, boy. I won't eat you," she said, although she nibbled on her cigarette holder, which he now saw was made of jade, as if preparing to do just that.

He longed to withdraw his arm but felt it would be rude to do so. She terrified him, a fact of which she was undoubtedly aware and in which she probably delighted.

"Nobody ma'am," he said at last, and indicated Fletcher. "I'm here with my friend. He wishes to, er, speak with his late fiancée."

Mrs. Cranshaw frowned. "Oh, but I am sure there is someone. We have all lost someone close in these dark times. A friend? A brother who might have crossed over? Someone in the war?"

Quinn glanced again at Fletcher.

"Are you afraid of death?" Mrs. Cranshaw asked with a hint of mockery.

Quinn thought about this. "No."

"You don't believe what we do here though, do you?"

"That's not for me to say."

"Very diplomatic, but you can tell me. I don't mind. You don't believe in the spirit world?"

"I don't think so, ma'am."

"But you look afraid. Are you afraid, boy?"

"I have no wish to hear what the dead might have to say. Besides, why would they come back here?"

Mrs. Cranshaw sighed. "The spirits are sometimes—how to put this?—unquiet. Restless. Death is not always the end of things for everyone. There is often unfinished business, especially for those killed suddenly and violently—like in war. Sometimes the dead are trapped in an awful halfway world until they can say something to those left behind. Indeed, the living are sometimes themselves trapped, until they hear what the dead might have to tell them. There are some things that cannot be left unsaid. But if you don't believe in it all, then there is no need to be afraid, is there?"

Quinn realised he despised this woman and, worse, suspected she was a charlatan preying on vulnerable families. It was rumoured she kept the girls—who were probably not her daughters at all—against their will. Everyone knew the Bible prohibited talking with the dead. He attempted to withdraw his arm, a movement that only prompted the woman to clench him tighter.

"You know who was here a few weeks ago? Doyle, that's who. Sir Arthur. Ask the maid if you wish. Or Mrs. Beecroft wearing the white scarf. She was here. Seeking word from his son or wife, he was. My girl Lizzie was able to help him out. Ever so grateful, he was. I'm surprised he isn't here this afternoon, but I suppose he's busy. He's a doctor, after all. A man of science, you know."

When Quinn offered no response, Mrs. Cranshaw lowered her voice. "You may think what you wish," she rasped, now staring at him squarely in the eye. "But these good people are all quite bereaved. They need to hear from their dead. Their brothers and husbands. Their sisters. There's millions of them, you know. *Millions*. It softens their grief. Besides, this is part of the war effort; we need to remember their killers so they might be brought to account. If we forget those beastly Huns our boys will have died in vain, don't you know. See that lady there with the pale shawl over her widow's weeds? See her? Mrs. Henry Dance. Three out of four sons gone." She held up three knobbly fingers. "Three out of four. Do you see the way she watches you and your grinning friend?"

Quinn shook his head. Indeed, he had not noticed the woman until that moment.

Mrs. Cranshaw was strangely triumphant. "Well, she *hates* you because you are alive while her sons are in a mass grave. In bloody France, of all places. Cold and alone. Quite dead. What would you say to her? What would you say to a woman like that, eh? What would you say to her husband?"

The woman in question was perched in a green armchair. Her thin and restless fingers wrung a pair of black gloves in her lap, as if to death. Her husband stood at her shoulder and each of them wore a startled, pensive expression like they had steeled themselves for bad news so many times that their faces were permanently set thus.

"They are tired of sympathy," Mrs. Cranshaw went on. "Of people's kind words and the newspaper chatter about honour and bravery and sacrifice. They need a sign from their boys. Would you begrudge them that? Where should they go, these people? To *church*?" And she let go of his arm as if ridding herself of an ungrateful child.

Quinn felt humiliated and prepared to take his leave, but a warm hush descended on the gathering as three girls filed in with heads lowered. They took their places at a long table upon which were scrolls of paper, one before each girl. The girls were similar, aside from the fact that two were blonde while the last, the prettiest, had hair the colour of damp rust. Again he scanned the room, hoping to depart, but at that moment a maid had closed the door, trapping him in the parlour.

⊰⊱

Quinn heard a soft crack behind him. He leaped to his feet and fumbled with his revolver. He faced the direction of the noise. It sounded as though someone were stepping about in the darkness beyond the fire's light. He aimed and cocked the weapon. "Who's there?" he hissed. "Show yourself."

He angled his head to give his right ear—which he perceived to be less damaged—the chance to detect something but heard nothing more. He stayed where he was, just breathing. The sodden sponges of his damn ears. Again he moved his head this way and that, straining to hear. There was only the sputtering growl of the nearby fire.

Then, to his right, in the fire's flicker, he made out something gathered about a low bush. It was several feet away, unclear in the darkness. He stared until he could see the glint of silver or brass. He tensed. A piece of cloth. A torn piece of cloth. Now a button. Two buttons. A man's uniform, English by the look of it. He blinked and peered further. A hand, unattached to any limb, the wrist a bloody tangle of wiry veins and gristle blackened where it had been ripped from the forearm. There was a muddy boot on the ground.

Then the snap of a twig behind him. Without thinking he wheeled and fired his gun, always surprised at the weapon's sullen buck. The revolver's blue smoke hung in the night air. A whiff of gunpowder. He stood unmoving. Nothing.

After several minutes, as he prepared to sit again, convinced he had imagined the entire thing, the crash of something thumping through the undergrowth some distance away, the noise of it growing ever fainter, retreating along the ridge. Quinn swore. Was it possible his sister's murderer knew already he had returned, and sought to kill him? His heart quickened. He checked his revolver. He waited. He prayed.

Part Two

THE GIRL

~

8

The next morning, Quinn opened his eyes from a tangled sleep before dawn. The light was thin, aquatic. The air was fresh and cold. He was lying on his side beneath his trench coat, hands clamped between his thighs for warmth.

The fire was now little more than a smoking pile of grey shards. Startled, he looked around. There, on the other side of the fire, squatted a rangy, blonde-haired girl, perhaps ten or eleven years old, who was watching him with frank interest. Quinn sat up and prepared to draw his revolver, but the girl didn't move. She appeared to be alone.

"Who are you?" he asked.

The girl sniffed and wiped a hand under her nose. She wore a ragged dress that might once have been blue but had faded to the colour of a week-old bruise. A pink cardigan, no shoes, toes like stubby shells at the ends of her feet. She had a sharp chin, hobnail teeth hammered into her gums.

Quinn's mouth was sticky with sleep. Dirt crumbed from his face. His neck was sore from sleeping on the uneven ground. He ran a hand through his hair. "Who are you? Have you been there for long? Watching me? Are you alone?"

The girl didn't seem to register the fact he had spoken at all. Not only were her eyes the dark brown of a moth's wing, but—even open, as they were now—they fluttered gently, almost preparing for flight. She stared at the surrounding trees as if listening to what they were saying, idly scratching one foot as she did so. She was perhaps not right in the head. Another simpleton, like that Edward Fitch.

Neither of them spoke. She made Quinn uneasy. He brushed himself down and set about rebuilding the fire, throwing on handfuls of dry leaves and blowing on the smouldering embers. He was hungry, although this was nothing new: he had been famished for years.

The girl watched him with her dark eyes. "What are you doing up here?" she said at last.

"I could ask you the same thing."

She pursed her lips and pondered this. "Go on then."

"What?"

"Ask me, then. What I'm doing up here."

"That would be idiotic."

"Not if you wanted to know it wouldn't be."

He snapped a branch in half across one knee and threw it on the embers. "To be honest, I don't really care."

The leaves had begun to burn and now the larger pieces of wood crackled and glowed. He drew unaccountable pleasure from this limited control over such a dangerous element. He blew on the leaves some more and tossed on another handful of bracken. The girl watched him in the manner of someone who knew a better way to do the task at hand but was biting her tongue. The fire took hold. He sat back on his haunches and decided to humour her. "Alright, then. What are you doing up here by yourself so early?"

"I can't tell you."

"Why not?"

"It's a secret."

Quinn smiled despite himself, then covered his mouth with one hand. Although the scar stained only the left part of his mouth and jaw, there was a certain tightness about his entire face when he assumed particular expressions. His smile, he knew, was now lopsided and somewhat sinister, as if one half of him were amused while the other unimpressed by the same joke. He stood and put on his trench coat.

"What happened to your face?"

Quinn blushed and kicked at the edges of the fire. "The war. I got injured."

"I always live up here. I live in these hills."

Quinn doubted this boast, but nodded by way of answer. He had wandered these ranges as a boy and knew there was little here apart from boulders and bushes, the dark and disordered press of trees. No people lived up here now the miners had gone.

The girl licked her lips. "I have a house. A *whole* house, hidden away where no one can find it." She looked inordinately pleased to have told Quinn this and said nothing more for a few minutes, before standing to stretch and yawn. Now she was upright, Quinn could see she was a bony cat of a girl, all angles and joints. "But you never answered my question."

"What question?"

"Why are you up here when your house is down there?"

"How do you know where I used to live?"

Her smile was thin-lipped, as if what she prepared to reveal pained her. "I know all sorts of things."

Quinn was suspicious, but the girl appeared guileless. She had probably heard whispers about him, from her parents or town gossip. People around here talked when they had nothing better to do and invented facts to fill the spaces in their knowledge, the way ancient cartographers surmised entire continents into existence. And children, he knew, were most susceptible to these fantasies, because their understanding of the world was so limited.

"Are you by yourself?" he asked.

The girl ignored him and untangled a twig from her hair.

"I'll make a deal with you. I'll tell you why I'm up here if you tell me if there's anyone with you."

That got her attention. She regarded him. "You go first then."

"I'm here to see someone. Someone I need to help."

"A friend?"

"A relative."

"Who?"

He paused. "I can't tell you that."

"That's not a proper answer."

"Now it's your turn. Are you up here with anyone?"

"No."

Quinn was not convinced. Had she been as vague in her answers as he had been? In the brightening morning light the girl seemed insubstantial, and he recalled fairy tales of wars between giants and men, how the still-warm blood of the dead villains was given to the few imps who remained so they could assume the shape of people. And in Europe after the war, orphans ran through villages stealing bread and firewood, planting curses on the old men and women. Although they were probably just tall stories, he suspected such mythical children were best kept at a distance.

"Where are your mother and father?" he asked.

She glanced away, muttered something.

"What?"

"My father left years ago."

"Did he go to the war?"

"Not to the war. Before I was born. Mother is dead because of the plague. There's a plague, you know."

Quinn flinched and mentally chastised himself. These days it was sometimes best not to enquire after anyone's family, lest the answer be one such as that. "Oh, I'm sorry. What about a brother or sister? Who's looking after you then?"

She scratched her arm. "I can take care of myself. I told you. I have a house. Over there." And she gestured behind her.

The girl was at once frail and self-possessed, and although he was intimidated by her, this was tempered by a curious compulsion to befriend her. "How old are you?"

"Twelve, I think."

"You think?"

"Well. How old are you?"

"I thought you knew lots of things?"

She tugged at the sleeve of her cardigan.

Quinn regretted his insolence. He had an idea. "Are you looking for a sheep? A lamb? I saw one yesterday down the other side of this hill. We could find it? I'll show you where I saw it."

The child shook her head. "He's not mine. I told you—I live up here. I'm not a shepherd." She added in a softer voice he could barely hear, "But that wasn't yesterday. That was days ago."

This took a moment to register. "You were watching me?"

She said something he didn't understand.

"What? What did you say? The guns have damaged my ears. You need to speak up."

"I said: He *told* me about you."

Quinn chuckled. His initial instinct was correct: the child was simple. "Right. The lamb told you."

"Said you hugged him, too."

"Don't be ridiculous. You must have been watching me."

"I wasn't. He told me."

He was incredulous. "You know how to talk to sheep?"

She pouted. "No. Only how to understand them."

"And how do you do that?"

"Listen. You just have to listen to them. I told you before. I know about lots of things. I know about the wind and stars, about what happens in rivers." The girl shrugged limply.

"What else did the lamb tell you then?"

She brushed back a tumble of hair from her face and withdrew a burning twig from the fire. She waved it around until the tiny flame was extinguished, then watched the thread of smoke unfurl from its glowing tip. The end of her tongue edged provocatively between her lips. "He told me what you said to him."

Quinn dug out his tin of tobacco and set about rolling a smoke. His fingers trembled. The tobacco was as friable as soil and repeatedly crumbled from the thin paper.

"And that you were *crying*," the girl added.

Quinn blushed and devoted unnecessary attention to his cigarette. The girl unsettled him. A magpie warbled nearby.

"You don't believe me, do you?" she persisted.

Quinn jammed the cigarette between his lips and lit it with a branch from the fire. It was a good question; he was no longer sure what to believe. It seemed equally that all things were possible and also that very little was. The cigarette smoke irritated his throat. He coughed.

The girl wandered off a little way, nudging at leaves with her bare feet, stooping here and there to examine objects she spied in the dirt. Quinn put his free hand into his pocket and fondled the revolver. He supposed he could withdraw it if he needed to.

By now the sun had risen over the lip of the earth, releasing its warmth. The day was getting underway. He wondered about his mother and father down there in the valley. The residents of Flint would be starting to go about their business, eating boiled eggs and drinking mugs of tea.

The girl approached him. "Are you going to shoot me now?"

She was bold, he would say that for her. Quinn withdrew his hand from his pocket. "Don't be ridiculous." He paused. "Was that you last night in the bushes? Were you watching me?"

Unsmiling, she made a gun of her hand, pointed her index finger at him and cocked her grubby thumb. "*Who's there? Show yourself.*"

They stood unmoving for several seconds before she dissolved into laughter and sauntered about as if she owned the place. Quinn drew on his cigarette. He flicked the stub into the fire and sensed—like waves building far out at sea—a coughing attack that, sure enough, started as a series of tight gulps before cascading into spasms of painful spluttering.

The girl leaned backwards. "Do you have the plague?"

He shook his head and sat on a log. He bent double, grasping his stomach and groaning with pain until the episode subsided several minutes later, leaving him sweating and his innards quivering. When he became aware again of his surrounds, she was beside him with a hand resting on his shoulder. He resisted the urge to shrug her away and instead spat into the fire and wiped his watering mouth and eyes.

"Did you get gassed?"

He nodded.

"Where?"

"In France."

"Tom Smith was gassed, too." She crouched again and tossed twigs one by one into the fire. "You shouldn't have fired at me last night. They hear shots right through the valley . . ."

He couldn't hear what she said next. "What?"

"I said: There's sometimes people hide up here."

"What kind of people?"

The girl shrugged. "People getting away from the nubonic plague—"

"*Bu*bonic."

"What?"

"It's bubonic plague. Not *nu*bonic. And it's not that, anyway. It's influenza."

She shrugged. "Swagmen hide up here. Criminals. Sometimes blokes afraid of conscripting. Down in Flint they're afraid of everything now. Shoot people, sometimes," she added, almost as an afterthought.

"Shoot people? Who does?"

"Mr. Dalton shot a swaggie two years ago, while he was out hunting. Buried him in a gully. Dogs dug him up later on. I saw a bit of him in a dog's mouth. An arm, I think." She made a face.

Quinn started. "Why on earth did he do that?"

She regarded him as if he were a dim-witted child. "Because he could."

"Does anyone know about . . . Mr. Dalton shooting that man?"

"Of course not."

"How do you know he did it?"

"I just know." She looked at him. "He does lots of bad things."

Despite himself, Quinn shivered. He considered the child for a long time, trying to determine what she really might know. "What were you doing up here last night?"

"I told you. I live up here."

The girl was no doubt a troublemaker; still, he couldn't help but be intrigued. "What else did the lamb tell you?"

She stood and grinned, pleased she had so piqued his interest. Then he recalled she was little more than a child making up stories. He set about packing his things, eager to get away. He turned his back on her to remove the revolver from his pocket and shove it into his kitbag.

"Why should I tell you when you don't believe me?" she demanded, circling until she stood in front of him.

Quinn closed his eyes, hoping that when he re-opened them, the girl might have vanished. In France, Fletcher had told him of an apparition that presented itself in the trenches one evening ahead of battle: a melancholy, ill-dressed officer who asked for directions to the German lines, only to dissolve once the barrage was underway. But when Quinn opened his eyes, she was still there.

"You will need to kill a rabbit today," she said.

"Oh, will I?"

"Yes. If you want to eat." She stepped closer. "I can help you. I'm good at those things. Good at traps. My brother taught me."

"So, you have a brother?"

She hesitated, as if caught out in a lie. "Yes. He's a pilot in the war. But he'll be back soon."

By now Quinn had gathered his things together. "Good. Then you'll have someone to take care of you. Well, I need to go. There are things I have to do. Cheerio."

"Are you going to see your relative now?"

He wondered what to tell her. "I'm going to see my mother. She is sick. Good-bye. Good luck."

The girl began to cackle and then, in a high-pitched voice, unable to contain her giggling, said: "*There there. I won't hurt you.* That's what you said to the lamb. *I'll protect you.*"

Quinn halted. No one could have heard what he'd said to that creature. The child was standing a few feet from him, out of reach. He considered grabbing her and, as if reading his mind, she stepped back and cocked her head to listen.

Quinn watched her. He strained to hear, too. There, faintly, the sound of someone clattering across dry leaves and through the undergrowth further down the hill.

The girl looked stricken. "It's Mr. Dalton."

Quinn's blood tightened. His uncle. He swore and bent down to pick up his bag, and when he turned back there was no trace of the girl. She had dissolved, like smoke or water. He wanted to call out for her but thought better of it. He hefted his swag and plunged into the undergrowth.

He jumped and bounded and ran, slipping on rocks and stones, managing to maintain balance only by some miracle. Behind him on the ridge, a man's voice yelled out. No doubt his uncle had discovered the fire. Quinn slithered down a dusty slope on his arse. Galahs flung themselves from trees and rose shrieking into the air.

His swag was awkward to carry while running. Branches snagged on his uniform and spider webs gathered in his hair. He came to a dry creek bed overhung with low branches and dotted with leaf-dark puddles. The air was filled with the euphonic throb of cicadas, hidden from view but everywhere, making themselves known to those who could hear. He panted and turned to look back up the ridge where he glimpsed his uncle blundering through the trees a few hundred feet away.

Quinn considered his options. The incline on the opposite side was far too steep and overgrown. Robert would surely catch him and drag him back to Flint, to his father who longed to hang him for what he thought Quinn had done. The only thing was to scramble along the creek bed and hope it led somewhere safer. With one arm raised to shield his face, he ducked beneath a tangle of branches to his left.

The bed was uneven, potted with holes and littered with dead branches. His breath came in coarse, leaden clumps. He bent to crawl beneath the lowest branches, his face only two inches from the ground, and came face-to-face with what looked like a thick and gleaming turd, but revealed itself to be a brown snake curled on a rock.

Quinn froze. Rivulets of sweat poured down his face and neck. He held his breath as best he could. He could feel the dry heat rising from the sun-baked rock, the same warmth that had doubtless attracted the snake. It was a fat King Brown, had probably been living here for years. Quinn and the snake stared at each other for several long seconds. Snakes never blinked, gave nothing of themselves away, might as well have been hollow.

Then, luxuriously, like a drowsy bohemian after a mid-morning nap, the snake uncoiled. Its blue-grey tongue flickered about, tasting the air, making its reptilian calculations. Quinn knew a sudden movement would prompt it to strike. His heart thrummed and his skin itched beneath his uniform. The creature began to flatten itself out and prepare for movement. The world around Quinn drained away. The abrupt disembowelment of sensation reminded him of that split second before the shell landed near him at Pozières. That same knowing and unknowing.

He reached into his kitbag for his revolver. He would shoot the creature, even if the sound of firing gave away his position. He had to. Then run. He would shoot it and run. Keeping his eye on the snake, he rummaged gently in his bag. Nothing. The revolver was gone. It must have fallen out when he fled. Bloody hell. *Bloody hell.* Still the snake unravelled. He began to shuffle backwards but his stuttering progress was stymied by a branch that snagged on the shoulder of his uniform. He felt faint. He mumbled a prayer.

Then, in an instant, a hand swooped to grasp the snake about its neck. The girl stood before him with the flailing serpent in a slender, two-fisted grip. The snake spat and writhed and looped its long body around her forearm. Grimacing with effort, she unwound it from her pale arm, stepped past Quinn and—measuring the throw several times before she released it—tossed the snake back down the gully in the direction Quinn had come. Her face was flushed with fear and delight when she turned to him, as if the experience were a lark from the *Boy's Own Paper.* "That should put him off," she said and laughed.

Quinn was stunned. He ran a hand across the mangled portion of his lip. His mouth was dry and his skull buzzed with heat and fatigue, as if in concert with the flies and cicadas in the trees around them.

The girl began to clamber up some rocks through a narrow break in the undergrowth he hadn't noticed. She paused to address him. "You should come with me."

He heard Robert Dalton advancing up the dry gully and scrambled after her.

9

The noises of pursuit soon fell away. His uncle had probably stumbled across the furious snake and retreated. Quinn smiled at the thought. He followed the girl with difficulty, crawling up steep slopes through dense bush litter into which he sometimes plunged as far as his knees. At times he lost sight of her altogether, but she would materialise nearby, chewing on a twig or peeling bark from a tree, quietly urging him on.

After Europe's perpetual autumn, which had been made worse by the clammy dust of war, the dry air of New South Wales scorched his lungs. He was forced to stop often to cough and catch his breath. The girl grunted with effort, hitched her dirty dress. They pressed on.

Quinn had once been acquainted with every gully and rise in these ranges, but the tracks along which she led him felt as if they belonged to a different part of the district altogether. He attempted to pinpoint a tree or another landmark by which to orient himself, but there was nothing recognisable, and he was too exhausted and too fearful to think clearly. The landscape afforded little in the way of a view. There were only the ragged regiments of trees with sheets of bark unravelling from their trunks, their oddly angled branches clutching at the air. Cockatoos screeched overhead.

They went on like this for more than an hour and then they stopped. The shack the girl led him to was so thoroughly encrusted with ivy and overhung with vines and trees that they were standing in front of it before Quinn even realised.

He looked up, panting and sweating. "Where the hell are we?"

Through the foliage he could see the place was a ruin. The girl wrested his bag from him, stepped onto the crumbling porch and went inside. Quinn bent over with his palms braced on his knees. After a few minutes, he followed. There was little else to do.

Despite the sunny weather, the interior of the ruin was dark and claustral, pierced here and there with fingers of light. There was a kitchen and one other room. Skeletal branches brushed up hard against the side of the cottage. Dust had collected along the skirting boards and on the few items scattered about. There was a filthy shelf of empty bottles and jars, discarded tins of food, a pile of bricks and rubble in one corner, and the unmistakable stink of animal droppings. A faded print torn from a magazine or annual was pinned to one wall. Apple peel, piles of chicken bones and other food scraps were strewn over the floor. Quinn had seen some curious sights in the years he had been away, but this house reminded him that the world was indeed full of strange and wonderful places. There was little doubt the girl lived here alone.

He shrugged off his coat and leaned against a doorframe. A fly droned about his eyes. He unbuttoned his grubby tunic and was overcome by a burning cramp in his guts. He felt as if he had swallowed broken glass. He doubled over and slumped halfway to the rotten floor, spluttering and groaning. The girl vanished and returned a moment later with a tin mug, which she pressed into his hand.

Quinn took the mug. The water tasted of mildew but eased the pain in his throat. He thanked her, this girl who was at times childish, and at other moments seemed prematurely aged. Sweat pebbled on her upper lip, which she wiped away with the back of one hand.

Now recovered, Quinn wrestled himself to standing and loosened the remaining buttons of his tunic. The girl explained that Quinn could sleep in the kitchen. He could make a bed of his coat, she told him, adding that no one would find them because no one ever came up this way and, even if they did, they never noticed this place. "It's a complete secret," she said.

Quinn shook his head. "I can't stay here. Maybe only tonight, I don't know.'

"What do you mean? Why can't you?"

"I can't."

The girl mumbled something.

"What?"

"Where else you going to go?"

He couldn't think straight. "I don't know. I'll camp out, find a room."

She laughed. "What do you mean? You can't go back to Flint. You can't camp because Mr. Dalton will find you."

"I'll leave town, then. I can't stay here."

"You can't *leave*."

"Why not?"

"Because why did you come? What about your mother?"

Quinn hesitated. "Yes. I need to be somewhere closer to her. She's very sick. How do I get down to Flint from here?"

"I'll show you a hidden way. No one will ever see you. I'll take you tomorrow."

"Can you take me now?"

The girl shook her head. "It's too dangerous with Mr. Dalton walking around." She was right.

"What is this place, anyway?"

"I don't know. Been empty for years. Old miner's shack, I suppose."

"Why don't you stay at your father's house? Somewhere better than this."

"I told you, my father left. My mother is dead. Mr. Dalton knows my old house. This is better, safer. He'll never find us up here." She crossed her arms and leaned against a crumbling wall. "You know what he's like."

Quinn did indeed know all about Robert Dalton. His mother's younger brother was ill-suited to life in a town as small and rudimentary as Flint. He thought the people were fools. He was always bothered by the heat and the flies, and would talk fondly of his former life in his beloved England, a life to which—for reasons that were unclear—he was unable to return.

"You should stay away from him," said Quinn.

"Oh, I do." She twisted her fingers. "He used to come around even when Mother was alive, when Thomas had left for the war. Said he was seeing if he could help us, but Mother told him we were fine, thanks all the same, *no one's taking my daughter away from me. Bloody do-gooder*, she used to call him. He came around a lot. I used to hide."

"Hide up here?"

"Other places, too. I have very good hiding places. He came again after Mother died but I ran off. Tried to catch me. Said he'd take me to a church place in Bathurst. He's been up in the hills searching for me. He can't find me by himself, but that tracker Gracie is away in Bathurst hunting for a bloke that killed his wife. He won't be back for weeks, they all reckon."

"When did your mother die?"

She grew pensive. "Couple of weeks ago. She was sick for only five days."

"What's your name?"

"Sadie Fox," she said, but without conviction. She pushed greasy hair from her face. "You're Quinn, aren't you?"

"How do you know my name?"

"Quinn *Walker*," she said with relish. "Everyone knows about you."

"What do you mean? I haven't been here for years."

"I know. They all think you're dead in the war."

Quinn thought of the telegram that his mother had shown him. He sighed and crouched to pick burrs from his khaki trousers.

"Do you know what they call you?"

He glanced up. "Who?"

The girl was thrilled at what she knew. She stepped from foot to foot in excitement. "In town. People in town. What they call you? They still talk about what you done. I hear them."

Quinn paced about, picking at the peeling walls and jabbing shards of broken wood with the toe of his boot. "What?" he asked, trying in vain to sound uninterested.

"There was even a reward, I heard them—"

"What?" he hissed. "What do they call me?"

She shrank back but remained defiant. "They all call you the Murderer."

He halted at the cold stove, partly sunken into the rotted floor and peppered with animal droppings. He ran a finger over its rusty surface. In fleeing this town and traversing the world he had imagined, foolishly, that he might be able to escape the major fact of his life; but there it was, contained in the prison of two words. It was both the reason he had never come back, and why he had now returned. *The Murderer.*

"They say you stabbed your sister," the girl went on. "Years ago. And other things, too. They say you did *worse* things to her—"

"I didn't do it."

"Then who did?"

He hesitated, wondering whether to tell her the truth he had never told anyone. "God, I would *never* do anything like that . . ."

Still she watched him, waited.

"You can't tell anyone. If I tell you, my mother can't know."

The girl took a step forward. "I won't tell. Promise. Cross my heart."

"It was my uncle," he said eventually. "And someone else. Another man, I don't know who"

Sadie did not look surprised. She cleared her throat. "That's what Mr. Dalton wants with me, isn't it?"

Quinn didn't answer. It was grotesque a girl should have even the barest inkling of what such a man would want with her.

"What happened? What did you see?" she persisted.

He shook his head. "I can't tell you."

"Are you here for revenge?" she asked.

"No—" He caught himself. "I don't know."

"You should be. Especially if everyone thinks you did it."

He waved her away. "Maybe I'll go to the police. I'll tell them what happened. Who it was."

She gave him a queer look and shook her head. "Didn't anyone tell you?"

"Tell me what?"

"You don't know?"

"What?"

"Robert Dalton *is* the police."

Quinn's heart grew limp. "I don't believe you."

She stared at him. Her eyes were lit with a fierce glow. "Robert Dalton is the constable in Flint. For the whole district. He took over from Mr. Mackey ages ago. No one will ever believe he killed your sister. You know that, anyway. They love him. They think he is honourable and upstanding. I have heard them. All of them. Even though he drinks grog. They talk about him like he was a saint. Even your mother. *Especially* your mother."

Quinn sat in stunned silence. He felt sick, as if the air had drained from the room.

"You were there, though," she continued. "That's what your father says."

He bent down until their eyes were level. "Why aren't *you* afraid of me then, if that's what they all call me? If I'm the Murderer?"

She stood her ground. "Because. Because I can tell you are as afraid of Mr. Dalton as I am."

❖

When it was dark, they ate cold beans and dry bread, and Sadie told Quinn of other things: Mrs. Taylor, who wept every night over the deaths of her three sons in the war; the McClaren boy, who died from the plague and how a slug of blood leaked from his ear when they carried him from the house; how the Reverend's daughter Casey Smail got pregnant by a travelling salesman and they took her to the Chinaman to drink a potion that dissolved her baby; the Harman boy, who came back from the war possessed by the Devil; that his uncle Robert Dalton sometimes visited the widowed Mrs. Higgins late at night. Who was dead, who married—the events that tangle and weave, over time, to make a town's history.

The girl spoke quickly, laughing, barking out details at random, as if desperate to divest herself of the information she had gathered. "I go down into town at night and peek in the windows," she said with a shrug when Quinn asked how she knew so much of the town's happenings. "I have for years. I listen to things. People don't even know I'm there. I hide under their house or in a bush. People talk about all kinds of things. I've heard all sorts of secrets. That's what I mean when I say I can help you. I'm good at finding things out."

She told him about her brother Thomas, who took care of her when their seamstress mother went to Bathurst for supplies or to run errands. He had gone to fly planes in the war. "I have to wait for Thomas to get back. The war's over, isn't it? He'll know what to do, he'll look after me. He'll be back any day now, I reckon."

Quinn tore off a hunk of bread and placed it into his mouth. "Yes, the war's been over for a few months."

She beamed at this. She said she had no other relatives she knew about, perhaps an uncle in Perth but she didn't know his name, and Perth was such a long way away, wasn't it? There was nowhere else for her to go. She had to wait here for Thomas, who must be delayed by this plague, that was why things were taking so long.

⁂

Later that night, as he lay in the darkness on the floor, Sadie began singing a hymn in the next room.

> *In the sweet bye and bye*
> *We shall meet on that beautiful shore*
> *In the sweet bye and bye*
> *We shall meet on that beautiful shore*

Quinn thought back to the evening of the séance when he had been trapped in that Marylebone parlour. Mrs. Cranshaw assured the gathering that the Lord was with them in their endeavours, reminded them not to approach her girls at *any* stage and launched into a ramshackle version of that very same hymn, turning from her piano keyboard to the audience with encouraging smiles at the start of each verse. The mixture of the theatrical and the pious was unsettling and powerful; by the time the last notes had died away, one or two ladies were weeping. Then Mrs. Cranshaw, formal, head bowed, stepped aside and vanished into the shadows, leaving the three girls at their table. Quinn's view was blocked momentarily by a shoulder, then by the ostrich feathers of a lady's hat. A young man whispered something to his companion. Fletcher stood with his hands at his sides and a hopeful light in his eyes. The room hummed with anticipation.

The three girls sat with palms flat upon the table and closed their eyes. They were about fourteen years of age, Quinn guessed. Each of them wore a white dress and had her hair tied back with ribbons. Their faces were pale as small moons atop their fragile necks. Quinn stepped from foot to foot. A carriage passed in the street outside. It would be dark by the time he and Fletcher got away from here. The damp washcloth of evening would already be falling over the London streets, and it was at that moment that Quinn yearned for Australia, where the light was sheer and full, without edges or mercy.

One of the blonde girls jerked upright and mouthed something. Then her entire body convulsed. Her eyelids quivered and she began, with eyes still shut, to scrawl on the paper with a pencil. Her blonde companion emitted a low hum and followed suit. Neither of them took much notice of what they were doing. The first girl allowed her head to bob about this way and that on her shoulders as if manipulated by unseen hands.

Despite Quinn's scepticism, the entire scene—with its flickering lamps and droning girls, its sharp fug of tobacco smoke—terrified him. He was aware of the prickle of sweat on his skin. The last girl, the red-haired one, just sat there and gradually the room fell away—the curtains, the furniture, the shelves of books—until it was as if she and Quinn alone remained. Her eyes were closed and her face upturned, catlike, as if whatever she hoped to detect would come through her nostrils. Her skin was lit by an inner light. After several minutes she opened her eyes, and her gaze settled on Quinn as if his had been the face she had sought all along.

She stared at Quinn for so long that people began to glance at him, whispering, as if he were the instigator of their mute exchange. Eventually, the girl bent to the desk and started to write, stopping every few seconds as if listening to and deciphering instructions. A limp curl of red hair fell across her face, but she did not brush it away. Her mouth puckered and twitched.

After fifteen minutes, the girls ceased moaning and fell still with their chins upon their chests. The audience watched in rapt silence as Mrs. Cranshaw detached herself from the shadows, roused each of the girls in turn and guided them away, uttering maternal sounds as she did so. Quinn was unsure what he had witnessed, but applause rippled through the assembly before it dissolved into twitters and exclamations of amazement. "*Extraordinary*," a nearby woman whispered. "My, my," said another. "Did you see how they looked?"

There followed a hubbub as Mrs. Cranshaw re-emerged with shards of paper that Quinn recognised as having been torn from the rolls on which the girls had been writing. She then proceeded to call out the names that were scrawled there: "Mr. Wright? A message for Mr. Wright. Thank you, sir, that will be ten shillings. Is there someone known to Emily . . . *Masters*, is it? Pasters? Marsden? A child, I believe. The . . . mother, perhaps? An aunt? No? Aaah, Miss Wilcox. Glad you were able to come this week. I *know*, it's rained non-stop, hasn't it? Still, it could be worse. Mr. Conroy. Mr. Conroy, is your wife feeling better? Good, good . . ."

Quinn backed from the parlour to wait for Fletcher in the hall. He was desperate to get away and only hoped Mrs. Cranshaw wouldn't confront him again. People bustled past, some clutching pieces of paper, their faces distorted by sorrow or joy. When Fletcher joined him, he was downcast, as there had been no word from his fiancée. He spoke already of visiting another medium, one that was particularly adept at conversing with young ladies who had crossed over.

Quinn was adamant that he would never let Fletcher persuade him to attend such an event again. They put on their hats, shuffled through the heavy door and were stepping down to the wet and shining street when they heard the thump of footsteps. A voice called out to them. Quinn turned to see the red-haired girl hurrying towards them along the carpeted hall, pinching her dress at the knee to forestall tripping on its hem. Her face was flushed and, before he could query Fletcher for guidance on what might be happening or how to respond, the girl had bounded down the stairs, pressed herself against him and flung her arms about his waist.

"Thank you ever so much for coming," she whispered before stepping back inside with evident reluctance. The whole episode lasted barely five seconds, but a fresh unease gripped Quinn's innards.

Mrs. Cranshaw herself then swung into the hallway behind the girl, eyes ablaze, her mouth as tight as wire. She looked from the girl to Quinn to Fletcher. Unsettled and confused about what had actually transpired, Quinn straightened his crumpled tunic and fastened the remainder of its buttons. His breath fogged out in front of him. Drizzle needled through the halo of a streetlamp. How on earth had he allowed Fletcher to drag him to this terrible place?

Mrs. Cranshaw had by now rested a hand upon the red-haired girl's shoulder—and not entirely maternally, Quinn thought. Indeed the girl stumbled backwards as her mother—if this woman really were her mother—shoved herself off and set sail down the wet stairs. Fletcher addressed the fast-approaching Mrs. Cranshaw with a remark that she should keep an eye on the girl, who seemed a trifle rattled after her experience with the dead. Mrs. Cranshaw ignored the comment as she placed herself before Quinn.

"What did she say to you?" she demanded in a low voice.

Sunk into the collar of his tunic against the damp air, Quinn wanted to be elsewhere, somewhere warm. He grasped a prong of the iron fence. The cold, wet metal reminded him that in two days he would be back in France and he sensed the pointless shrug of his heart.

Mrs. Cranshaw stepped closer. Rain gathered on her eyelashes. "I must ask you again: did she say anything to you, sir?" Her breath hung in the air between them as thick as candle smoke, an impression augmented by its waxen scent. She looked him up and down, as if expecting to notice something that might alert her to what had occurred between him and the girl. "We charge for messages from the other side, you know."

Over Mrs. Cranshaw's shoulder, Quinn spied the girl still standing in the hallway, her body hunched as a question mark.

"Mr. Walker, isn't it?"

"Yes."

"Well, sir, what did Margaret say to you?"

"Nothing. She didn't say a word."

"Are you sure, boy?"

"Yes. Quite sure."

Mrs. Cranshaw dug out something from her lower lip with her tongue. Again she inspected him but, eventually, muttering under her breath, waddled back up the steps. "No need for you to come here again,

Mr. Wakefield," she announced to an astonished Fletcher from the top step, before slamming the heavy door behind her.

It was only later at their barracks at Abbey Wood that Quinn had discovered the note the girl Margaret must have stuffed into his pocket when she embraced him. But even now, on a hot night in an abandoned house thousands of miles from that London parlour, he could conjure her quivering gaze that, were it the sound of an instrument, would be akin to a violin's deepest low.

10

Sadie was as good as her word. The following morning she led Quinn to his parents' house, down gullies and through stiff tangles of wattle and grevillea.

It took more than an hour and, when they arrived at the ragged edge of the property, Quinn wondered how he would find his way to the shack again.

Sadie tied a length of blue wool several times around the lower branch of a large bloodwood tree. "Meet me under this tree," she said, as if reading his thoughts. "I'll be here in an hour or so, and we'll go back to the shack together. It's safer that way. I'll go now and try to find some food for us."

"Wait." He still had no idea why he had chosen to trust this strange girl. "What about Robert Dalton?"

She waved a fly from her face. "I'll be careful. He'll never catch me. He's hopeless. Remember, one hour." Then she scampered away like a sprite and ducked into the undergrowth before he could think of another thing to say.

❧

His mother was asleep when, again clutching a fistful of lavender, Quinn entered her room. Her features were slick with sweat. When she opened her eyes, she mouthed something unintelligible, then, gasping, said, "My poor, prodigal boy. So smart in your uniform."

Quinn smoothed a hand schoolboyishly down his front. The uniform felt stiff and unwieldy here, without purpose. He needed to find some civilian clothes and rid himself of the stink of war.

She looked at him for a long time. "I have sometimes wondered, if I longed for you enough, whether I might be able to produce you, the way a magician does his scarves and rabbits. Remember that Houdini chap we used to read about? A foolish thought, of course, although you *are* here now and—don't tell anyone this because they will think me mad—I swear I have seen a little girl pass by in the hall. A fever has its benefits, perhaps. There are reasons to be fond of grief, as someone wiser than I once said. What do you think, Quinn?"

"About what?"

"Would you think it possible to imagine someone into being? With nothing but love?"

It was a good question. Quinn couldn't answer. His mother held out a hand to him, and he understood she wanted to touch him as she had on their first meeting, to prove to herself that he was physically present and not an angel or phantom concocted by her sorrow.

She licked her lips. "I hoped we would see each other again, but I never imagined it would be in this life."

Quinn had also pondered this meeting on countless occasions and had fretted over his mother's possible reaction to the news that it was actually her own brother who had killed Sarah. With bitterness, he remembered what she had told him on that first visit: *Robert has been my saviour in all this.* And he realised there was no way he could ever tell her the truth of what he saw on that afternoon, for it would surely kill her. It would have to be enough for her to know it wasn't Quinn.

"Even my firstborn isn't near me," his mother said. "William became a farmer. Married. He couldn't stay here, not after what happened. He took it very hard. He writes to me sometimes, but not often. He has a new life now."

It was difficult to imagine William married. He had always been more comfortable dealing with objects than people, one of those boys rarely without a hammer or screwdriver in his grip. He had built bird houses that hung from the boughs of trees and fashioned figurines from wood, each with jagged eyes and mouths scratched out with his knife. When she was a few years old, the two brothers had vied for Sarah's affection as they might for that of a pet, but William soon retreated to the predictability of machinery and wire. He would watch Quinn and Sarah from beneath a lick of blond hair, leaning against a fence post while their father expounded on something he'd heard from a bloke down at The Mail.

"Were you married, Quinn? Did you have children?"

He shook his head. Indeed, after losing Sarah, he had found it impossible to countenance the notion of loving anyone with such abandon again, for fear they would be taken from him. Once, there was a girl, Emily, the daughter of a farmer he'd worked for before the war. She was dark-haired, pretty, and had even run a finger down his cheek one long-ago dusk. Sometimes he tried to imagine what she was doing now but was satisfied, almost, with this dream of her.

His mother sighed. "It is a strange bargain one makes with the gods—that in return for the purest love imaginable one must endure the constant fear that something dreadful will happen to your child, and that it will be your fault for bringing them into the world. The number of times I thought of you. Mothers never believe their children are dead. I have seen it in others, the ones with sons killed in the war. God, it's awful. Months after they have received those telegrams they still stand at their kitchen windows and watch the gate for a sign of them. I wake in the night. One's child," she went on in a trembling voice, "is always one's child, no matter what age they might be. You worry when your child makes a noise, when he doesn't. It's a terrible kind of love. Terrible."

An awkward silence followed. Her tearful gaze fell to Quinn's hand. "Have you brought me something?"

He handed her the flowers, by now soggy from his grasp.

His mother mouthed a mute expression of pleasure. She fingered the rosary of camphor balls at her neck. "I'm sorry about the smell. It's for my illness. This . . . influenza, or whatever it is. It is supposed to cleanse the air." And with a gesture that reminded Quinn of afternoons fifteen years earlier when she would secretly spoil him and Sarah with freshly baked biscuits while their father and William worked outside, she flicked one hand contemptuously. "I don't think it's doing a thing, but your father insisted. Half the country is dying from it. The half not already dead from the war, that is. He made it himself, you know. He's very proud of his handiwork."

Quinn imagined his father tying the camphor necklace by candlelight with his stubby, soot-stained fingers, applying himself with the same concentration he brought to any task he thought would benefit his family. His throat swelled with emotion.

She held the lavender flowers to her face and closed her eyes to breathe in their scent. "Lavandula. An ancient flower, you know. It's mentioned in The Song of Solomon by another name, I can't recall what. Do you remember the name, Quinn? I'm sure I told you. Begins with S, perhaps. I'll think of it later, no doubt."

Mary dozed, then jerked awake. As though fearful he was preparing to depart, she said, "Tell me where you have been. For all these years."

"I have been many places, Mother. Where would I start?"

"From the beginning. I want to know everything."

He paused. "That's a long time ago."

"I know. Of all people, I know. Ten years of days. You have no idea." She spluttered for a minute, then regained her composure. "You know, I used to creep into your room when you were all sleeping—when you were small—to watch you, to listen for your breath. You and Sarah used to breathe in time."

Quinn's face contorted with grief. He bowed his head so his mother couldn't see the hot tears that squeezed from his eyes and rolled down his cheeks. It was too much to bear. He should never have come. He clamped a hand to his mouth as if to prevent the escape of his stale sorrow. His fingers smelled of nicotine.

"The day," he began, but his words were soon drowned in grief. He continued to weep, a kind of unravelling he was unable to halt now that it had begun. "I only ran away because I was scared," he said between sobs. "I didn't know what else to do. I was too late to save her. I was too afraid. I ran and ran. Mother, I couldn't even speak."

It was true. In the months afterwards, words had caught like bones in his throat. He had roamed the country alone, staying well clear of people, watching only his shadow as it rose before him in the morning and slid about his forever-moving figure until, at night, it gathered itself again to him. Mumbil, Coolah, Curlewis—place names that might have been the words for crimes in unknown languages. He spoke with no one. He bathed in rivers and dams, and ate grass or fruit stolen at night from orchards or gardens. For three days a pair of wild dogs loped after him as they might a lame kangaroo, during which time he slept in a tree. A barren time.

His mother coughed and held out a hand flecked with her own blood. "Hush now. It's alright. You can't bring her back, Quinn. It's a long time ago. Let's talk of happier things," she said with enforced cheer. "The war is ended, at least. We are here together. That is good enough for now. Why don't you tell me how you came to be here."

Quinn collected himself and wiped his eyes. "I was in Sydney."

She attempted to sit up. "Oh, how lovely. It is many years since I was there. The harbour? Is it still beautiful?"

"Of course. It was crowded. There were many boats on the water. People are glad the war is over. They can get back to their lives."

"And were you there long? What did you do there?"

Quinn blew his nose and allowed himself a shy smile. "I tried to find an orange." His mother laughed. "But without any luck."

"An orange. You always adored them. For a time you lived on them. But I haven't seen one in a good while. Yes, an orange would be lovely. The war, you know. It's meant there's been little to eat. Farmers off at war. Killed, I suppose."

She closed her eyes again. It was now obvious to him she was dying. She was right: half the country was stricken with this influenza. In Sydney, the newspapers had been full of predictions of further outbreaks, of mountains of dead. As if a war were not enough for the world to endure. Quinn stooped to take her muggy hand in his own. She dozed, and in the ticking silence he wondered what he could tell her of the war, of his life. He became aware of a distant rumble through his boots on the wooden floor. Horse hooves. Horses approaching. He straightened.

His mother muttered something.

"What?" Quinn asked.

"What day is it?"

"Monday, I think."

"That might be Doctor Fraser with your father."

Panic squirmed through Quinn's chest. Even with his limited hearing he could tell the horses were close, perhaps at the front gate. He wondered if he could leap through the curtained window and escape unseen, but his mother reached out to him.

"Quinn. Hide next door. In your old room. Quick. Your father won't come into the house."

"You won't tell him I'm here?"

"Of course not. Quickly now."

Quinn did as she told him. Like a trespasser, he stood behind the closed door of the room he had shared with Sarah and William. His heart pounded and he strained to hear. Woolly voices, his father's and that of Doctor Fraser. There came a knock on the front door. The doctor calling out, his footfalls along the passageway, his mother greeting him. Quinn pressed his ear to the wooden door but could only make out mumbles, a forced cough, the jingling of glass bottles being placed on the dresser. Soon, Doctor Fraser went back outside and chatted with Nathaniel for a moment before leaving.

Quinn relaxed enough to consider his surrounds. His mother was right; the room was unchanged. It was as if he had been transplanted into a memory. There was the same chipped dresser, a shelf with several tattered children's books and Sarah's Lucy Doll. Everything was furred with dust, which floated through the light in curlicues. Under the bed he saw a sack of tools. On the floor beside her low bed was Sarah's cigar box in which she stored her treasures. The box exerted a strange magnetism.

Quinn had never resolved himself to Sarah's spiritual whereabouts now she was gone. Even though he found it impossible to imagine the pastoral version of heaven people talked about, he was even more uncomfortable at the thought of his sister cold and alone in her rotted coffin. He had often found himself narrating out loud the particulars of, say, tying a knot or checking a sail as if for her benefit. Mostly, he imagined her in some way to be alongside him—twirling her hair, trying to balance on a fence, leaning down to whisper a secret in his ear.

He squatted, picked up the cigar box and opened it. It contained a stamp, a rock shaped like a kangaroo's head, a length of barbed wire, an imitation pearl, three pebbles of gold, the magpie feather his mother had mentioned, and a large red button. The button Quinn recognised immediately as one of three or four that Sarah had insisted their mother sew onto her dresses—including the white dress, in fact, she was wearing on the day she died. He stared at these things in horror, as if they might assemble against him. If he could have fled at that moment, he would have done so.

From the box he took the red button, held it to his lips, then his forehead. "*I had a dream which was not all a dream,*" he whispered. "*The bright sun was extinguish'd and the stars did wander darkling in the eternal space.*"

He dropped the button into the cigar box and returned the box with its other treasures to where he had found it. He crept to the window that overlooked the veranda, careful to remain invisible to his father, who was sitting on a chair by Mary's window with his head in his hands. He appeared confounded, and the shock of seeing him like this infused Quinn with a fierce melancholy. His father had shrunk in the intervening years, had become altogether more human in scale.

His father raised his head and spoke into the open window. "The doctor says you are both better and worse today."

Mary's response was inaudible.

"Agitated," Nathaniel went on. "What? . . . Well, you should do as he says. He is a doctor . . . Of course he knows what he is doing. Mary? Are you wearing the camphor? Mary? They say it works. Do you at least have it close by?" He paused to listen. "Very well. I won't go on about it but make sure it is nearby at all times . . . I know it smells. I expect it cleanses the air. But there is something else I have ordered from Sydney. A new product should arrive any day now. Hearn's Bronchitis Cure it's called, and they assure me that it will help with . . ."

Quinn could see his father's face was smeared with soot and his arms were ripe with muscle. A moustache darkened his upper lip. His elbows were slack on his knees, fingers knotted in an attitude of exhaustion or prayer. He raised himself every so often to adjust his position or speak more clearly into his wife's open window. In his father's slumping shoulders, in the expressions that flitted across his weathered features,

Quinn saw something of their family's terrible story, the way wind was visible when it ruffled a field of wheat.

His parents ceased talking. His father fidgeted and glanced about. Quinn's legs grew stiff from staying still for so long. After about fifteen minutes, Nathaniel stood to leave. "Did you see the food the Auxiliary ladies left for you? . . . Will it be enough? . . . Are you sure? . . . And you *are* eating it, I trust? You need your strength. I should go now. Oh, I nearly forgot. Your brother said he would call by today. Said he's been busy. Some orphan girl up in the hills he wants to find." He slapped his hat against his dusty thigh and laughed. "He told me he saw her a few days ago but that—listen to this, Mary—he said that she turned into a *snake*. Probably dreamed up the whole thing, you know what an imagination he has. It might have been rabbiters or something. Lot of people moving about these days. Anyway, he fell and cut his hand so I expect that held him up a bit."

Mary said something Quinn couldn't hear.

"Course he's alright. Your brother is charmed. But I'll tell him. I'll make sure he stops by. Don't worry, Mary. Save your strength."

Quinn heard his father step off the veranda and he sat up to watch him retreat back up the road on his horse. When he was sure he had left, Quinn slunk from his former room, down the dim hall, and out into the afternoon that was bursting with sunlight.

As promised, Sadie was waiting for him in the shade of the bloodwood tree. He was unaccountably pleased to see her and had to restrain himself from embracing her. Together they tramped back through the afternoon heat to their shack, but only when they were halfway there did Quinn realise she was not carrying anything.

He stopped. "Did you not find any food?"

Sadie paused with her hands on her hips. She shook her head and wound a strand of hair behind an ear. She looked exhausted. "I couldn't take anything. Too many people about. Tomorrow I'll go out even earlier. Don't worry, I know what I'm doing. Come on, let's go."

11

That night Quinn lay on the floor of the shack bundled in his trench coat, his thin hands a cushion of twigs beneath his head. The cooling night creaked outside, and the years he had been gone didn't feel quite so long. He was hungry. He listened out for footsteps, for voices, for those who wished to hang him from a tree. After some time, the night settled and grew quiet. Wherever she was, the girl made no noise.

Spikenard, he thought suddenly. Was that the name by which lavender was known in the Bible, the word his mother had been trying to think of earlier that day? It was unlike her to forget; for a time he had been certain his mother knew everything there was to know: the names of King Henry's wives, of all the planets, the dates of the French Revolution. She herself was a curio in these parts where, by and large, people understood little of the outside world and cared even less about its goings-on. When asked how she knew the Latin for *Men learn as they teach* or that the first governor-general was a chap called Hope, she would smile, tap her head and say she had slept with the encyclopaedia under her pillow as a girl and the information had seeped, entry by entry, into her brain.

Of course this was just another fanciful story. In fact, she'd worked her way through her father's substantial library after her wealthy parents perished on a boat to Hong Kong when she was nineteen. Quinn remembered her balancing an open dictionary on her palm as she carried the laundry to the line, or fetched flour from the pantry. "Listen to this, children," she would announce before declaiming a line of poetry or an obscure historical fact. "*You'll* like this, William. Do you see this fellow hanging upside-down from a crane, above a road? See that? Houdini, or some such. Good God. Breaks out of padlocks, you know." She alerted them to the wisdom potentially contained in books. "A story is a wondrous invention," she would say. "A glimpse into another place altogether. I like sometimes to escape from here."

She had moved from Sydney to western New South Wales early in her marriage, although she would have preferred to stay in the city, and it was naturally to such environs her imagination drifted. While she had never visited them, she told the children tales of watery London and darkly smoking Cairo. She read to them anything that came to hand— the Bible, newspapers, stories of the Trojans, incomprehensible poetry stuffed with *thee* and *thou*, even advertising pamphlets she picked up in Flint (*Life drops are the great household remedy for asthma, bronchitis, colds, dysentery, fevers, spasmodic affection, toothaches etc*). Even when baking or sewing she passed on to her children a thousand curious odds and ends, and—although Sarah was by far the most adept at retaining facts and figures—Quinn often found himself, such as now, regurgitating a scrap of information or line of poetry that was almost certainly told to him by his mother on a distant summer's afternoon. *My spikenard sendeth forth the smell thereof.*

The next thing he knew it was dawn. Glimmers of light flitted through the interior. It reminded him of swimming in a deep and muddy lake. The barrage had stopped some time in the night and for once he couldn't even hear the distant lolling of artillery. He resolved to take advantage of the silence and lie there as inconspicuous as a rock beneath his coat. Soon enough someone would stumble over him, curse him or otherwise rouse him, and there would be no more sleep until God only knew when. *Come on, Walker. Come on, Meek.*

He was aware of his breathing, but from within. The moist pull and draw of his ragged lungs. He loosened a splinter from the wooden floor. On the ground in front of him an ant zig-zagged in and out of his focus. It amazed him that such a tiny creature should have its own shadow. He heard the click of his blink. He squeezed the splinter lengthwise between his thumb and forefinger until the skin of first his forefinger and then his thumb was pierced. Twin balloons of blood swelled and burst under their own weight. What a thing. To be alive. To be alive in a time of war was to be charged, as if with electricity, with light, with violence and mercy, all those things of which men were capable.

Then he heard the sounds of birds and realised where he was. The war was over. They had won. Of course. Now anxious, he sat up. He wiped his mouth, which was spongy with drool on the damaged left side. Where was the girl? She'd told him there was a price on his head. Dear God. Of course.

He detected something moving around outside. Footsteps, voices. Sadie, if that were even her real name, had probably told them where he was. Told Dalton. They would kill him. His uncle would string him from a tree. He was a fool to have trusted the child. He was addled, that was the problem. What with the heat and everything, his distress at seeing his mother in such an awful state.

He took up a plank of wood and stood, half crouching, like a large bird preparing to take flight, his coat puddled on the floor beside him. The girl arrived in the doorway, clutching a bulging flour bag to her chest. Quinn raised the length of wood as if to strike.

A look of childish betrayal passed over Sadie's features. "Don't hurt me," she said.

The words were almost inaudible but their meaning was clear to him in the begging of her eyes.

"Who's with you?" he demanded.

"No one."

"Don't lie to me."

"There's no one."

"I heard voices."

The girl mumbled something.

"What?"

"I was singing a song."

Quinn paused. He angled his head the way the half-blind did to better make out shapes or movement, but heard nothing more. If the girl had brought Dalton or his father, they would have shown themselves by now. He relaxed but kept the piece of wood at the ready.

"Where have you been?"

She hefted her sack by way of answer.

"What's that?"

"I was out getting food for us. Early morning is the best time."

"Who gave it to you?"

She laughed humourlessly. "No one *gave* it to me."

Quinn wiped his mouth and approached her. She was watching the length of wood, as if preparing to leap clear should he attempt to strike her with it. He grabbed her by the wrist and pulled her hot body against his own. Then he dragged her squirming and wriggling outside.

She was telling the truth: there was no one there. He released her.

She stood rigid, head down, her hair a lank curtain across her face. The knuckles of the hand holding the bag were white with anger. A floral bruise marked the skin of her inner wrist where Quinn had gripped her. He dropped the wood to the ground.

She flung the bag at him and several items tumbled out. She said something, but it was only when Quinn failed to respond that she looked at him. Her eyes glittered like water at the bottom of a well. "Don't touch me again or I'll cut the eyes out of you."

Ashamed, Quinn stared at the ground to see what had fallen from the bag. A loaf of bread and a tin of jam. Inside, he could see a small bottle of whiskey, a tin of tobacco, some flour, four apples and there, resting against his boot, two oranges. He raised his head to speak to the girl—a *sorry* or *thank you*—but she had gone.

12

For twenty minutes, Quinn called out for Sadie and searched the bushland around the shack, but there was no sign of her. She was gone. He chastised himself for his mistrust, packed the food back into the flour bag and left it inside the shack. With some effort, losing his way now and then, he stumbled down to his father's house alone. He sheltered in the shade of the bloodwood tree until he was sure there was no one around, then went to his mother's bedside.

His mother's eyes fluttered open when he entered, then she fell back asleep. Quinn mopped her brow. Her health seemed worse than ever, and he despaired at the possibility that his visits might have been doing more harm than good. There were several bottles of tablets on the dresser by her bed. Quinine, aspirin and Dr Morse's Indian Root Pills—*Keep clean inside and out and minimise the risk of influenza.*

After several minutes, she woke again and smiled. They talked of trivial things. Through the morning he told her palatable bits and pieces from his years at war: the excitement of joining up; of becoming friends with a soldier from Adelaide called George Kenward; of crossing the English Channel at night, its sickening chop and yaw under low clouds.

"Parts of France are beautiful," he told her, hardly aware of what he was saying, speaking to fill the vacuum, hoping to rejuvenate her somehow. "The parts away from the war, that is. Such old buildings. They have woods there. Forests, like in the fairy tales you told us when we were children."

His mother didn't answer, but he was heartened to see her nod.

"We walked through one at night," he continued. "It was dark, of course, so I didn't see very much. There were hundreds of us walking along the road. On the grass and through the trees. Men and horses and mules, as quiet as we could be, talking only now and then to save our energy. The next day we were due to attack a village full of Germans."

His mother whispered something.

Quinn leaned in. "Pardon, Mother?"

"Were you afraid?"

"Yes."

"But you went on?"

"There wasn't much choice. I prayed a lot."

Mary opened her eyes. "When you were small enough to hold in my arms, your heart used to beat so fast I wondered if, in fact, you didn't have *two* hearts in your chest. You were always brave."

Quinn flinched. "Well," he said after a silence, "there were a few hundred of us trudging along. It was cold, and we could see our breath when we exhaled. It was like smoke, as if we were already on fire. Mainly you followed the fellow in front, kept walking, didn't think too much."

Quinn recalled seeing an owl on the sheared and blackened stump of a tree. The bird gazed at them dispassionately, as if it had stood on that very spot for centuries and watched passing armies. The Gauls, the Romans. Bridles clanked in the darkness. Every now and again someone tripped on a tree root or a piece of wreckage and cursed. Quinn kept his eyes down, concentrated on his footfalls. The air smelled of muddy leaves, of damp wool and of horse sweat.

"After a while the darkness changed colour. We thought we had entered a valley, or a large dip in the landscape because the night became misty. It was too early for morning. We checked our maps. Then we heard several hollow sounds, a sort of *pot*, followed by another, then another. There was a curious smell—almost recognisable, but not quite—a bit like wet hay. I remember a fellow stumbled to his knees to pray. Then more men did the same. There were lots of men on their knees in the mist, as if the lower parts of their legs had sunk into the mud."

He wiped his mother's hot brow. "Gas. We were being shelled with gas. We got on all fours, down low, the way we had been taught, but some blokes panicked and couldn't get the masks on. They aren't always easy to put on. Your hands shake and the strap catches on things. And it was dark, of course. Some men breathed the gas in and had to be carried the rest of the way through the night, to the battle."

The gas had stewed in ditches and wreathed about them as they marched on. They waited for another, louder assault that never came. Some men threw themselves to the ground and had to be coaxed to standing again, so keen were they to enwomb themselves into the earth. Quinn's own breathing was hot and loud and close in his ears as if, with the mask and its eye shields and tubes and clasps, he had been transformed into a sinister machine. They walked on through the toxic gruel, and those who had been boastful became solemn.

The ground around them was littered with broken equipment, with empty boxes of ammunition, scraps of uniform, books, rubble. He saw a large wall clock. Bicycle wheels and motor-car tyres. The inert bodies of dead men. Crockery, wooden boxes. Papers blew about here and there. A collection of muddy boots, dozens of muddy stretchers. An officer sitting cross-legged on a table watched them as they trudged past and, although his face was obscured by his own mask, his expression was one of grim mockery as he drew a finger across his throat. A pair of chairs, helmets and hats, bully tins, trees stark and broken against the pale sky.

After some time, Quinn became aware of objects crunching beneath his boots. When he crouched to investigate, he discovered they had been walking on small birds that had fallen dead from the trees. Their bodies were plump and stiff. They looked the size of a child's heart, and he carried one of them in his palm, God only knew why, through the long night until they came to a field at dawn, whereupon he lay down and slept. When he woke hours later, the bird was still cupped in his hand. Its red feathers blew about in the breeze. Its tongue was a pellet of lead. A minister was moving through the coughing and groaning men, among boys suddenly made old. He assured them God was with them in their struggle. Someone wept, another man called out over and over until he was taken elsewhere.

Quinn and his mother sat in silence for several minutes. "I'm sorry," he said, "I shouldn't have told you that. You don't need to know those things." He felt foolish, ashamed.

She waved away his concern. "I take it you didn't see Little Red Riding Hood, then? Or that damn wolf?"

He grinned. "No. They are just stories, Mother."

"Stories are rarely only stories," she chided him.

He told her of the battle for the village of Pozières, or what he remembered of it (a blue flare wriggling back to earth, the grunt and shriek of artillery) before a shell had exploded near him and thrown him to the ground. It was perhaps that incident that had prompted the inaccurate news of his death. There were worse things that happened, in the weeks and months that followed, but of these he told his mother nothing. There were no words to convey the horror of what he saw during the war or, rather, that to describe it would require every word of the language, all of them at once, until they no longer made sense.

Quinn had a sudden thought. "Mother? Do you remember a family called Fox living in the district?"

Mary repeated the name to herself, dipped into the well of her memory. "*Fox*. Yes, I do remember something. Out on Sutton Ridge. Terribly poor. I think the mother was a seamstress. Father ran off. Yes." She snorted. "That's right, your father heard somewhere the woman was involved in magic, which I very much doubt. Probably heard it down at that fool Sully's place. In fact my brother told me he had tried to help them recently, but the woman told him to shove off. Why do you want to know, Quinn?"

"Curious, that's all. I met a man in France who knew them." He kissed his mother's forehead, and stood to leave. "I have to go. You're tired. I'll come back tomorrow."

Mary closed her eyes. She looked better for his visit. Perhaps the conversation did her good, after all? Before he passed through the doorway, she called to him. "Quinn. What was it Sarah used to call you? That funny name, when she was young and couldn't say your name properly? I was wondering about it the other day, racking my brains, trying to remember."

"Pim."

"Ah, yes. Dear thing she was."

13

Quinn lit a candle, a puny defence against the darkness. Outside, insects thripped in the warm night and bats hung from branches in heavy clumps. He had shed most of his uniform on account of the heat and wore only trousers and a singlet. His exposed arms and ankles were thin and hairless. About him on the floor was an archipelago of discarded uniform: his trench coat, boots, tunic, the satchel with the gas mask.

Sadie was in the next room singing some popular song to herself and playing a game that involved slapping something against the floor. This was followed by the scrabble and shake of small items. Slap and scrabble. Slap, slap. It was extremely annoying, but he had resolved to let her be following the incident that morning with the bag of food. She had only returned at nightfall and still not spoken to him. The girl was unbalanced; it was obvious in the slide of her gait and the drift of her eyes. Orphans, Quinn suspected, were usually possessed of cunning and frailty in equal measure, each of which was a form of desperation. Sadie was no different. He had pondered leaving her but resolved to stay, for now at least. He supposed the girl needed him and, besides, he had to remain, for his mother's sake.

She began singing again with the pegged-nose intonation of a phonograph singer he had himself recently heard. *Smile and the world smiles with you, weep and you weep alone. La la la la clouds have silver linings la la la la getting through.*

From a trouser pocket Quinn took a battered match-safe, and from the tin tube drew a piece of paper that had been folded and refolded like a minuscule map. He had carried this note from the girl Margaret ever since that London séance. He knew what was written on it, but couldn't help checking it every so often—as one might a note from a sweetheart—in the hope the words could be experienced anew or that another, hidden meaning should become apparent. In the bedraggled scrawl, by now almost illegible, was the same phrase he'd read on the scrap of paper all those months ago. He stared at it for several minutes.

"What's that?"

He looked up, startled. Sadie was in the doorway. He thought to hide the note but realised there was no point—she had probably been watching him for some time. Besides, he wanted her to stay; he was remorseful about what had happened.

"A message," he said.

"Who from?"

He stared at her. That long-ago evening at Abbey Wood, Fletcher had asked him the same question, which he had waved away with a dismissive mutter. But now he felt compelled to tell the truth. "It's from . . . a girl."

"What kind of girl?"

He swallowed. "It's from my sister. It's from Sarah."

Sadie came closer, tentatively, the same way a cat sidled into a room. And it was clear that, like a cat, she would have to be coaxed in, step by step. Indeed, her entire body flickered in the candlelight as if she might vanish at any moment. She brushed hair from her face and frowned. "Have you been carrying that around since . . . since she died?"

Quinn stared up at her from where he was sitting cross-legged on the floor. "I didn't do it, you know. It's wrong what they call me in town. You must believe me. My uncle was the murderer."

She watched him with her dark, pooling eyes. She had a girlish habit of running her thumb along the seam at the hip of her linen dress, up and down, up and down, indecision made manifest. She was doing it now. That portion of the fabric was grubby and worn.

"You really don't need to be afraid of me," Quinn said. "I won't hurt you."

Her lips moved.

"Pardon?"

"Do you *promise*?" she said.

"Of course."

She pouted. "Cross your heart and hope to die?"

Quinn refolded the note, placed it back into the match-safe and returned that to his trouser pocket. "Alright. Cross my heart. Hope to die."

Sadie was somewhat appeased. She looked about as if for useful scraps of conversation and continued to worry at the seam of her dress. The candle flame trembled in a breeze. Eventually, she edged completely into the room and rested against the wall. In this light she looked remote, haunted, both near and far. On her knees were patches of dirt where she had been kneeling to play her game. The hem of her dress was torn, her hair was unruly, but this was tempered by her innate elegance and defiance. Quinn felt tender towards her, concerned not only for her future but also for what might have already happened in her short life.

"I have a letter, too," she announced. "From my brother. Do you want to see it?"

Quinn smiled with relief. He felt he had recovered her trust. "Yes. Of course."

She bolted back into her room. He heard her rummaging around, the rattle of a tin. Then she was back, flushed and beaming. In her hand was a rumpled sheet of paper. She cast her eyes over it, as if to confirm it was the correct letter, and handed it to Quinn.

The letter was in a careful, sloping hand.

Dearest mother,

Well here i am doing flying training. Cannot tell you where i am or the sort of planes I am learning to fly because of the sensorship but everything is well. Good fellows training here one is even from Bathurst! We work hard and are keen to getting into the action and giving the hun something to be sorry about. On the boat here i was frightfuly sick. I am getting to see the world in Egypt. I tried to ride a camel but the creature refused to move anywhere with me. I tryed and tryed. Gippoes had a good laugh at my ekspense i tell you. They are devils always tryeing to sell you something cant be trusted. I had better say fairwel now. Do not worry about me as I am sure I will be alright this war will not be long. Can you send me some socks pleese it is cold here. Look after my darling sister tell her I will send her a pcard soon.

Your loving son Thomas

The letter was dated June 1917, almost two years ago. It was most likely a letter from a dead man, mailed from England during his training. It had a ring of innocence about it; only those yet to go into battle still thought the war would finish quickly.

Sadie snatched back the letter. "See? He'll be home soon."

"You could go to Sydney, if there is no one else to take care of you. They have organisations now that look after children like you. Orphans. You're an orphan now. The Red Cross could take care of you."

She shook her head. "You're like Robert Dalton."

Quinn was appalled. "No! No. I'm not like him at all. Don't even *think* that. Please. Not ever. I'm not like him."

The girl was silent for a time until he realised, with horror, that she was weeping. He stood and crossed the room to comfort her, but she wriggled out from his embrace.

"I don't want to live with strangers," she said. "I want Mother back, I want my brother home. Thomas will know what to do. I want it the way it was before."

I want it the way it was before. Quinn knew what she meant.

Sadie said something unintelligible.

"What?" he asked.

"Are you going to stay here?"

"In Flint?"

"I mean with me."

He sat down again. "I'm not sure I did the right thing coming back. I don't know what it will achieve. I can't tell my mother who did it. She is already so sick, and the shock of seeing me—"

"You can't leave!"

"Maybe you should come with me? It's not safe here. They'll kill me if they find me. And you. If Dalton finds you, then . . ."

"It's safe for now. I'm waiting for Thomas. We have a few weeks until Gracie is back, and Dalton will never track us by himself. I'll work out when the tracker is home. We're safe until then."

"But how will you know when this Gracie is coming back?"

"I'll find out. I hear everything around here. Besides, my mother taught me things."

Quinn thought of what his father had heard at Sully's. "What? Magic things?" She glanced at him. He was unconvinced, but nodded anyway. There was no arguing with the girl.

She sat on the floor beside him. "Maybe you could kill Constable Dalton."

"What? You really think I could do that? Kill my uncle?"

A languid shrug passed across her shoulders.

Quinn could only stare at her. At last he found his voice. "In the war they gave me a medal for bravery. I can hardly remember what I did to earn it. War is noise and confusion. They said I saved two men who had been injured and would have been killed. But I have never been brave. The medal was a bloody joke. I'm terrified of my uncle. I know what he is capable of. I caught him spying on Sarah once when she was washing and he told me he would cut my throat if I told a soul. And I never have. Until now. Besides," he said, recalling his mother's words, "revenge is not our business. It belongs to God. I've seen a lot of dead men these past few years."

She leaned forward. "Then what is one more? It is nothing. God isn't even watching."

Quinn shook his head. The girl was so fervent for retribution that he wondered if she had been waiting all along for him to set it in motion. "I can't do it."

"Edward Fitch will tell people he saw you. Gracie will help Dalton find you. He'll find me. They'll hang you."

"How do you know I saw Fitch?"

"I *told* you," she said with theatrical exasperation. "I see things, I hear things."

Again Quinn was reminded that Sadie was a girl, only twelve years old, ignorant of the world. "No one believes Edward Fitch. He's a simpleton. Besides, if Dalton is as hopeless as you say, why are you so worried that he'll find us? It was just a coincidence he nearly caught us."

"What's that?"

"Like luck. Chance."

"There's no such thing."

Quinn laughed uneasily. "Well, it was luck I ran into you, although I'm not sure if it was good luck or bad."

"It wasn't *luck*."

"What, then?"

She murmured something Quinn couldn't understand.

"What?"

"I prayed you here. For someone to come and help me. Here on this floor. Right here on this floor." She jabbed herself in the chest with a finger. "*I* brought you here."

"I thought you said God didn't pay us any attention. Isn't that what you said before?" He was shocked to detect an unappealing, triumphant note in his voice.

She gave him a queer, scornful look. "Yes. But there are others that do."

Quinn shivered. Scattered about them on the floor was the food she had procured that morning: the loaf of bread, the apples and oranges. He took a swig of whiskey and grimaced as it seared his throat. Alcohol had never agreed with him—it always made him sleepy—but if there were ever a time for a man to have a vice, then it was war and its aftermath. He exhaled and wiped his mouth with the back of a hand.

"You should grow a beard," she said after some minutes. "That way you can be certain he won't recognise you when you go and get him."

Quinn caressed his face. During all his years of travel, through the war and beyond, he had kept up shaving with priestly devotion, as if it might safeguard his humanity among such terrible scenes. It was a small, civilised act, not always easy to accomplish. Now he touched the scar at his mouth. Perhaps the girl was right. Perhaps, out here in the middle of nowhere, there was no longer a need to shave.

He held out one of the oranges. "Here," he said, eager to change the subject and cement their friendlier footing. "Are you hungry? Let's eat this."

"No. They're for you. They were gifts."

He balanced the fruit in his palm. It had cost him some restraint all day not to eat it. "No. We'll share it, you and I. Food is meant to be shared, isn't it? That makes it a meal, that's what my mother always used to say." And, already feeling the effects of the liquor, he set about peeling the orange with fumbling fingers.

Quinn had eaten a lot of oranges in his life, but this was the best so far. They devoured it, rind included. Sweet and sharp it was, the way an orange was supposed to be. He savoured each mouthful, careful that no juice escape. Sadie licked her fingers and smirked with the sheer pleasure of it. The sight of her smiling made him happy.

"Who did you steal all this from?" he asked.

In the candle's light her teeth fluttered like a line of ragged laundry. She told him that she took something from most residents at one time or another. People followed their daily routines, and she only had to watch them for a few days to see when they would be out. Some homes she stayed away from, of course. She had been doing it for years. Her brother had taught her plenty of tricks. It was easy, and most families didn't miss an apple or a couple of slices of bread. "I could get you anything you wanted," she boasted.

"Like what?"

"I don't know. A horse? Hammer or nails. A gun."

"I think someone might miss their horse. Besides, stealing is wrong."

"Better than starving to death. Wasn't *my* fault my father ran off. Or the war. How else are we supposed to live? Look around." She sneered and made a gesture that encompassed not only the battered and peeling room in which they sat, but the rise of the Bolsheviks, the flu plague, the Great War with its gas canisters and flame throwers, and the murder of his sister by her own uncle. The girl was right. In the face of such moral catastrophe, theft was not so serious.

"So, what should I get for you?" she asked after a pause.

"I need some ordinary clothes. I hate this uniform. And more tobacco."

Sadie looked him up and down as she picked orange pulp from her teeth. She seemed disappointed at his prosaic request. "Alright then."

"An orange was what I really wanted, actually. Even during the war I tried to find one. I asked every farmer, harassed the quartermaster. Mother said I used to live on them when I was a boy. I've always loved them."

Sadie nodded. "Yes, I know."

Quinn looked up. "How do you know that?"

Sadie froze with glistening fingers halfway to her mouth. A globule of pulp hung from her lip. "You talk in your sleep."

"I talk about oranges?"

"Yes. And other things, too. Things I can't understand. About gas. Lots of mumbling. Sometimes," she said, smiling, warming to the odd direction their conversation had taken, "you make a sound like a dog."

"I bark?"

"No. Not barking. Like a—I don't know—an injured dog. Whimpering, sort of."

"Why were you watching me when I was sleeping?"

She tucked a strand of hair behind her ear. "I have to be sure of who you are."

"And how can I be sure of who *you* are?"

She smiled again.

Quinn reached out with one hand towards her, but she arched away so rapidly that she kicked over the candle on its metal plate. The flame guttered and spat, was extinguished. The room collapsed into darkness and was filled with the waxy stink of wick. He knocked aside a chair or box and swore. He fumbled about in his pockets for matches and re-lit the candle. Hot wax pricked his hand. It took several seconds for his eyes to adjust, and when his vision returned he saw Sadie standing on the far side of the room with a large knife in her fist, her wrung-sheet features drenched in fear. "I *told* you not to touch me," she warned in a low voice.

Quinn hardly moved. He raised a finger to indicate his own lip. "You've got some orange on your mouth, that's all."

But Sadie had gone.

❧

Later, Quinn lay awake as long as he could, but finally succumbed to sleep. In the night he woke gasping for breath, the remnants of unpleasant dreams still cobwebbed about his hair and neck. His first thought was that she had stabbed him. He unbuttoned his tunic and expected to feel the dull stick of blood on his fingers. It was dark. Hot and dark. Dark and hot. A churning pain in his guts. He curled up as tight as he could on the wooden floor, made a fraying ball of himself, the way he'd seen injured men do. He heard the dull *pad pad pad* of the girl's bare feet. The mad girl, whatever was her name. Sadie. Shit. Coming for him. Imagine surviving all he had survived to be stabbed in the stomach by a crazed orphan girl.

He floundered about for something he might use as a weapon but could find nothing. He was hopelessly disoriented. He bumped his head against the iron leg of the stove. He slithered over the boards, aiming for the corner. The revolver. Where was his revolver? Still he fumbled in his pockets. That's right. The revolver was lost.

Then she was beside him, visible at first as an outline, the dull shine of her face against the greater darkness, saying things he couldn't hear above the clamour of his breathing. He shuffled backwards and flung out a hand to ward her off, but she was stronger than he would have thought—or he, weaker—and, as his breathing slowed and he gave up struggling, he heard beyond the roar of his partial deafness that she wasn't saying anything in particular, at least not words, just a soft *shhh shhh shhh*.

The girl scampered away and returned a minute later. She lit the candle and stirred liquid in a tin mug with one finger. She held the mug to his mouth. "Drink this."

The mug contained a murky fluid that smelled of nothing in particular, perhaps the slight whiff of a chemist's.

"Bicarb and water," she said. "Best thing to take if you've been gassed. I heard Tom Smith talking about it. I got a whole box of it for you."

Quinn sniffed it, then drank. The mixture was mildly bitter, but the pain in his stomach eased. Sadie had a hand cupped against the back of his head to help him drink. Her hands were still redolent of the orange they had eaten earlier, her breath a freshly watered orchard. Weeping now and spluttering, he gulped the concoction. His gratitude was pathetic. He could not recall the last time anyone had cared for him in such a manner. Even the nurses at Harefield were brisk, their English jolliness stretched tight across the wards. And fair enough: men died all the time, were trundled out daily under sheets or sent back to France as soon as they could walk.

Some minutes passed before Sadie shifted herself free of him.

"Thank you," he said.

She shuffled across the floor and he heard the granular strike of a match as she lit another candle. A halo of light pooled around her and threw her shadow high onto the wall behind. The knife was still in her fist.

"Now you have to do something for me," she said.

14

Quinn kneeled on the floor, bare-chested, his dirty singlet beside him. Sweat collected in the folds of his stomach. With his left hand he pulled his chest skin taut against the hull of his ribs. Sadie, girlish again, squatted nearby, watching him, chin cupped in her hands. He didn't know why he had agreed to her request but hoped it might, at least, ease her evident distress. He held the knife in his free hand and motioned with it, two quick strokes above his shining chest. "Here? Like this?"

She nodded.

"Are you sure I need to do this? Can't you take my word—"

"No."

"This is rather strange, that's all."

"Come on. Do it."

Bats squeaked in the trees outside. He imagined an ancient man rapidly opening and closing dozens of tiny cabinet doors on rusted hinges, seeking something he had misplaced. Very little was out of the question these days. He pressed the blade to his skin and carved a jagged cross into his chest. Nothing for a second—then black blood.

On the troopship to the Middle East for training, soldiers had carved designs into their skin and filled the wound with a paste made from soot and oil, a scrimshaw tattoo forever on their bodies. They engraved the names of their sweethearts, their mothers, the town they were from or the battalion to which they now belonged. But this, what Sadie demanded of him, this was different—part punishment, part promise.

He gestured for her to pass him the moist cloth she had ready to wipe away the blood, but she shook her head.

"You got to say the words or it doesn't mean anything."

Quinn was reminded of Sarah and the way little girls always had elaborate rules for things that were impossible to know in advance. Often, games were only excuses for a new set of behavioural guidelines, and often stalled on the finer points of the correct way to play hide-and-seek or snap. One spring day, Sarah refused to eat or drink until Quinn and a furious William had dressed as sprites so they could act out a poem she had written about a troupe of acrobats who encountered a mysterious tribe. As always, the thought of his sister prompted in him an odd sensation, as if a trough had opened inside him, one so deep it might swallow him altogether.

By now the blood from his two cuts had dribbled down to his stomach. Still on his knees, he straightened to prevent it staining his trousers, but it was too late. The wool at his waist was already darkening. "Cross my heart and hope to die," he said. "Now pass me that cloth."

Sadie grinned and crawled over to him. From a shallow tray of water she drew the soaking cloth. This she applied to his skin, tenderly at first, barely touching him, then harder, wiping away the blood that had begun to coagulate in the hair of his chest. The wounds were not painful and felt to Quinn like some sort of release. As he watched Sadie bent to her task, he half expected to see steam sighing from the two raw gills now carved into his flesh.

⁂

The following morning, Quinn noticed an odd bundle strung from one of the eaves, the unravelled remnants, or so it first looked, of a bird's nest. Closer inspection revealed the package to have been constructed from several thin bones, indeed perhaps those of a bird, bound together with black hair and lengths of dried wheat grass. The frail, prehistoric-looking object crackled in his hands. He scanned the porch eaves and located two more, each hanging like the first by a length of cotton from a beam. Sadie was out somewhere. He had not seen her since he woke. He took down the bundles and pondered them in his palm before putting them back.

When she returned later that afternoon, he asked her about them, but she offered no explanation. She stared at him with her sooty eyes. "You didn't do anything to them, did you?"

"No."

"Don't touch them. They're important."

"But what are they?"

She put down the apple she had been eating. "Leave them exactly where they are. Don't even touch them."

With his vision now attuned to the offerings, he began to spy them everywhere. She must have been fashioning them for years. Here and there in the bushland around the shack, he stumbled across Lilliputian cairns of rocks and stones. Clumps of hair, fingernail clippings and torn shards of photographs leaked from the gaps between them. He found clusters of bones arranged in patterns on the ground, the cuticles of insects. Once, even a brass candlestick, its stem stuffed with wax and shredded cloth. An old medicine jar crammed with animal teeth and kangaroo paws. Arranged on windowsills and the shack floor were patterns of string and dry grass, mounds of desiccated snail shells. A red marble hung from a tree on a length of twine where it glowed in the afternoon light like a globule of blood.

One day, several hundred yards from the house, he found a wattle tree adorned not only with its brushy yellow flowers but also with what he took to be dozens of children's fingers. He remembered what his mother had said about Mrs. Fox's involvement in witchcraft. He approached with trepidation and was relieved to discover the pale cylinders to be rolled pages of the Bible, bound with hair. The ends of each were crimped shut.

He stood there for some time admiring her handiwork, which must have taken hours to accomplish. The air shrilled with cicadas. He plucked a tube from the tree, picked apart the seam and poured the contents into his palm. It contained ash, seeds and pebbles, an empty silver locket. The page was from the Book of Jeremiah. *I will not cause mine anger to fall upon you: for I am merciful, saith the Lord.* Mindful of her warnings, he placed it back as carefully as he could. Sweat coursed down his face and dried gritty as salt on his lips.

⊰⊱

Sadie stole some civilian clothes for him. A white shirt, dark trousers and a jacket. Each item was worn, faded in places, but in reasonable condition. The clothes were light against his body, insubstantial. He didn't ask where she got them.

He visited his mother every day. Her health continued to deteriorate and mostly she was unable to carry on any conversation. He read to her, as she had to him and his siblings when they were ill, but it was unclear what she understood or whether his visits were beneficial. Often they sat without speaking, and it was these occasions that Quinn feared the most. Not only was he terrified for his mother's health, but during these grim silences he was most aware of phantoms pressing against the outer panes of his memory.

At dusk, Quinn and Sadie sat outside to catch the last of the light. It was the best time of day. Birds frolicked through the air and the hot afternoon grew sleepy and docile. Sadie often sat on a stump with her chin cupped in one hand and told him stories: of the blackfellas she had once seen dragging the carcass of a kangaroo through the bush, how they gibbered and menaced her; that Kimberley Porteous talked every night to a photograph of her late husband, Reginald, who was killed by Germans in France; how Billy Davis sometimes met Miss Haylock by the river on summer nights. She knew everything private of the townsfolk, hoarded lives, could see into the very chamber of people's hearts.

Later, when the moon rose, they went inside, lit candles and devoured whatever food they had. Quinn still slept on the bed he had made of his trench coat while Sadie, he'd since discovered, nestled in a crawlspace she had dug out beneath some broken floorboards, with a blanket and a knife for comfort.

He still feared this mysterious whelp, this Sadie Fox, in ways he was unable to define. In the middle of the night he heard her talking to herself, praying, whispering phrases she had half heard from church services. *Pray my soul to keep. Though I walk through the shadow of the valley of death. Lord is a shepherd.* Sometimes he lifted the broken board and watched her sleeping among the scraps of clothes and apple cores and chicken bones. He observed the twitch of her brow and the flex of her toe, the Morse code of her dreaming that played along her body.

But she watched him, too. Sometimes he opened his eyes at night to see her, visible at first as two large, milky pearls blinking in the dark. Then, depending on the size of the moon, perhaps the outline of her jaw or the dull shine of her hair, the glint of her knife. The first time this happened they watched each other in silence: Quinn on his side on the floor; she, a dislodged gargoyle by the door with her arms wrapped around her knees. Although he was certain she knew he was awake, they didn't acknowledge each other then, or the next day.

After several nights of this, she sidled deeper into the room, inch by inch, until she was so close Quinn could smell the tang of her unwashed skin. One morning, he woke to discover her folded into the curl of his body, her sweaty hair tickling his throat, her heartbeat hard and fast against his own. Without discussion, this became the way they slept every night.

The summer days droned on. They settled into a pantomime of domesticity: tidying the shack; gossiping about Flint residents; sharing meals; dozing through the long afternoons, one of her thin arms flung across his chest. Day and night, the opiate tide of heat moved through the wreck of the ramshackle cottage.

The cross Sadie had demanded Quinn carve into his chest started to heal over, but there began to appear all over his body—particularly about his torso and arms—other wounds, a barbed-wire galaxy of dark planets and stars, of tiny moons adrift over his pale skin. Some were deep and painful, others mere nicks. Of making them himself he had no memory. Most mornings he would wake to discover one or two more. Perhaps Sadie did it as he slept. Who knew what she was capable of? If she noticed them when they bathed or slept, she didn't mention it. He pored over them in the morning, trying to determine which were new. He kept his shirt sleeves rolled down when he visited his mother but was aware at all times of their minute keening.

They swam sometimes in a nearby creek, washed their clothes, and dried them on rocks or flung across branches. Quinn's beard itched as it grew. At night, when the house and surrounding bush were still, he heard the whiskers growing through his cheeks with a sound like that of countless nails being prised from wood. Inspecting himself in a shard of mirror he was surprised to detect in his bristles spatters of grey, as if the beard were that of an older man grafted over his more youthful face. Absently he stroked this new feature, finding in the action a curious pleasure.

Sometimes Sadie vanished for hours, whereupon he would pace around the ruined house or sit marooned with his back to a crumbling wall and listen, just listen, trying to pick through the bird calls and rustling leaves, straining to hear a sign of her return. On several occasions he attempted to follow her but was never able to keep up, and each time she disappeared he feared she'd left for good. He fretted over the things that might happen and became certain with every passing hour that disaster had befallen her: she had slipped into a mine shaft, been caught by his uncle, been bitten by a snake.

But always, regardless of how stonily he waited, she would appear from nowhere, approaching with no audible footfall and no explanation as to her former whereabouts. He was surprised at the desperation he felt at her absence. Over the years he had inured himself to solitude and often found it preferable to be alone. He had become a man who kept himself aloof, but now this. This strange longing.

Sadie didn't talk much or, rather, she didn't reveal much more about herself. If Quinn asked about her parents, she shrugged and made indeterminate noises of regret. If he continued she became sullen, then angry, causing Quinn to feel guilty for pressing her so. He shuddered to imagine all the children of the world left defenceless, abandoned by war or disease to fend for themselves. He pictured a crusading army of them storming over the land with Sarah at their head, seeking retribution from those who had failed them.

He saw her sometimes when he was out collecting wood or returning from visiting his mother. She would be kneeling in the bracken apparently engaged in conversation with an insect or lizard he couldn't see. Once he saw her standing with her entire body pressed to the trunk of a paperbark tree, in communion with its peeling surface. He watched her from ten feet away until she turned to him as if she had known of his presence all along, blinked, ran a hand through her greasy hair and said, "This tree says it will rain tonight. The ants say the same thing. They know everything, of course. They talk with everyone here. You see how they stop and chat with each other?"

Rain seemed unlikely: overhead the sky was blue and cloudless. That night they ate boiled potatoes and bread smeared with honey. The shack was lit by numerous candles and a gas lamp she had picked up somewhere.

Later, he heard the dark rumble of thunder, followed by the spatter, only a purr at first but increasing in clamour like an applauding audience rising to its feet, of rain. He went outside and onto his outstretched palm fell large, sluggish drops. A surge of comfort and fear overwhelmed him as he sensed Sadie behind him in the shack watching him. Rain, just as she'd said. Rain.

15

The air in his mother's room was warm, narcotic. As usual, she was asleep. Her profile was queenly, her neck marmoreal. The curtains were drawn against the summer sun.

He thought about how, in France during the war, he was billeted with several other Australian soldiers at a farmhouse in a village that was home to about a hundred families. The village had cobbled streets and houses with thatched roofs, a tatty square of yellow sand in which old men gathered to smoke in the afternoon. There was also a church rumoured to contain, among other things, the immaculately preserved body of a shepherdess beheaded hundreds of years earlier for spurning the advances of a scoundrel, but who had carried her severed head several miles before dropping dead. The village might have been just as it was hundreds of years ago were it not for the persistent thump of artillery from the Front twenty miles away.

An elderly couple managed the farm. Their eleven-year-old grandson Philippe lived with them: Philippe's father was away fighting, and his mother was in Paris for reasons that were never clear. The boy would linger in the doorway as the soldiers played cards at night. A fellow called Bill Spark named him The Watcher. "Look out, boys," he would say with a wink. "The Watcher's 'ere. Better mind your *langwidge* now."

It was late winter, 1918. The air swirled with news and rumours: the Germans had captured one hundred thousand men on the Eastern Front; the British were advancing on the Jerusalem–Nablus Road; hundreds were lost when a cruiser was sunk off the Irish coast; Billy Hughes had typhoid. Quinn's own battalion was down from one thousand men to around three hundred. He had expected some atonement from his war experience, but it had offered nothing of the sort. Men died and were replaced by others. They huddled underground in trenches, in hollows, in ruins, many of them so muddied and grey about the gills they might have been fashioned from the earth itself. By this stage they didn't fear death so much as they feared living this way forever. War, he had discovered, blighted every sense a man possessed: if he closed his eyes to the sight of ruined trees and bloodied men, he still heard guns and screaming; if he covered his ears he still felt the jolting earth; the smell of gas lined his nostrils; everything he touched was wet or bloody. Even when asleep, he dreamed of flickering explosions of light, of torn clothing, of grunting laughter. And on and on it went.

And his sister was still dead.

One cold afternoon, squatting with his back to one of the barn's stone walls, Quinn became aware the boy was watching him and, in time, Philippe tore over to him through a gaggle of geese. He had blue eyes and freckles across his nose. Quinn was fond of the boy. He wanted to assure him his mother and father would be fine and that the war would soon be over, but he didn't know the language and, besides, he might well be wrong. False assurances were certainly more harmful than none at all.

Philippe sized him up and started talking. "You want," he said in his fractured English, "you come with me. I show you . . . something."

Quinn shook his head. He wanted to stay where he was, with his back against a wall that had probably been standing for three hundred years. But the boy was insistent. He tugged at Quinn's sleeve and, eventually, he relented.

The village smelled of manure and of bread. They passed an old woman dressed in black who scowled at them. They arrived at a large, wooden door. Philippe knocked and implored whoever was on the other side to open up. After a few minutes, there was the sound of a bolt sliding back and they slipped through. A man ushered them into a stone portico that led to a courtyard. Quinn could now see the man was wearing a cassock: a priest, then. Quinn was becoming impatient. He was cold and hungry. He blew into his cupped hands and stamped his feet.

They stepped into a stable that was empty save for straw scattered over the ground. Philippe and the priest crossed to the far corner where they kneeled to sweep a space on the floor with their hands. They ran their fingers along the seam of what resembled a cellar door, which they hauled open by means of a brass ring. The priest was displeased, but lit a candle and descended grumbling into the cellar. Philippe indicated that Quinn should follow.

He paused. How was he to know these Catholics weren't intending to murder him? He had heard rumours of such traitors. Had anyone seen him leave with the boy? He jammed his hands under his armpits and stared back to the trapezoid of sunlight aslant in the courtyard. But when Philippe urged him on, Quinn climbed down the wooden stairs.

The cellar was dank but bloomed with an incongruous tropical smell, like that of overripe fruit. The priest busied himself lighting extra candles and drew back a curtain before turning to Quinn with shy pride.

Quinn gasped. Lying on a low table was a girl dressed in white. In the uncertain light the table was indistinguishable from the gloom, and this gave her the appearance of hovering unsupported at waist height. On the wall above was pinned a card of the Virgin Mary and on a nearby shelf was an assortment of crosses, unlit candles, silver cups and trays. Philippe smiled and nodded. "Saint Solange," he was saying. "*C'est Saint Solange.*"

The saint was young, with dark and brittle hair. Her hands, resting on her stomach, were thin and desiccated, more like claws, with fingernails the colour of port. A pink ribbon was tied around her neck, and attached to it by a tiny clasp was a silver cross partially hidden behind her high collar. Her dress was torn here and there, but most touching of all were the brown socks that covered her tiny feet.

Quinn was overcome. His throat quivered and burned. He clamped a hand across his mouth not only to prevent the escape of sobs that gurgled up from within, but to halt the very intake of breath. His eyes streamed with tears. The unmistakable dark, wet sounds of grief oozed through his fingers.

If a single image were to remain from Quinn's time at war it would be of this saint who had been dead for hundreds of years but whose face—cracked and sallow as it was—lent her the look of mere sleep, as if she might open her eyes at any moment, turn to him and smile, as his mother now did in her airless room.

"Ah. My long-lost boy." She fumbled for the glass of water on her bedside table. When she had drunk, she reached out to him, as was her habit. Around her on the bed were half-a-dozen books, some splayed open to reveal blocks of type. "Do you remember Ulysses? How during his adventures some of his men were given a plant to eat that made them forget all thoughts of home—of the past—and wish to remain exactly where they were? On an island, I think."

Quinn did not remember, but nodded nonetheless. His mother was delirious.

"Lotus plant," she went on. "Of course Ulysses also claimed to have had an encounter with a mob of Cyclops, so I am unsure how much we should believe his stories, you know."

Quinn flicked through the pages of a book he had picked up. He sat on the edge of the bed. "Should I read you something?"

But she had descended into the labyrinth of her memory. "I remember how Sarah loved to play that game—what was it?—that one with the sheep bones. Knuckles! Balancing them on the back of her hand. She played it for hours, didn't she? A sound through the house like rodents. That is what I remember of her, one of the things I remember about her. The damn things are probably still in her room. In that box, perhaps."

Sarah had often nagged him to play that game with her and he had done so countless times—under the shade of a eucalypt, on the veranda when it rained, even in the dirt beneath the house when it was hot. The game remained a constant passion among so many passing fancies; she even had a particular set of the bones, each marked with a crude *SW* in blue ink that wore off and had to be re-lettered every few weeks.

They sat in silence for several minutes. The clock ticked.

"You have new clothes?" she asked.

"Yes."

"Where did you get them?"

Quinn fidgeted. He hated lying to his mother but told her he bought them.

"Not here, I trust."

"No. In Sydney."

His mother seemed satisfied. "Quinn, I was thinking. You should go away. Don't stay here. Go to Queensland where you will be safe. Stay with your brother." She rummaged under the bedclothes and produced a crumpled envelope that she pressed to him. "Here. It has his address on the back. Take it."

"What does he think?"

"About what?"

"Does he think I did it?"

Mary hesitated. "We don't speak of it, but I could write to him, I could tell him what you told me."

He took the envelope but didn't look at it. The paper was much handled.

"Why did you come back?"

He was dismayed. "I thought you would be glad."

Mary looked stricken and coughed wetly. "Oh, Quinn. I am. I am. I told you: I would give anything for you all to be back here. You and William and Sarah. But what happened has happened. Everything has changed."

The speech had drained her. She slumped back into the pillows. She coughed again, and Quinn held the glass of water to her lips. "Even the water tastes different," she said when she had drunk. "This place has been poisoned. That's what a murder does."

His mother looked worse than on any previous occasion that Quinn had visited. She licked her lips over and over, and her face contorted as if the muscles beneath her sallow skin were operating under a malign influence.

"You are thin," she said, as if now conducting a different conversation. "And ragged. Some think it might be the end of the world. The minister was here recently. He visits me on the veranda, too. Said it was in the Bible, as if that would make me feel better. *The Lord shall smite thee with a consumption, and with a fever.* Pestilence. It's one of the four horsemen, you know."

Quinn batted dust from his trousers. Rumours of the end of the world had been rife in the past few months. Men on the *Argyllshire* spoke nervously of the Virgin talking to girls in Portugal, of swarms of locusts in Palestine, of strange lights over all the waters of the world. It was something he didn't wish to consider.

"What do you think, Quinn? You think this might be the end?"

He saw in his mother the expression that haunted those who feared they were soon to die, but wished to be reassured nonetheless. "I don't think so," he said at last, but without conviction.

"It is no matter. At least I will see my beloved Sarah." She drank again from the water glass before continuing. "Widows, widowers. Orphan—and you know I was already one of those. Do you know, Quinn, there isn't even a word for a parent who has lost a child? Strange, isn't it? You would think, after all these centuries of war and disease and trouble, but no, there is a hole in the English language. It is unspeakable. Bereft."

Quinn didn't point out that there was no word, either, for a brother who has lost his only sister.

"*Blessed are they that mourn,*" she murmured, "*for they shall be comforted.*" His mother knew a Bible verse for most things.

She looked at him anew. Something had occurred to her. "Should I fear you, Quinn?"

"Please, Mother."

A dry breeze edged through the heavy red curtain. She coughed. "If we didn't believe in our children, the human race would be lost. When everything else is in ruins, family is all we have. And God, of course."

She sighed and gestured at the books on the bed. "Your father brought these in this morning before he left. I asked him to fetch me something to read and he grabbed this armful. Can't blame him, I suppose. Didn't want to stay here with me too long."

His mother fell still. Quinn examined the book in his hand. After a few minutes, he began to read out loud from a random page.

"*How do you know that?*" he read. "*Have you been there to see? And if you had been there to see, and had seen none, that would not prove that there were none . . . And no one has a right to say that no water babies exist, till they have seen no water babies existing; which is quite a different thing, mind, from not seeing water babies . . ."*

He continued to read for another ten minutes until his mother was asleep, but when he closed the book to leave, she opened her eyes and drew him towards her.

"Don't go yet. Please."

"Mother. You are unwell. I have to go before Father comes back."

"Tell me where you were before the war. Tell me something of your life."

He sighed. "Before the war I worked for a bloke on his farm," he said. "And I built railways for a while near Grafton—"

Nathaniel's voice called out from the yard. His mother gasped. Quinn heard the clump of his father's boots on the veranda outside.

16

Panicked, Quinn stepped behind the wardrobe. His father leaned partway through the open window. Quinn shrank back further. His heart clattered beneath his ribs but his father didn't see him in the shadows.

"Are you alright, Mary?"

"I'm fine."

"But I heard talking."

Mary shooed Nathaniel away from the window and he lurched backwards and fell into the chair on the veranda. It was clear he was drunk. His breathing was stolid. He asked again how she was.

"The doctor," he was saying over and over, "the doctor can only do so much." There was fear and trembling in his voice. He said the other medicine he had ordered from Sydney, whatever the bloody thing was called, was yet to arrive but it would come any day now. Things were so bloody slow.

After a few minutes he calmed down, and he and Mary talked of other things, but hesitantly, as if afraid of hurting each other. They spoke of the heat and of the goings-on of a Melbourne gangster. He told her further rumours about the epidemic: Joe Ryan saying he had heard it was, in fact, scarlet fever. Mary scoffed.

The wardrobe Quinn cowered against smelled of polish and was tacky to the touch, as if it were sweating out the coats of varnish applied to it over the years. Outside in the hot wind a gate creaked and slapped, creaked and slapped. He made out the *pop pop* sound of his father tapping his pipe against his palm to dislodge charred tobacco. Although he couldn't see him clearly, Quinn knew his father would now lean forward and fill the pipe while staring into the middle distance, perhaps gnawing on his moustache as he did so. Despite his passionate nature, Nathaniel Walker was a man reluctant to engage in argument and this ritual of pinching tobacco from its tin, tamping it down and then searching for a match had always been effective in stalling an inconvenient interlocutor. There came the pleasing sweet smell of burning tobacco. His father rambled drunkenly about this and that.

Mary's eyelids sagged like two flowers overburdened with dew, then her unhinged gaze drifted across the room and alighted, as if with reluctance, upon Quinn. Her skin gleamed with fever. "Tell me," she said, not taking her eyes from her son. "What is it exactly you saw that day, Nathaniel?"

"What?" Nathaniel sat forward in his chair.

Mary licked her lips. "What did you see?"

"When, Mary?"

"On the day you found Sarah."

From where he stood, Quinn was able to observe not only his mother lying supine on her bed as if upon a funeral barge, but also the spectral shape of his father behind the curtained window. He panicked. He wondered if this were a trap devised by his mother. Had she planned this all along? He shook his head at her, urging her to halt her queries.

Nathaniel grunted to himself. "By God. You never wanted to know the details before, Mary. Why now?"

"Perhaps it's time."

His father muttered something, to which Mary repeated her wish to hear exactly what had happened all those years ago.

Quinn shut his eyes. On the troopship back to Australia after the war there had been men made blind and deaf by their injuries. He had seen them shuffle forlornly around the surf-slick decks of the *Argyllshire*. They were stoppered vessels, wrapped in bandages, closed off, each inhabiting a landscape unto themselves as they faced an ocean they could neither see nor hear. Everything to them was black and noiseless. There was a private called Little Thommo who chested the railings as if checking they would bear his weight and who, sure enough, was one of those soon lost overboard. Quinn had watched them with fear and envy. What a terrible freedom, he thought, to be so sealed off from the rigours of the world.

Like a child reluctant to be discovered, he kept his eyes shut. Through muddy hearing he discerned the curtain flapping in the hot wind. He felt sure the beat-beat-beating of his heart could be heard several feet away and placed a hand on his chest as if it were a skittish animal he might quieten with his touch. He sensed his mother's gaze still on him.

"It's so long ago," his father said at last.

"But you were so sure at the time—"

"I still am."

"Then tell me."

Quinn's father belched. "I would rather not. You are ill. It is so many years ago."

"Does it feel that way to you, Nathaniel? Does it? For me it is as if they are still here with me, both of them, *all* of them. Sarah and William and Quinn. All of them here moving around, coming in and out of my room, asking me things. Do you remember when Quinn went through that phase of insisting his name was *duck*? Over and over you used to ask him what his name was, just to hear him say it. *My little duck*, you called him. Do you remember? And how serious and quiet William was, even as a boy? And poor Sarah . . ." Mary lapsed into weeping.

Quinn's father smoked his pipe. His silence made it clear his wife's tears were nothing new to him.

After several minutes, he spoke. "I came down the road on the mare we had at the time. Jenny. It was late—I'm sure you remember that—and Sarah had been gone for hours. The pair of them had been gone all afternoon. You know how they were together, always plotting at something like a pair of bloody savages. It was the boy's fault, of course. Sarah was too young to be left in his care so much—"

"Don't be ridiculous. They looked after each other."

His father harrumphed. "Do you remember when they went missing once, a year or so before . . . before Sarah died? When they were meant to be at school? And they got it into their heads to steal something from Oliver Sharp's place. *That* was the boy's idea. And someone found them down there with my spade and dragged them home. Lucky old Sharp didn't know what was going on."

Quinn recalled that morning vividly. It was a bright, crisp day in spring, three years before Sarah was killed. William, at eighteen, was helping Mr. Greely in his orchard most days. All three of them set off early, walking together to Greely's place, from where Quinn and Sarah would make their own way to school.

Sarah loved school because it multiplied the pool of children available for her to organise into troupes for her various games. Passers-by chuckled at the sight of her standing on a fruit box, from where she would dictate the rules of her latest endeavour to half-a-dozen squirming children. In her boldness and in her quest for novelty, she was more like their father than anyone divined.

Most mornings, Quinn would pause at a scrappy track near their home to throw stones at a tin sign hammered to a tree twenty feet away, on which were scrawled the words *no shoot*. From five attempts he usually hit the sign at least three times.

Sarah watched him throw with a critical eye. "No chance," she said as Quinn released the first stone, which indeed sailed wide of the mark. "You always throw much too far to the right."

Quinn tried again and was this time rewarded with the satisfying *clank* of rock striking tin. Sarah clapped in delight and urged him to throw again. Quinn succeeded in his next three efforts. William was by now a fair way off and called out for them to hurry, but they ignored him. Excited, Sarah told Quinn that if he hit the sign on the next throw it would be five times in a row.

Again William called out to them that he was going. Quinn waved to show he had understood, and William vanished into the trees.

"If you hit it five times in a row you get a prize," Sarah said as she handed him a suitable rock.

"What's the prize?"

Sarah looked down at a blade of grass in her hand. "You got to do it first, Pim."

He paused, then wheeled around and threw the rock without even taking aim. The throw was perfect. *Clank*. Sarah squealed and flung her arms around his neck.

"So what's the prize?"

"An ad*ven*ture."

Quinn shivered. "No. We should go to school. Miss Haylock is probably waiting for us."

Sarah scratched her eyebrow and affected no enthusiasm one way or the other, as if it were all the same to her. "Oh. Suit yourself."

Quinn squinted about at the surrounding trees. The morning had begun like any other—oats for breakfast, letting the chooks out of their coop, being bustled out the door by their mother—but now, suddenly, the day had cracked open like an egg. This was Sarah's terrible gift: her ability to infuse the world with possibility.

As always, Quinn relented, and ten minutes later they found themselves by the Flint River crouching beneath the drooping fronds of a willow tree. The bank was muddy and the seat of his trousers was soon wet. He grew uneasy as Sarah indicated Oliver Sharp's bark-and-blanket humpy fifty yards away. She told him that Mr. Sharp had fifty pounds in a sack buried beneath a tree.

"He sets out for his claim near Sparrowhawk at the crack of dawn," Sarah was saying. "Actually it's probably *more* than fifty pounds. Imagine."

"How do you know?"

"I just know."

Quinn didn't like the sound of this. His sister often spoke most authoritatively when her information was at its least reliable.

"Now," she went on, "it's Mother's birthday soon and I thought we could take a bit of Mr. Sharp's money and buy her something. Only *two pounds*," she hissed over his protests. "Enough for a shawl at the store."

"We can't do that. Stealing is wrong."

But Sarah had shuffled over to a nearby bush and produced from behind it a spade that she handed to him. "Here. Use this. Let's go. No one will even know."

He recognised the implement as one of his father's tools. "How did this get here?"

"I put it there last night. You have to plan these things, Quinn. Now —"

At that moment, her eyes and mouth opened wide, synchronised, like those of a marionette. Quinn had rarely seen Sarah show fear. Still on his haunches, he swivelled to see Mr. Sharp looming above them with a mattock over one shoulder, his rheumy eyes pinched into a bitter squint. Sarah squealed, lost her footing on the greasy bank and—arms windmilling, grasping at a willow frond that snapped off in her hand— she tumbled backwards into the river.

Their father was furious with Quinn when the pair of them showed up shamefaced at the house later that morning escorted by Constable Mackey. The incident was a minor scandal in Flint, but Sarah was resourceful and within days she adapted the adventure into a tale of derring-do worthy of a penny dreadful. Perched on her fruit crate, she spellbound the children at school with the account of her narrow escape from old Mr. Sharp who by this time had developed a hunched back and claws and—rather than kindly helping her from the river, as had really happened—had attempted to split her skull with his mattock.

Quinn opened his eyes. He was disoriented. It felt as though his sister was with them again; he and his parents had conjured her with the combined force of their imagining. From the quality of their awkward silence, he knew his parents had sensed it, too. But it was only a few seconds. Then she was gone.

"That day, it was raining fit to flood." His father was continuing his account. "Thunder and all. Jenny always hated thunder. And I asked around town. No one had seen her, but I ran into Jim Gracie and he said he had seen them by Wilson's Point. Gracie looked terrified of the storm himself."

"See, that is strange," Mary interrupted. "The children never played down there, not after the Gunn girl drowned there in '07. And that other girl—do you remember?—not long after we moved here. Sarah hated Wilson's Point."

"Well, the boy dragged her there, I suppose. Why do you doubt me? Do you not trust what I saw with my eyes? I wish as much as you that none of this happened. My God, to have a son like that."

"Do you really think he did it?"

"It is what I saw."

"But you didn't see him . . . you didn't see him *do* it?"

"You are blinded by your love for the boy."

"Did you see him do it, Nathaniel? It's important."

Quinn's father exhaled loudly. "No."

Mary closed her eyes, exhausted, whittled down by her twin vices of prayer and hopelessness.

"But you saw them together, Mary. You saw how they were . . ."

"They were brother and sister."

". . . always hiding, playing games. Disappearing under the house. You know what they called them down The Mail, because they were together so much? Do you even know? Romeo and Juliet. Romeo and *Juliet*."

"Don't be foolish. Only you called them that."

"No! Your brother did, too. He said as much to me later. Said it was clear all along what was going to happen."

Mary coughed long and hard. "You're being ridiculous. Robert would never say such a thing. He loved that girl as much as we did."

A hot silence thickened in the room. *He loved that girl as much as we did.* A faint wobble insinuated itself into Quinn's knees. He wanted to slide down the side of the wardrobe to the floor but feared his father would notice him. The urge to do so was almost irresistible, but he remained standing, shoulders slumped like those of a man at the gallows. He wondered if God could see into the broken bones of his heart.

"Anyway," his father continued, "William was home with you, in fever. I left Jenny tethered by the reeds and went over the low embankment. The lake was high. I was drenched to the skin. And I went to that old shed and the boy was there and he was . . . He had the knife in his hands and Sarah was on the floor and he looked up at me with an awful expression." He re-lit his pipe. "Mary? Let's leave this. Please? It is better that way. It has taken us all this time to forget it. Let's leave the past alone."

Mary gasped for air. Her fingers scrabbled at her bedding. "But it will not leave us alone, Nathaniel. Will not leave *me* alone."

Quinn's father got out of his chair and approached the window. "Are you alright? For God's sake."

Quinn shrank deeper into the shadows.

"Stay away from the window," Mary said. "Please. You'll catch it. Stay away."

Nathaniel reeled back. He dropped his pipe, swore and bent to retrieve it.

"But what next, Nathaniel?"

Quinn's father sighed with exasperation. His step was heavy on the boards as he paced. "The boy said not a word, but he had a look as if he had learned something terrible. He was pale and he was covered in blood. And that's when your brother showed up and said something and the boy shook his head and threw down the knife and ran off. He didn't say anything, but he ran, Mary. By God, he ran like a bloody rabbit."

Part Three

THE CAVE OF HANDS

17

The following day, Quinn watched his sleeping mother for some time. Already she resembled a creature not of this world, as if the greater part of her had been drawn away, like a tide, during the night. Her face appeared to have shrunk and there were flecks of dried blood on her upper lip. After some minutes, she opened her eyes and muttered, "Quinn. Tell me what you saw. On that day."

"I saw nothing, Mother."

"You heard what your father told me. Yesterday, or whenever that was. Were you here?"

"Yes."

"Why did you run off that day?"

He wiped her brow with a wet washcloth. "I don't know. I was afraid."

"But where did you go?"

Quinn toyed with the cloth in his hands. "I woke at some stage, Mother. I don't know how long it had been since I left here, perhaps two weeks? Long enough for the initial terror to dissolve but not long enough for me to make a plan of what to do. I had cuts all over my body from sleeping on the ground and from falling over. My back was bruised and sore. I thought I would probably die out there and, you know, the idea of it didn't really worry me too much. Death was not so frightening. I wondered how I would survive without Sarah, how I would survive after what had happened to her. I didn't even know then that anyone thought it was me who did it. That was too monstrous. It was only later I heard about that.

"I don't know what I did. I stared at the heavens, waited for the stars to fall from their orbit. Time passes, regardless of clocks. I slept on rocks. I watched clouds break and re-form into new shapes overhead. A scowling cat, a roll of fog, one day a herd of pale horses billowed over the sky. The world had never seemed so huge to me before. I was used to this place. To Flint. I had never wanted to leave. I never had to.

"I was followed by dogs for a few days. They barked as though encouraging me to join them and I thought about *The Jungle Book* you had read to us. Do you remember that? I imagined running with them like Mowgli as they scoured the countryside, and of huddling with them in their cave. I thought at least they would keep me warm at night. But I slept in a tree and they vanished."

He remembered that much of the time was spent trying to find food. He'd stumbled across rabbits in traps and stolen fruit from orchards. A man could get used to hunger. He learned this in the war, too. One could always survive, if survival was all that was required.

"The days became as mad as a dream," he continued. He'd seen incredible things: an ocean liner carving through fields of wheat. In the morning he sometimes heard breathing close by his ear. The harsh cry of birds all night long. He'd imagined he was taken up by two Arabian merchants who led him to their cave of treasure, and that he sailed on a boat that was destroyed by a sea monster in the Persian Gulf. He'd been mad with hunger and grief. With anxiety. He'd believed he had entered another, stranger world where anything was possible, which perhaps was true.

He looked down at his mother, who had hardly stirred these past few minutes. "When I first left Flint all those years ago it was not through choice. You must believe me on this. I hadn't *done* anything. I wandered aimlessly and my only thought was of escape even though I had done nothing wrong. An elderly couple found me insensible on their property and cared for me until I could walk. My voice was lost so I wrote them notes to explain where I had come from, or what I could recall. They were kind to me and I helped Mr. Tucker around his property—cutting wood and tending his sheep. Then I heard that I was the suspect in Sarah's murder. God, how awful. I moved on and worked on other properties as a roustabout or looking after horses. I was good with animals, and they liked me and trusted me. In truth I preferred their silent company to that of the stockmen or farmhands who drank and staggered in late at night, swearing and carrying on, tripping over their swags in the dark.

"People gave me odd jobs in exchange for board. I learned how to build a house, how to sink a well. I worked in Tamworth for a blacksmith lugging material. I met many kind people. No one asked how I came to be travelling alone."

Quinn stopped speaking. His mother didn't move, made no sign she had even noticed. Although relieved to feel her exhalation against his cheek when he leaned down, he was dismayed at the sour smell of rubbish on her breath. Melancholy swelled his heart. "I went to Newcastle after a while," he continued when he was able. "And I joined a boat that took goods to Brisbane. A steamer. It was hard work, but it was satisfying. I learned many things. There were a few of us on board, but the solitude was immense. At night I stared out over the universe and I thought I might hear the breath of God who scattered the stars of the Milky Way. Orion, Dog Star. It was comforting and terrifying. I joined other boats and travelled the world. I saw the markets of Cairo and the deserts of Spain. Thick smoke in the shadows, the smell of charcoal. Women in rattan cages, lizards tethered by their tails hanging from the ceilings of crowded stalls. I saw camels in the markets of Tangier. Mother, did you know they have a herb in Shanghai that smells exactly like lightning? And there are men who press secret powders into vials, who can make a man disappear without a word? That there are dragons in the Far East? I worked for a few months building rail lines near Grafton. Then the war, of course. The Great War, which erased everything that came before."

Quinn collected himself. "It took a long time to come back here, Mother, but you were never far from my thoughts. Even during the war, *especially* during the war when I feared I would die at any moment. In those freezing trenches I thought of you and Father and William, and of Sarah and what had happened. The idea that you considered me a killer was unbearable. I tried to imagine myself back here. I wished I had a magic carpet, a genie from a bottle who might grant me a single wish. Anything. I'm sorry at the way everything turned out, Mother. My leaving was unforgivable. I'm sorry."

Mary Walker made no sign she had heard him but, at last, she opened her swollen eyes and faced him. "Thank you," she said. She picked at her sheet. "Give me some water, please."

Quinn did as she asked, then she beckoned him close.

"Listen to me," she whispered. "I have been thinking, you know. Quinn, I thought I would learn everything from books. Not only of the present, but of the past as well. They enabled me to talk with interesting people and know things of other places. And I have learned many wonderful things about the world away from here. About ancient wars and lost cities, of strange kings and queens. I know all about the Seven Wonders of the World." Here she coughed for some time. "But, as much as they can be a way to learn about the world, I think perhaps stories are also a way of hiding from it. Do you understand me?"

Quinn felt tears boiling behind his eyes. He nodded.

"After all," she went on, her words by now almost inaudible. "After all, what good is it to me now to know about the Hanging Gardens of Babylon? Or that Henry's fifth wife was Catherine Howard now that I'm here on my deathbed—"

"Mother! You are not on your deathbed. Don't say such a thing. Please."

"Tell me. What good are stories?"

From the enamel dish on the bedside table Quinn took the wet cloth and pressed it to her fevered brow. His hands shook as he returned the cloth to the tepid water.

"Do you know what I mean? Quinn?"

He stood. "Mother, you are feverish. I will freshen this water. It is no cooler than you are."

His mother gripped his leg with her pathetic fingers.

He stared at her, horrified, as it dawned on him. "My God. You still don't believe me, do you?"

"It's not that . . ."

"Then what?"

She took a long time to answer. "A mother knows when her child is keeping something from her. Quinn, tell me what you saw that day. I need to know. Before I die. What did you see?"

He paused with the dish in his hand. It was a request he had been dreading.

"Quinn?"

"There is nothing more to tell you. I found her and she was already dead. Whoever did it was long gone."

"Very well." She fumbled beside her and pressed a tea tin to him. "Here. Take this. It's thirty pounds, maybe more. All we have. Take it and go, Quinn."

He opened the tin. Sure enough, inside was a roll of notes bound tightly with string.

"You should get away from here before they find you. Leave us, my son. Go and live your life. You are free. This place has been no good for us—"

"But I can't leave you. I can't take this."

"You can and you will. I prayed for your return but now I want you to leave while you still can. You have done all you needed to by coming back. They will kill you if they find you. I need to know that you will be safe. Please. I have already lost one child, I cannot bear to lose another. Can you not see that, Quinn?"

He took the roll from the tin and held it in his palm. He had never seen so much money. It was a small fortune. He stared at it for a long time. She was right; it was only a matter of time before his uncle found him and Sadie, and then everything would be lost.

He leaned down to kiss his mother's hot forehead. "Are you sure, Mother?"

"I am sure." She gasped for breath.

"Will you be alright?"

"Leave as soon as you can. Promise me."

He thumbed the roll of money.

"Quinn, do you promise?"

"Cross my heart."

He said goodbye and waited for her response, but she said nothing further, whether from exhaustion or despair he couldn't tell. He changed the water in the dish and refilled her glass. He lingered at her side for several minutes until, finally, he crept away.

·⁂·

When he returned to the shack an hour later, Sadie was sitting cross-legged on the floor gnawing on a chicken leg. She failed to notice him for several seconds, then glanced up.

"How is your mother?"

He squatted on his haunches. The meeting with his mother had drained him. He felt exhausted. "She's not well. I don't think she has long to live."

"You have been crying."

"Yes."

Sadie tossed away the chicken bone and licked her fingers. She grunted sympathetically. "Before my mother died she said some curious things. Told me our father had flown in to see her." She mimed this by flapping her crooked elbows against her ribs. "They have fever, you know. They don't always realise what they are saying. Ginny Reynolds raved for two days about little blue men she had seen running around her bed and—"

"Sadie. We have to get away from here. We have to leave. Now."

"I can't. I'm waiting for Thomas. I told you that."

"But what about the tracker? He'll be back any day and then Dalton will come after you. After us. They'll kill us."

"We have time to wait a bit longer."

The girl was so infuriating. "What if the tracker gets back before Thomas?" he demanded. "Then what will we do? Then it will be too late."

She frowned. It seemed she had not even considered this.

"I have some money," Quinn went on, eager to press his case. "We can get away from here. Go to Sydney. To Queensland, even."

She looked at him. "I have a special way to find out exactly when the tracker will be back."

"How?"

She dismissed his query. "In any case there are things we need to do first."

"Like what?"

She sauntered over and squatted before him, bringing her odour of lemons, of soil and of girlish sweat. She inspected him closely with her dark, watery eyes before raising a hand and caressing his beard. Quinn shrank back. Sadie Fox, so febrile with energy he feared she might scorch him with her touch.

"A few things," she said.

She trotted away, rummaged in the next room and returned to rearrange herself on the floor before him. She took his face in her hand and turned his head this way and that. Then with the slightest upward pressure on his chin, she tilted his head back, leaving his throat naked to the air. From the bottom edge of his vision, Quinn caught the fishtail flicker of his razor in her hand.

He drew back and moved to protect his throat but the steel was already at his neck. A handful of his shirt in Sadie's grip forestalled any sudden movement.

"What"s the matter?" she asked.

Something small meandered down his bare neck, an ant or spider perhaps, a dribble of sweat.

"Did you think I might kill you? Cut your throat? Would you even care, Quinn Walker?"

They stayed like that for some seconds, she smirking, he frozen, until she pressed the blade against his skin and trimmed the edges of his beard. This she did in silence, pursing her mouth in sympathy as Quinn stared at the water stains and cobwebs on the ceiling. The razor crackled against his cheeks and neck. When she was done, Sadie loosened her grip and removed the blade. Quinn slumped back on his heels.

"I needed to tidy your beard," she said, closing the razor and handing it to him. Then she brushed the tiny trimmed hairs from his shirtfront and collected them in her palm as one might a handful of iron filings. "You're almost ready now."

"Ready for what?"

But she only smiled at him, as if it were a foolish question to which surely he knew the answer.

18

Quinn lay on his back. It was late afternoon, hot. He wondered once again what he was doing in this strange house with Sadie Fox. He heard her singing. Despite the wretched quality of her voice, her earnest quavering made him smile. She had told him the Donovans had a phonograph player and when they wound it up on Sunday evenings she sometimes hid in the rose bush beneath their window. The thought of her huddling against the wall of a stranger's house broke his heart.

What's the use of worrying?
It never was worthwhile, so
Pack up your troubles in your old kitbag
And smile, smile, smile

Her singing devolved into exuberant humming before she launched into another verse. Clearly, she had not been paying attention to the words.

Private Perks he went a-marching into Flanders
With his smile
His funny smile . . .

She paused and there followed the noise, faint at first, of what sounded like a family of well-shod mice skittering a short distance over the boards. Startled, Quinn sat up. Again she hummed, followed by a few half-sung words. He jammed a finger into his ear. His rotten hearing was still no better. He stood and went to the doorway of the next room.

Although she had her back to him and appeared to be absorbed in what she was doing, he was sure she was aware of him standing there. She always was.

She scattered something to the floor and, smiling, turned to face him. "You want to play?"

"Play what?"

She laughed, revealing a glint of teeth, like a shiv tucked behind her lips. "You know."

Quinn felt queasy. His palms were clammy.

Sadie scooped objects from the floor and held out her hand. In her palm were five or six lumpy bones, sheep's vertebrae. "Knuckles, of course!"

He shook his head. "I don't think I know that game."

"You do."

"No. I don't."

"You *do*."

"How would you know?" His tone was more aggressive than he intended, and he regretted it at once.

Unperturbed, she demonstrated it for him. "Everyone knows this game. It's very common. You throw them down, then pick them up, one after another. Like this. Then over hand ones, over hand twos. Oh. Like *that*. You probably forgot, that's all. Then that one, there. Like that . . . and *that*. Then . . . on the back of your hand. Remember now?"

Quinn watched as she showed him again. She tossed the half-a-dozen bones into the air and caught two on the back of her hand. Those two she threw into the air and caught in her palm. The idea was to throw those already caught into the air and attempt to pick up as many of the others as possible before catching them again. He knew there were more complicated versions according to one's expertise. Horse in the stable, over the jump, threading the needle.

Quinn found himself drawn into the room, as if the room—indeed the whole house—had shifted on its meagre foundations to re-situate him within it. A flickering trickery of light and he was on his knees beside her, breathing hard. She took his hand, which he gave up without protest. Her palm was soft and moist as bread dough, and her nails were bitten to the quick.

She prattled on for several minutes, saying how good it would be if they could play together. "It passes the time and it helps with your coordination. People have played it for thousands of years, you know."

He watched her as she spoke. Her lips were cracked and she had a mole on her left cheek he had not noticed before. "Who are you?" he asked in a quivering voice.

Sadie laughed and picked over the bones. "I told you."

Quinn sensed the hard heat of her thigh alongside his own. He coughed into his hand. He felt puzzled, excited. "No. Who are you, *really*?"

She looked at him as if caught in an act of mischief, before her mouth—her entire face—exploded into a grin.

"I'm a little reprobate!"

"What?"

Now serious, Sadie levered herself to standing and looped a strand of hair behind her ear. "I'm Sadie Fox. That's all."

"Where is your family, Miss Sadie Fox?"

She smoothed the front of her dress, which was stained with dirt and food and dried chicken blood. "Dead from the plague. I told you that, too. The bubonic plague, or whatever it's called. My mother died from it, and my father left before I was even born. My brother looked after us, then I did when he went to war. But he'll be back soon and he'll know what to do, even if you don't. He'll help me."

He ignored her implied taunt. "Does Thomas know about your mother?"

She fixed him with her dark-eyed gaze and said something under her breath.

"What?"

She tilted her chin, only a fraction, but enough to make plain her sudden disdain for him. "If you can't help me, why don't you leave?"

"No, I—"

"You *know* what he did to her."

"What? Who?" Quinn began rolling a cigarette with uncooperative fingers. The atmosphere in the room had altered, as if yanked tight. The gas lamp growled.

"Don't you even care what happened to Sarah?" she persisted when he didn't answer.

He threw down his cigarette. "Of course I do. She was my sister."

"You can't hide up here forever. They'll get you, they'll get *us*."

"You're mad."

"And you're scared."

He ignored her and retrieved his ill-rolled cigarette from the floor. He lit it. The smoke irritated his throat but calmed him nonetheless.

Sadie didn't move from the doorway but lifted up her left foot and picked at its filthy sole, removing splinters long embedded in her flesh from going about barefoot. She brushed hair from her eyes. "He took her," she began in a droning voice, "to Wilson's Point, you know where that old shed is?"

"Of course I know. I told you, *I* found her." He sucked again on his cigarette and felt his heart list in the swell of his chest. He wished the girl would shut up; she talked all the bloody time.

"She was by herself because you were supposed to be taking care of her. She was young. Was she afraid of thunder? Of the storm? Perhaps your uncle said he would take her somewhere safe, and she went with him?"

Quinn stood and shook the pins and needles from his left leg. He crossed the dim room, almost leaving the penumbra of lantern light. On the wall was a crumpled print not much larger than a postcard. It was a watercolour painting of a green and benign English countryside, complete with cows and sheep, a ruddy farmer ploughing a field. Puffy clouds dotted the blue sky and in the judder of gaslight, if he squinted, Quinn could animate the scene—observe the farmer's awkward progress, hear the whistle of birds, inhale the loamy scent of the earth. It looked peaceful, a million miles from here.

"And perhaps they played some games?" Sadie went on. "You know how she loved to play games. But then he made her take her clothes off and she tried to get away."

Quinn charged across the room until he towered over her. He longed to strike her, strike her hard, but instead threw down his cigarette and jammed his hands deep in his pockets. "Shut the hell up!"

Sadie said nothing, but looked smug. She fiddled with a twig, twisted it this way and that in her hands.

"How would you know?" he hissed. "You weren't even born."

"I was."

"Barely."

She slumped against the doorframe. "I told you. There are things I *know*. I hear stories. I know about the Mimi spirits that live in rocks, that there is a wind they call the Mistral that makes men mad. About the spider that whistles. About how your father found you with her. I know odd things. There is a plant that screams when you pull it out of the ground, the meek will inherit the earth, the first man to fly ten miles in an aeroplane was Delagrange on June 22nd, 1908, in Milan."

"That's no answer."

Sadie shrugged, breathless after her outburst.

Quinn put his face even closer to hers this time. He could detect her bitter smell. There was dirt on her neck. "Who the hell are you?"

"She fought better than the other girls he killed. Alice Gunn and one before her. Ages ago. That's why he had to use the knife on your sister."

"Shut up."

Sadie was unmoved. "Why did you come back here? Why don't you leave?" She paused. "Well?"

Quinn rubbed at his beard. The gas lantern crackled as if preparing to go out, but rallied. *Why did you come back here?* It was a simple question. He stared at her slouched in the pearlish light. This girl. This curious girl, who waited defiantly, gnawing on a thumbnail.

"I didn't want to come back," he began. "I knew they thought it was me. But I was called here. *She* called me back." He wiped his sweating face. He was embarrassed. He dug about in his pocket and withdrew the match-safe containing the note scrawled by the Cranshaw girl at the séance. Sadie pushed herself off the jamb and licked her lips, as if she expected him to produce a tiny delicacy.

With trembling hands, Quinn uncapped the match-safe and withdrew the note. After such fervent folding and refolding, the paper was thin and crumbling. The safe slipped from his fingers to the floor. He held the note unopened in his hand, unsure what to do with it.

Sadie came closer. She stared up at him, then uttered the words that Quinn had read so often in the past months that they were engraved on his memory. "*Don't forget me. Come back and save me. Please.*"

Quinn's heart fell away. He stood there foolishly with the scrap of paper still folded between his fingers. He bent to retrieve the match-safe from the floor and, watched closely by Sadie, slid the note back into the tin. There followed a lengthy silence.

"Don't you see?" she said. "You're here to help *me*."

Quinn experienced a headlong plunge of sensation—a crack of thunder, a man's laugh, the glint of a belt buckle. There it all was, in a single sickening punch of memory. His sister's grubby knee, the rotten smell of rain-soaked wood, a red button popping from her dress. He reeled, steadied himself. Shapes bobbing in the half-light.

"You have to make him pay for what he did," she murmured conspiratorially. "Especially when everyone thinks you did it."

She lifted a broken floorboard and from the darkness produced a tobacco tin, which she prised open with some urgency. She scrabbled around inside it, then held out her hand. "Here," she said.

He squinted down at her palm. A red square button and a soiled length of lace. Dumbfounded, he shook his head to indicate that he didn't understand.

She held up the button between thumb and forefinger. "You don't recognise this?"

He reached out to take the proffered button but drew back, afraid. Would there be no end to this?

Sadie shoved it at him. "Here. Take it. It's your sister's button. You remember how your mother sewed this onto her dress? For luck. Your uncle keeps these things. Like treasure."

"You went to his house? Are you mad? You must stay away from him. He's an animal."

She held up the length of lace. "And this is Alice Gunn's. Part of her dress. It got torn. He killed her, too. Years ago. She didn't drown, the way everyone thinks. He killed her, then threw her in the reservoir."

By now the button was in his own hand. He studied it. Sure enough, it resembled one of Sarah's favourites. One corner was chipped. It was some time before Quinn was able to say anything, as if the memory of that horrific day were once again lodged in his throat.

"I could have saved her," he said, aware of how pathetic it sounded after all this time, "if I had been braver."

Sadie shuffled forward, eager. "What happened?"

"We were playing her latest favourite game—pirates marooned on an island with giant monsters. It was a sunny day, and we were out in the area north of Sparrowhawk, you know where there's that clump of pine trees, about a mile from our place? We'd been out all morning, and I went back to my father's place for some food. I stole some raisin cake that Mrs. Smail had brought around. Father was at work. William was sick in bed with fever, and Mother was reading *Huckleberry Finn* to him. I didn't let her see me because I knew she would call me in, but I waited by the door listening. William was asleep and Mother was reading the bit where Huck finds the canoe in the river. I always loved hearing my mother read, so I stayed there. I got distracted." Quinn recalled the warm lilt of his mother's voice.

"And by the time I started back, the day had changed. A storm was rolling in. I remember hearing thunder from the west. You're right— Sarah was afraid of thunder. About the only thing she was afraid of. And when I got back to where we had been playing, she was gone." There had been the blunt howl of the wind through the pines and the prickle of needles thrown into his face. On the ground, almost buried under leaf litter, he saw one of Sarah's shoes, the red one with the rusted buckle. There were scuffs in the dirt.

He rolled another cigarette. "And I was terrified right away, I don't know why. Just a feeling. I found her shoe. There were ants all over it, you know how they move about when it is going to rain?"

"They might have known where she went."

"And I sat down. I had no idea what to do. I called out but it was no use. It was as if she had been taken by the wind. It was impossible to hear anything, the way it was sometimes during the war. The terrible noise, thunder so close." He tapped the side of his head. "That sound right between your ears."

He lit his cigarette. From behind the tears pooling in his eyes, Sadie looked immaterial, as if she might dissolve at any moment. He drew on his cigarette and coughed. "After a while I began searching for her, going in wider and wider circles. I went to the top of the ridge from where I could see the valley, but it had begun to rain so hard that it was impossible to see very much. I was drenched. Then lightning exploded over the church and in its flash I saw them, three people hurrying through the paddock alongside Sully's place."

He closed his eyes to better recall the scene. "There were two men dragging Sarah along. But by the time I got down to Sully's paddock, they were long gone. I jumped the fence in the direction they had been heading. I thought I heard someone screaming, but it might have been the storm. It could have been anything, animals, the wind—"

"Maybe it was Mrs. Crink—lightning burned out her eyes that day?"

He nodded and fell silent. Despite her persistent questions, he was unable to tell her how, after about fifteen minutes, he did locate the source of the screams in the old shed at Wilson's Point. How he had crept up through the driving rain until he could see through a gap in the timber wall, had spied his uncle grinding into his kicking sister while the other man held Sarah's arms and tried to clamp her mouth. His sister's thighs were as white as milk. On the floor nearby was a pair of wet rifles. When he was done, Robert drew back and hitched his trousers, laughing, and at that instant Sarah screeched and lashed out, whereupon his uncle thrust a hunting knife hard into Sarah's chest. Quinn had stifled a cry and fallen away from the knothole. Thunder had crackled and rolled. He had listened to the futile thump and scrape of Sarah's shoe on the rotted floor, the breathing of the two men inside as they bickered over what had happened like a pair of goblins. *She would have recognised me anyway*, Robert was saying over the objections of the other man. *I had to . . .*

Quinn's inability to speak now reminded him of how it was afterwards as he wandered the countryside sleeping in hollows and trees. He drew on his cigarette.

Sadie scratched her cheek. "Why didn't you save her then? If you were right there?"

Quinn stared at her, through tears. Surely it was clear enough. "I told you. Because I was terrified. I am afraid of my uncle. You will laugh and think me even more of a coward on this, but the only thing that protected me from him was Sarah. She stood up to him. She knew his real nature when no one else did. And he *knew* she knew. And now I am terrified of everything.

"If I had been braver I might have grabbed their rifles and shot them. It would have been justice of some sort. My God, you know what my uncle said? He said, *Good day's hunting, after all. Much better than rabbits.* I heard him say that over the rain, when my hearing was still good. And the other man said something. They argued and the other man's voice was hoarse, like a rusty hinge. I don't know who he was. A stranger, I suppose. No one I knew." Quinn shuddered at the memory of it.

"And then they left. I watched them go and went inside when I was sure they weren't coming back. I pulled the knife out of her. She was in my arms. And that's when my father found me. Then Robert came back, and I ran without even thinking. I was so scared, you have to understand, I was so afraid . . ."

Neither of them said anything for some minutes. Sadie propped by the door where she ran the fingers of one hand along the ragged jamb. "What will you do now?"

"I don't know. I can't tell my mother. I can't tell anyone, they would never believe me. And I have no proof. I know what I saw but—"

"Then you have to kill him."

"I told you: I can't *kill* him."

She edged away. "But you promised to protect me. What if he comes after me? You said you wanted to be braver, but if you can't look after me, then leave. Get out. I'll wait here by myself for Thomas. Your uncle won't find me. I'll live in the caves." She pointed outside. "Go, then."

Quinn dreaded wandering the country again, stopping here or there for some work, eating with strangers, part of nothing. The thought of it. The wreck of his life. The very thought of it. And, worse, she would be alone here forever, waiting for a brother destined never to return—at the mercy of the creatures and the weather, Robert, all the menaces of the world. No. It was too late for all that. They needed each other.

"Do you remember?" he asked. "Do you remember the time we took a spade and tried to find the money you thought old Mr. Sharp had buried along the riverbank? And you slipped and fell into the river? We were going to buy Mother a shawl for her birthday at the general store."

The girl shrugged.

"Don't make me go," he said.

She remained silent, petulant.

He ran his fingers through his beard. "How is my beard growing?"

The girl's expression altered. She looked pleased as she admired its growth. "You look like a bushranger, an avenger." She turned, but stopped and glanced over her shoulder at him. "Oh, I have a question for you. What is a lucifer?"

Quinn's hand traced the bristly edges of his beard. He was caught unawares by her question but felt a surge of pride at his opportunity to enlighten the poor girl. "It's the Devil, of course. The fallen angel, who was cast out of heaven by God. His job is to tempt us away from faith in God. To lead us into sin, to abandon our better selves."

She was unimpressed. "Why?"

"It's his nature. Didn't you ever go to church, didn't your mother take you?"

"Not really . . ."

"Originally, Satan was in heaven with God, but his heart was full of iniquity an—"

"What's that? Inquity?"

"Ini*quity*. Evil."

He couldn't make out her response.

"What?"

"Why doesn't God stop him from doing bad things? If he's so powerful, that is. He could have stopped the war, no one would ever get sick or die. My mother would still be here, Thomas would be back. Even your sister . . ." She trailed off.

Quinn sighed. "I don't know. I don't remember. I mean, there is an explanation. I don't . . . It's been a long time since I went to church. The war, you know, interrupted everything."

This was not quite true; the auxiliary hospital at Harefield conducted services every Sunday in a nearby hall but the few times he'd attended he had been unable to concentrate and instead found himself staring out the windows, at the pretty nurses, at the backs of soldiers' heads. At the Front, too, there had been chaplains assigned to battalions. Once he might have been able to recall some Bible passage by way of explanation, but no longer. After all, it was an excellent question.

"I don't remember," he repeated.

She appeared dissatisfied with this stuttering response but waited politely. Clearly, she expected him to solve this problem for her.

"Why do you want to know, anyway?" he snapped.

"Oh, you know. It's in that song." And she spun on her bare heel and left the room.

Quinn had no idea what she was talking about. Which song? He picked up one of the knuckles from the floor. His ankles throbbed from squatting for so long. He lit no candle or lamp. Darkness silted around him, gathering in drifts along the windowsill, in the folds of his clothes and in his hair. Dusk was his favourite time of day because there was always a moment when he could imagine it might soon become lighter, not darker.

But the moment was brief and when it was almost too dark to see, he opened his hand and held his palm to his face where he could make out, much faded, a pen marking on one side of the knuckle. *SW.* He stared at it, relieved, disquieted. The girl began singing again.

> *Pack up your troubles in an old kitbag*
> *And smile, smile, smile*

While you've got a lucifer to light your fag
Smile, boys, that's the style

And, indeed, like a river creeping its banks, Quinn smiled. Somehow, in ways probably best not imagined, they had conjured each other. He shivered with strange pleasure.

19

L ater that night, after eating a meal of tinned meat and stale bread, Quinn was sitting outside on a log, smoking a cigarette, when Sadie materialised beside him. As usual she was wearing her grimy dress and no shoes. Her brown limbs were almost invisible, and she initially resembled no more than an indistinct face atop a hollow dress. She had taken to wearing his abandoned khaki satchel slung over one shoulder. It gave her an idiosyncratic air, as if she might at any moment ask him for identification to process his entry into her childish land.

She handed him his army tunic, flaccid as an animal pelt in her grip. "Here. Put this on."

"What? Why?"

"I need your help. We need to go get something. We need to be prepared for anything. It's an adventure, a mission. Like in the war. And if you wear this you can't be seen."

Quinn drew the last from his cigarette. He could hear around him the persistent whine of mosquitoes. Despite himself, he felt a thrill. An *adventure*. He put on the tunic. "Alright. Let's go."

Sadie clapped her hands in delight and, perhaps for the first time since they had met, she smiled with joy rather than suspicion. To Quinn's further surprise, she leaned down and pecked him on the cheek before yanking him upright. "Let's go."

"Where are we going?"

But she had already spun on her heel and run away, legs flashing in the dark. He had difficulty keeping up with her and lost sight of her on several occasions, but she always reappeared to guide him on until, after about half an hour, they emerged onto a low hill where they slumped to catch their breath.

It took Quinn a while to orient himself, but after several minutes the bulky, indistinct shapes of Flint emerged from the gloom to his right. He made out the spire of the Anglican church on Main Street and the mechanics' institute. He heard the trickle of the river and saw lamps burning in windows. They must be on the north-west side of town, between the river and the old shafts. A dog barked, then another.

From her satchel Sadie produced an army-issue water bottle from which she sucked a noisy draught, then held it out to him.

"Where did you get that?"

"Jack Fraser. Want some?"

"You stole that, too?"

She turned to face him. Water glistened on her chin. "Mr. Fraser died in the war. It's been in a drawer for ages."

She announced his death as if it were of no more importance than, say, if poor Jack had lost a loaf of bread. He supposed it was more unusual these days to hear of a young man alive and well.

He took the canister and drank. "Who else died? In the war, I mean."

Sadie made a world-weary face. As a girl might skitter about in her mother's shoes, it was an adult expression she was yet to master, and it could have been comical were it not for the fact that it indicated the dead were too numerous to name.

"Well," she began, ticking the names off her fingers, "Billy Quail got shot. Robert Sully. Mr. Gollings from out near Jersey Creek. Jack Fletcher and Graeme Fletcher, the butcher's boys." She clamped a hand over her mouth to smother a nervous giggle. "One of the Williams boys came back, but his face is all *melted*. I saw him and he looked at me, and I screamed and ran off and tripped. I hurt my wrist." She held up the underside of one hand to show him.

Quinn recalled seeing similar cot cases. Men with pummelled faces. Gowned creatures being wheeled down halls. The limbless and the mute. The wards at Harefield were kept dim, but he sensed the swaddled creatures watching him with their begging eyes as he passed. He had heard doctors were fitting masks of tin on which were moulded and painted with those features blasted off—eyes, noses, chins, cheeks, ears—and he was appalled at the thought of men being transformed into likenesses of the very machines that had mutilated them.

Sadie produced a brass tube he recognised as a folded-up telescope. Expertly, she extended the three drawers, lay on her front and scanned the town for several minutes, grunting every few seconds with recognition. Then she passed the telescope to Quinn, who raised it to his right eye.

It took a few seconds to adjust to the vertiginous sensation of seeing the world so enlarged and unwieldy. He saw a blur of light, a bicycle wheel. A limp Union Jack on a pole. Moonlight shone on Sully the blacksmith's roof on Gully Road. Three men were standing on the street outside The Mail Hotel under a gas lantern. One of them laughed and leaned down to slap his thigh. No sound reached Quinn, of course. Another fellow gulped his beer and went back inside with a rollicking gait he would have assumed was of drunkenness but for the realisation the man tottered on a wooden leg.

Sadie stood and brushed grass from her dress. "Come on," she said as she grabbed the telescope and stuffed it into her satchel. Without speaking, they trotted in the damp shadows of a stand of pines and skirted an open field before sneaking through a paddock and plunging into the empty streets of that village of widows.

Sadie led him along the lower end of Main Street where it dwindled almost to nothing. They cut through the orchard beside the Anglican church. She waited for him to wriggle though the wire fence and, when he was through, took his hand and smiled, twin gestures that prompted in him an almost unbearable stab of joy. He felt like laughing. Her hand was hot and small and fierce in his own. The air in the orchard was heavy with the smell of overripe fruit. Although he had no idea what they were doing, he was having fun for the first time in years.

Hand in hand they moved—over another fence, through the dusty schoolyard, across Church Street and into rambling gardens on Orchard Street. Quinn heard the flutter of chickens. Crickets suspended their chirruping as they passed. Then across Fletcher Street and through another fence. Sadie paused on her haunches and placed a finger to her lips. Quinn crouched beside her and was at once overwhelmed by a sharp perfume. They were beneath an apple tree, and the ground was littered with flowers and fruit.

Quinn brushed a spider web from his face and peered up through the darkness. Beyond the shelter of the apple tree was a lawn that glowed frosty grey in the moonlight. After a minute he made out the pale banisters of some back steps and the glint of a window behind a bulge of a daisy bush. A white chair on the veranda. He turned to Sadie. "Where are we? What are we doing?"

She didn't answer. Instead, she headed towards the house, skirting the lawn by keeping to the ragged flowerbed. Quinn followed. They stopped again on the veranda.

"Mrs. Higgins lives here now," Sadie informed him. "But she plays bridge tonight with the minister's wife." She crept forward, opened the back door, motioned for him to follow and slipped inside, as if into water.

Quinn looked around. He was nervous. The cross on his chest itched. Nearby, perhaps only a few houses away, a dog barked. The slap of a screen door, then silence. He stepped into the cool house, closed the door behind him and waited to acclimatise to this fresh darkness.

Mrs. Higgins' house smelled of wood polish and dried roses. Sadie emerged from the gloom, took his hand and led him down the hall. Crockery on a sideboard rattled as they passed. By now Quinn's eyes had adjusted. On a mantel over a fireplace was a cluster of silver-framed photographs. Sadie drew him over to a corner where she tugged at something from underneath a glass-fronted bureau. Their twin shadowy reflections bobbed in the glass in front of them like apparitions.

"See," she hissed, "it's stuck."

Quinn kneeled on the wooden floor and grasped a small, brass handle. "What is it?"

"A box."

"I can see that. What's in it?"

"We got to drag it out to open it."

"What's inside?"

"Pull it *out*."

Exasperated, Quinn yanked until he freed the box. Something tumbled off the bureau and rolled behind a curtain. They paused instinctively before wrestling again with the box. When it was free, he undid the metal hasps but discovered it was locked.

From her knapsack, Sadie produced a large screwdriver. "Here. Try this."

Quinn was impressed. He jammed the tool's narrow point beneath the lid, stood and rested his weight on the handle until the box splintered open. Sadie shuffled forward on hands and knees and rummaged through its contents.

But then, even through his dulled hearing, Quinn heard the noise of a shoe scraping against a step. Then another. Mrs. Higgins, presumably. Sadie must have heard it, too. She stood. He felt the trembling heat of her body. He sensed her watching him, the pale glow of her face in his peripheral vision. She held a bundle of clothes or sheets to her stomach.

"What about that bloody bridge game?" he whispered. The rattle of a handle, followed by a door creaking open, the front door of this very house, only ten feet away. Then, most chilling of all, tittering voices. Not a person. Worse. *People*.

20

Quinn looked at Sadie for a clue as to what on earth they should do. Her elfin features were pinched with fear. On the other side of the wall, a woman giggled and said, *Watch out there*. A low voice. The front door slammed shut and prompted a fresh round of laughter. Again the other, deeper voice. A man's. Quinn was unable to move. An oblong wedge of moonlight fell across the dining table and illuminated a basket of fruit.

Silence. Had they been caught?

Then voices again, shuffling footsteps followed by a knock, perhaps that of a shoe heel on skirting board. The man spoke. Quinn was unable to understand but recognised the sticky drawl at once, and knew by the way her head snapped to one side that Sadie did, too. Robert Dalton. His heart clenched.

More laughter from the hallway, muffled words. Quinn made out the shape of the doorway across the room and then the glint of a mirror in the hall. Perhaps they could run for it and escape—through the door, along the hallway, out the back door and into the garden? The woman's voice, low and suggestive. *This way, Constable* . . . Footsteps, a grunt and the unmistakable greasy squeak of a mattress. More laughter, now uninhibited and the thud of a boot landing on the floor.

Sadie's tiny chest heaved. She licked her lips and, as if handling a newborn child, she held out the bundle she had taken from the box. He shook his head at her to indicate there was no time for that now, but she pressed it to him. Something in her manner brooked no refusal. He took it and was surprised to discover it was much heavier than he expected. He picked apart the wrapping and released a smell of machine oil.

A revolver, a Webley by the look of it, probably the same make as the one he had lost. Sadie handed him a box of ammunition.

From the bedroom came further squeaks, ravenous murmurs, whispers. Quinn blushed. During training in Cairo, he had been dragged to a brothel by fellow soldiers and, although he'd refused the entreaties of the dark-eyed women there, the experience instilled in him a horror of anything suggestive of the sordid intimacies between men and women. The place had been lousy with incense smoke and the stink of alcohol. He was reminded now of that hot night, just as then he had been reminded obscurely of the afternoon of Sarah's murder; the dim particulars of each occasion melded into a kaleidoscope of churning limbs, sinister laughter and the flash of a stranger's crooked teeth.

He cracked the revolver open, fitted three bullets into chambers and snipped it shut. The action was remarkably satisfying. He and Sadie crept through the door and stood in the hallway. The floor creaked underfoot. They froze. Quinn realised he was shaking with terror. He heard his uncle's guffaws. He indicated for Sadie to stand by the back door, and she nodded and did as she was told. Although he was unsure how to proceed, Quinn imagined he might step into the bedroom and shoot his uncle where he lay. That other time, that time with Sarah, how he had wished he'd had a weapon such as this in his grasp. He inspected the revolver. Perhaps vengeance did, in fact, belong with him?

Suddenly a shape in front of him in the hallway. A woman, dressed in a filmy undergarment. It was Mrs. Higgins. Moonlight glanced off her sweating forehead, lending her the appearance of having been dipped in milk. Her fingers fluttered in the air. "Dick," she was whispering. "Dick, is that you? My God I'm so sorry, I thought . . ."

Quinn stared at her, mesmerised, unable to speak. The woman was familiar. *Evelyn*. Evelyn Kingston, whom he had known at school. A feisty girl who once, upon being excluded from a cricket game the boys were playing, stole their ball and flung it into the orchard bordering the schoolyard.

He felt a draught of night air and understood at once that Sadie had opened the back door behind him. There was the intimation of movement from the bedroom, followed by a muffled query. Robert.

Evelyn Higgins was still speaking in her plaintive voice. "Dick, you had been gone so long now, for so many years I thought . . ."

Quinn spun on his heel and ran straight out the door and onto the veranda. He leaped onto the lawn, lost his footing and tumbled forward onto his face with a dull grunt. Blood blossomed in his mouth. There was the smell of bruised grass in his nostrils, grit coated the end of his tongue. Sadie was up ahead urging him on. Her limbs glimmered beneath the apple tree.

From behind him in the house he heard footsteps, raised voices, a curse. *No, please don't* . . . .

Quinn stood. Sadie glided across the lawn from right to left. "This way," she hissed, and vanished through the wooden fence.

Heart fumbling for rhythm, revolver in hand, Quinn staggered after her but was unable to locate the gap in the fence through which she had gone. He floundered on his knees in the garden bed. The ground was spongy and moist and stank of chicken shit. A branch scratched his cheek. At last he found the break in the fence and fell through to the other side. Sadie hauled him to his knees and sprinted across Fletcher Street and skidded around the corner.

From the other side of the fence, Quinn heard Dalton's querulous voice and Evelyn Higgins' placating one. *There's no need for your gun . . . Robert!* Dogs barked all around.

Quinn tried to get to his feet but was hampered by something tugging on the sleeve of his army tunic. He thought of the malevolent creatures that lurked in the puddles of the Flats, but it was only a rusted strand of barbed wire nailed to the fence. He twisted this way and that but was unable to detach himself. A knot of wire cut his knuckle.

Dalton's furious voice again from the other side of the fence. His uncle was getting closer, kicking through the undergrowth, seeking the intruder. *Get here, you little bitch . . .*

Quinn shrugged out of the tunic, staggered to his feet and bolted around the corner, where he almost collided with Sadie coming back the other way.

"What are you *doing*?" she whispered, out of breath.

"I got stuck."

"Where's the revolver?"

He showed it to her, still wrapped in its strip of oily cloth.

Her eyes glowed. "Now's your chance. Go back and shoot him. Do it now."

But Quinn just stared at her. He didn't move.

When it was clear he was not going to act, she pulled him by his shirt sleeve. "Come on, then."

They fled through the lower part of Flint. Dogs yapped and threw themselves against fences. They kept to the grassy verge. Quinn imagined wives waking their sleeping men, creeping to bedroom windows, wondering at the noises they heard so late at night. He and Sadie jogged past orchards and continued until they crossed the soggy pastures at the edge of town and plunged into the bush.

They made it back to the shack an hour later. Exhausted, nerves jangling, they collapsed to the floor. Quinn lay and stared at the ceiling. Neither of them spoke. Sadie sat against the wall.

Quinn fell into an uneasy sleep punctuated by dreams of tangled tree limbs and muddy fields. Then the hollowed-out room, Sadie, a guttering candle flame, the taste of mud and blood in his mouth.

She gripped his upper arm. "Wake up," she was saying. "Wake up. Where's your tunic? Quinn? Where's your tunic?"

He sat up and rubbed the heels of his hands into his eyes. "What?"

"Your tunic. Didn't you bring it back with you?"

After a stunned silence, he said, "I left it by the fence. I told you. I was caught on barbed wire."

Sadie sat back on her heels and put her face in her hands.

"What?" Quinn asked.

"That's how they'll find us."

"What are you talking about?"

"That's how the tracker finds people for Dalton. And his dogs. They track people by their smell. On clothes and things. If there's no tracks. They can find anyone like that. You should have killed him when you had the chance."

Quinn swore to himself. The girl was probably right. How could he have been so stupid, so cowardly? At least he had ripped his name tag from the tunic. At least he had done that. The taste of blood prompted him to run a finger along his front teeth. Sure enough, his left eye tooth felt loose. He waggled it, and it broke off between his fingers. He wiped it free of blood and held it out in front of him, where it gleamed.

⚶

The next morning, wearing only trousers, Quinn filled a bucket with water from the tank and stood outside to bathe. Dragonflies darted about, trapping the sunlight in their blurring wings. The morning was cool but held the promise of another scorcher. Cupfuls of icy water shattered across his head and coursed down his face and chest. He inhaled short, stabbing breaths and washed his shoulders and shrugging neck, folding his arms about his head as a bird might do its wings.

He heard the door slapping shut and turned to see Sadie standing several feet away watching him. Her blinkless eyes flickered across his wet torso. Who knew what went through her mind? They observed each other for several seconds before she picked her way over to him through the long grass, raised a hand and, in a movement at once tender and savage, tore loose the vertical scab of the cross he had carved into his chest some days ago. So shocked was he, and so sudden was the act, that he hardly registered what had occurred until he noticed a dollop of woolly blood unravel from the wound and make its way down across his ribs. The pain was brittle, exquisite, and he shuddered with it. Something loomed at the edges of his memory, vanished, then returned. Blood. Sarah's blood, on her, on him. The weight of her, the dull coins of her eyes. By the time he thought to look up again, Sadie had returned inside.

21

When Quinn woke the following morning, he was alone. He lay on the floor with his trench coat for a pillow. He felt weak; he suspected the water they were drawing from the rusty tank was poisoned; that perhaps a possum or a koala had died in there. Their diet of scrawny rabbits, old bread and stolen tins of beans didn't help. He heard the dull chatter of artillery in his head, but the war now seemed a million miles away, in the way that winter was unimaginable in the height of summer. A mouse skittered across the floor and vanished into a hole. Gone, just like that.

He lapsed in and out of sleep for most of the day and was woken by a coughing fit that racked his body. When he was again sensible to the world, Sadie was crouching over him holding a cup of bicarb and water to his mouth. She always showed up when he needed her. He gulped the mixture and, when he could sit up, she took his hand and led him outside. There, tethered to a tree by a length of ragged rope, was the lamb he had seen when he first arrived. The creature bleated and shook its bony head. Sadie kneeled to kiss the lamb's face, untied it and led them—Quinn by one hand, the lamb by its length of rope—into the bush.

Although he didn't protest, the girl must have sensed his hesitation. She tugged his hand until he was bent almost double. She fitted her lips to his ear and the words she uttered circumvented his sense of hearing and instead plumbed his heart.

"Pim," she whispered. "You need to trust me."

Quinn stared at her face, her cherry-black eyes and the slice of her mouth. She licked away pearls of sweat that had already formed on her upper lip. She let go of his hand, muttered encouraging words to the lamb and led the creature into the undergrowth. Quinn waited a minute before hurrying after them.

They tramped for two hours, rising higher and higher into the hills, panting with the effort of it. The way was rocky and steep. The lamb was reluctant and had to be cajoled to make the ascent; it suspected, perhaps, that something unpleasant would be required of it. They arrived at a cave set high into the rock. A wind hummed through the surrounding trees, and when they stood on the granite lip of the cave they could see the pattern of the earth normally denied them, right over the western plains of New South Wales. Fields and roads; dozens of brown dams; clumps of trees; the wink of sunlight on tin roofs; the shiver of streams.

The cave entrance was massive, had perhaps served as a handhold for God as he clambered about the earth inspecting his handiwork all those years ago. Quinn wondered what it might be like to have the vision afforded God: to see the whole planet and all its people, their futures and pasts in one single moment. It was a terrible and magical thought. The cave's prehistoric air cooled the sweat on his back as he and Sadie stared out over the horizon.

"This is the Cave of Hands," she said when she had caught her breath. She tethered the lamb to a tree. "I used to hide from Mr. Dalton up here."

Mesmerised, Quinn watched the girl. She was so capable, so certain of her place in the world. She kicked away some bracken. The lamb gazed around with its wayward eyes and expelled the occasional quavering bleat.

"No one knows about this place except me and the blackfellas. It's the unknown terror."

"The what?"

"You know. Terror incognito. Means unknown."

He laughed. "It's *terra*—spelt T-E-R-R-A. Means ground. Unknown land."

She looked at him askance for several seconds before allowing herself a sly smile. She took his hand. "You're funny. Come on."

She led him about fifteen feet, to the rear of the cave. The rocky ceiling sloped, and they were forced to waddle for the remaining few feet. The light of day didn't seep this far, and the recess was cool and dim. Quinn's head brushed the ceiling. They sat on the cold ground and waited for their eyes to adjust. The girl was beside him, picking at a scab on her bare shin, absorbed in her childish task. Quinn could scarcely believe the truth of her and, as if compelled by an inner force not his own, he reached out one hand across the few feet separating them. She stopped what she was doing and glanced up. She didn't move. She allowed him to caress first one cheek, then the other, to run his fingers through her long hair. He sensed, percolating up within him, the urge to weep.

He withdrew his hand, coughed into his fist. His ankles were aching from kneeling. Then, there, right in front of him, as his eyes acclimatised further to the darkness, he made out a galaxy of painted hands all around them. There were dozens of them spread over the walls and ceiling—not only hands but kangaroos and snakes, all daubed in ochre and black. He laughed with sudden recognition and scanned the hands until he located one proportionate to his own and pressed his palm to the cold rock.

He took his hand away and smiled at Sadie. "But what are we doing up here?"

"We need to find out when the tracker is back, like you said. Especially now Dalton has the tunic. There are magic ways to find out these things, but you have to help me."

She scrambled from the cave, only to return a minute later with the lamb in tow. She insisted Quinn grab the lamb around its shoulders with one hand cupped beneath its chin. Like a hirsute infant the lamb struggled against his chest, wrenching its rocky head this way and that, bleating.

With a nub of chalk, Sadie drew a circle on the ground around them. "Holding tight?"

Quinn smirked. The whole thing was ridiculous, but he nodded anyway. He would indulge her for the moment. "What happens now?"

With eyes screwed half shut, Sadie mouthed something and plunged her knife into the lamb. She sliced open the creature's belly with a sound not unlike the shredding of a canvas sack. A humid smell of shit and innards filled the cave. Quinn's thighs became warm with blood. He swore. The lamb struggled against him, bucked desperately, until it lurched free and stood a few feet away and stared at them with an expression of startled reproof. Its intestines ploppered to the cave floor, followed by other, purpled innards. The creature collapsed to its front legs then its hind and, after emitting a plaintive ruckle, fell over, stiffened and died. The entire episode only lasted a minute.

Quinn rubbed at his bloodstained trousers. He attempted to stand and banged his head against the low ceiling. He kneeled again. "What in hell are you doing?"

But the girl, herself blood-spattered, was already squatting beside the dead lamb with her back to him. She commenced her divinations, nodding to herself as she separated the innards with her fingers and clucked with recognition or surprise. She raised a finger at him to forestall interruption and, discomfited, Quinn shuffled back into the light of the late afternoon.

He sat on the shelf of rock, scored with odd symbols—perhaps even illegible words—that did not appear to have been done by the same people who did the cave paintings. He noticed objects littering the ground around the cave mouth. There were piles of stones and bones, pieces of string, hair, even a pair of cast-iron soldiers wedged upright between stones with their rifles pointing out across the land. He shook his head. Sadie.

It was getting late. There was a fizz in the gloaming. It was his favourite time, when it was possible to see those things not usually visible in the flattening light of day: whorling clouds of insects; flecks of pollen; feathers gleaming; tiny parachutes of dandelion eddying in the wind. Smoke rose along the horizon from a distant bushfire. How amazing, he thought, to be in the world. To be in *this* world. Where nothing was out of the question, where anything was possible. He felt a curious and liberating exhilaration. Far below him sun glinted on metal, and he imagined if someone were to scour the side of the mountain with a telescope at that very moment, they would not even notice him, a rough beast crouching in the shadows.

Sadie emerged half an hour later and squatted to wipe her hands on the rocks at the cave entrance made moist by a trickle of water. She stared out over the darkening country as if digesting what she had discovered, then sat beside him with her head on his shoulder.

"So," he said, "what did you find out?"

"Nothing yet. It's not always so simple. The information sometimes comes in unexpected ways."

"I see."

"You don't believe in this, do you?"

Quinn shuddered to hear an echo of Mrs. Cranshaw in the girl's words. "We might not have time, that's all."

"The answer will come. I heard them talking at Sully's yesterday, and they said there was no sign yet of the man who killed his wife. The tracker won't be back for a week, at least."

Quinn sighed. It was hardly scientific. God only knew how he could persuade her to leave this place. He thought of his dying mother down there in the shadows.

With a bloody finger, Sadie pointed out a smoke-hued mountain range in the distance. "Is France past those mountains? Where you were?"

"Yes. And over the sea, too."

"The sea?"

"The ocean. Full of water."

"You mean like a lake?"

"Much bigger than that. Larger than you can even see. I was on a boat for weeks to get there."

She did not seem convinced but nodded anyway, and squinted out over the plains as if she might spy this mysterious body of water. "Is it nice in France?"

"Nice?"

"Not like here."

At once Quinn understood. Australia was an in-between place, without order, where trees were forced to grow anywhere they could. Their poor roots clawed the ground. The animals were lumpen, wobbling and slithering. Even the birds didn't sing but, rather, cackled and hooted and laughed like so many lunatic inmates. And overhead, always, that sheer, blade-sharp sky.

"No," he said. "It's not like here at all."

"What about Kensington Gardens? Is that a long way?"

He laughed. Sadie knew all sorts of esoteric details about the world, but she could be ignorant of basic facts. "It's in London. That's quite far. Miles."

"As far away as France?"

"Yes. Why do you want to know?"

"I thought me and Thomas would go there when he gets back. Mrs. Babcock reads to her children about it. I even dream about it. There is a lake there. Fairies as small as your thumb, a world under the water. Imagine that. They have parties where all the creatures are invited, all the squirrels and birds and so forth, rabbits and crickets." She seemed to feast on this memory. "I have prayed that we will get there."

Quinn had indeed spied her at night on her knees with her slender hands steepled against her bony chest, a pale and earnest mantis in the moonlight.

"You could come with us to Kensington Gardens," she said. "With me and Thomas. The three of us. You'd like Thomas, everyone likes Thomas. He's very funny."

Clouds of insects swarmed in the hot and trembling light of dusk. She draped an arm around his shoulders. A dry wind whipped her damp hair about and at that moment she resembled a girl suspended underwater, patiently holding her breath with waterweed plastered across her face.

Darkness flooded the land. Quinn gathered wood and built a fire inside the cave. With Sadie's knife they butchered the lamb and cooked pieces over the fire. She told him that he needed to eat as much of the lamb as he could, that it would help them find out the date of the tracker's return. He didn't believe her, but he was hungry and happy enough to gorge himself on the charred meat. Lying on their backs on the cave's undulating floor, they watched the firelight animate the ancient Aboriginal hands and animals, and Quinn had the sense that, without his having noticed it, a grain of happiness had lodged by his heart.

⊰⊱

In the middle of the night, he heard Fletcher Wakefield's clotted breath in the cot alongside him. He, too, had been gassed at Pozières. A shaft of sulphurous light fell through the window onto his own bed. The windowpane glimmered with rain. The dormitory smelled of carbolic. There were ten other soldiers around him in the near-dark and he was comforted by their slumbering presence. They were good men, mostly. Those not ruined by it were made decent by war. To survive one tragedy was to learn you cannot survive them all, and this knowledge was both a freedom and a great loss. But now they had lived through much of the war, many, like Quinn, lay awake at night, untethered from the fear that had sustained them for so long. At the other end of the room a cigarette tip flared and faded, flared and faded.

He thought about the girl and, after half an hour of indecision, he rolled onto his side. "Fletcher," he hissed. "*Fletcher.*"

Fletcher woke but was clearly unhappy about it. His thin pillow tumbled to the floor. "What?"

"We should go back."

"What? Where? Jesus, Meek. What are you talking about?"

"That young girl."

"*What* girl?"

"The Cranshaw girl."

"Oh, God." Groggy, Fletcher propped himself up on one elbow. "Margaret, you mean? Did she . . . Did she say something to you?"

Someone *sshhed* them from the darkness.

"What did she say?"

Quinn rolled onto his back and stared at the ceiling.

"Well. What happened? Quinn? Jesus, you can't wake me up like that then clam up . . . .."

He wanted to tell Fletcher about the note, suggest they go back and take Margaret away from the grasping Mrs. Cranshaw, that to do so would be a decent act with which to arm themselves against the century's dark tides. They might need it, considering all the men they had probably killed with their bullets and grenades. But instead he ignored Fletcher's entreaties, and Fletcher rolled over, disgusted, and fell silent. After all, how to explain such a thing? And Quinn lay there until a watery English dawn leaked into the room.

❦

He woke abruptly from his dream. His skin was slick with moisture, and he cast about for something with which to orient himself. The stink of viscera filled his nostrils; a pebble pressed into his cheek. There. Fire embers, like a burning town seen from a vast distance. He coughed. Pain gripped his innards. Then someone was beside him. Sadie. She nestled against him and whispered reassuring words. Her body was without guile, mere breath and bones, the branches of her limbs. There was a nub at her wrist where the joint underneath pressed against her skin and, further along her arm, down like that of a peach.

They stayed unmoving, folded birdlike about each other as they had on many nights, listening to the traffic of the stars and the shift of the earth. The night was complete, would not become any darker. He wondered what would become of them, not only tonight or in the next few days but over the months and years to come.

She wriggled tighter against him. "You won't let them take me away, will you? You'll wait until Thomas comes back for me?"

The embers of their fire wheezed. "Yes. Of course I'll stay. I won't let them find you."

"You'll protect me? Do you promise?"

"I cross my heart."

He rebuilt the fire, and they spent the rest of the night huddled against the cold. In the morning, they constructed a bier of branches to which they tied the eviscerated lamb, and dragged it back down the mountain to their shack.

22

The day ripened hot and hard. When they arrived at the shack, Sadie collapsed to the floor and fell asleep. By now her dress was tattered all about the hem. Her hands were still stained with the lamb's blood and there were spatters of it on her upper arm. Quinn washed the lamb's blood from his clothes and dried his shirt over the limb of a tree.

Restless, Quinn went to the cemetery and drifted among the graves throughout the afternoon. He recalled that he had doubted Sadie when she claimed to have seen rain fall only four times in her life but, judging by the state of the land hereabouts, she might have been telling the truth. The ground was hard as rock, and the leaves of the eucalypt trees so dry he wouldn't be surprised if they ignited. Of course they had learned nothing all day about the tracker's return. *The information sometimes comes in unexpected ways.* Madness.

He was stupid to have imagined her magic could help at all, but he was desperate. His first impression of her was correct; she was barmy, probably didn't even have a brother. His uncle would find them sooner or later; they couldn't hide up here forever. He should go to Sydney, where no one knew him. He should leave, and at that moment regretted promising to wait here for Sadie's brother. He thought of what his mother had said: *It's a terrible kind of love. Terrible.*

He found the grave of Sadie's mother, Edna. There was a plain, white cross on the mound with the date of her death—February 1st, 1919, a couple of weeks before he had returned to Australia. Poor Sadie. It was dreadful to be so alone.

He made his way to Sarah's grave and removed a branch that had fallen across her headstone. He touched the place on his chest where his cross had scabbed. Beneath his shirt he could feel its faint texture, along with those of the other, more recent wounds. Something in the grass beside the headstone caught his eye, and he stooped to peer more closely. A white seashell the size of a grape. It was bound a dozen times with a length of cotton that might once have been red but was now faded to a pink so pale it was barely a colour. Sadie must have left it here. It was beautiful and pathetic, a tiny thing made sacred by a girl. They were so useless, these charms she constructed to assist passage through the worlds. With faith, with imagination and love, he thought, one could transform anything into something. He picked up the shell.

He remembered during the war seeing a young private named Shaw inhaling from a shell held to his face. Upon enquiry, he was told the boy had carried it from his birthplace in Western Australia, and claimed to be able to detect in the shell the aroma of the beach where he had swum the night before he enlisted. No one mocked the boy; the conditions of war permitted men to behave in unusual ways, not all of them barbaric. At the time Quinn thought it fanciful but now, squatting on a hill in the middle of nowhere, he lifted the shell to his nose and breathed in. At first nothing, just the sweat and eucalypt embedded in his palms, but soon he was able to discern other scents secreted in its tiny curl—the sea, sulphurous winds, even seaweed's tasty reek. The mere presence of the shell—so far from the beach where it must have been gathered— moved him unbearably. Hot tears tumbled down his cheek. What on earth would he do now? Where could he go?

He crouched there for some time, weeping, hunched as if bearing a weight. What was he doing here? Why had he returned at all? Around him the world revolved, went on its way. He caught a glimpse of himself as others might see him—a pathetic man, little better than a mendicant, in a cemetery, afraid to leave, afraid to stay.

Another sudden memory of war: of hearing a shot one otherwise peaceful night and learning the next day of a fellow who had somehow jammed a rifle barrel into his mouth and pressed the trigger with his toe. How he and some others had shrugged, not only with ambivalence at yet another wartime death, but with understanding as well. *Why not?* was the unspoken thought. *Why the bloody hell not?*

He wiped his eyes. Then he heard the crackle, unmistakable even beyond his impoverished hearing, of someone moving through the grass behind him. He straightened and was horrified to see his uncle grimacing with effort as he manoeuvred between the gravestones. Quinn drew breath. His body flushed with terror. *The Murderer.* With dismay he thought of the stolen Webley six-shooter stuffed into a pocket of his trench coat lying on the floor of the shack.

23

Robert Dalton was blond and barrel-chested, with a square forehead that shone pink in the late-afternoon sun. He stopped about ten feet from Quinn with one hand resting on the broken stone shoulder of an infant-sized angel. His uncle was sweating profusely, his eyes screwed tight against the glare. He undid several gold buttons of his blue police jacket and wrestled the collar loose, revealing at his throat the frayed edge of an undershirt. His police bicycle rested against a gravestone behind him. He had grown fuller about the waist in the time since Quinn had last seen him and would now be about fifty-five years old. Despite the uniform and the intervening years, he was still the same man who used to pinch Quinn hard on the arm for no reason when no one was looking and then mock him if he complained. *You could tell your mother but she'd never believe you.*

Quinn longed to flee but knew that to run was tantamount to an admission of guilt. His uncle approached.

"Well," Robert said after a minute, when he had caught his breath, "what have we here?" With a faint, unctuous smile he inspected Quinn.

Quinn realised the question was not rhetorical. He dropped his gaze. A skink flickered over his boot and vanished beneath a rock, as he would have liked to have done at that moment. His chest filled with blood and he thought of Sarah lying in the cool, subterranean dark a few feet away listening to their exchange. "I'm resting in the shade here. Passing through."

Robert drew a sleeve across his sweaty brow, then leaned over and squeezed from between his pursed lips a coin of spit that sizzled on a rock. It was clear he was drunk. "Unusual spot to take a rest, I would have thought. Fond of graveyards, are you?"

His uncle had not recognised him, at least. Quinn took a step back. "Well, it's peaceful here."

"It is that. Not a whisper out of them. Dead men tell no tales, eh?"

Quinn noticed his uncle's gaze drop for a second to Sarah's headstone. He saw also that Robert's left wrist was bandaged and remembered what his father had said about him falling when he had pursued Quinn and Sadie that morning two weeks ago. "I'm on my way to Bathurst," he stammered.

"Oh, are you? That's a long way."

"Yes."

Dalton indicated Flint, then scratched at his whiskery chin with his good hand. "Well, can't be worse than this place, I suppose. What a bloody dump. What a country. You know, most countries they start because they want to make something better, but not here. Australia was started to make something worse for those poor convicts. It's hard to picture it but, you know, the day I came to Flint it bloody snowed. It was actually quite pretty, believe it or not. The only time in history, they reckon. Hell froze over, you might say." He laughed at his own little joke, then sighed, as if getting down to business. "Where'd you say you came from?"

"Sydney. The war."

Dalton sniggered. "You don't look like a soldier."

"I am, I was—I mean, not anymore. The war is over."

Dalton's eyes widened in pantomime surprise. "The war is *over*? Why, thank you. You think I'm simple? You see this uniform? I'm the constable here, in case you didn't realise. Of course I know the war is over. I probably knew before anyone around here did, not that that's saying much. I probably knew before you did, mate. I'm the constable here. I get told all sorts of things that the general public isn't privy to." He paused. "Where did you fight, then?"

"In France. At Gallipoli. 17th Battalion."

Quinn hoped this information might mollify Dalton, but it had the opposite effect. His uncle became enraged.

"*Gallypolly*, eh? I suppose you reckon you're pretty brave, do you? Well, some of us had to stay here and keep order. Home fires and all that. Take care of the women. The children. We've had all sorts of blokes come through here, hiding out up in the hills. Lot of coves about these days. It's not all glory, mate. Not all bloody glory."

With exaggerated ceremony, Dalton unbuckled his revolver from its holster and waved it in Quinn's general direction. He stepped closer and pressed the revolver barrel into Quinn's stomach. "I could shoot you, you know. So very easily."

Quinn flinched and looked away. If his uncle recognised him now, he would doubtless kill him. *Imagine surviving what we survived and then ending up going like that? Bloody crazy.* He recalled suddenly his uncle's attempt to join him and Sarah as they played a game on the back veranda. Years and years ago, maybe a year before the murder. William and Nathaniel were out, and their mother was running errands in Flint. His sister, never inclined to waste energy on niceties, shrugged off Uncle Robert and sauntered away. *Let's go do something else where we won't be disturbed*, she'd said. And as soon as Sarah's back was turned, Robert, livid, had rapped Quinn so hard with a knuckle that there formed above his eye a lump the size of a walnut, which he had to explain away to his mother as the result of a tumble from a tree.

"I've done it before," Dalton went on in his rum-soaked whisper. "No one cares about people like you. One more dead. One among millions. Leave you here for the crows. Get my little mate to get rid of you. It doesn't matter. What's your name, anyway?"

Quinn was paralysed. Sadie had warned him not to venture out too much during the day and to stay away from anywhere he might encounter people. The residents of Flint, she had said, were suspicious and had been made more so by the twin disasters of war and disease. It was a rule he had followed as much as possible. Until today. Until now. He clenched the shell in his palm. "My name is Fletcher Wakefield."

"Wakefield, eh? Funny name. You got your papers there? We got to keep track of people coming through here and make sure no one's infected. You got one of those certificates? Are you allowed on the train?

You know the borders are closed? They'll shoot if you try to cross, you know," he added with relish.

Quinn didn't move. He gripped the cotton-bound charm so hard in his sweating hand that, if he survived this encounter, he knew there would be in his palm a wound shaped like a crescent moon. He untethered his heart and prayed.

To his amazement, there appeared over Robert's shoulder, at first as a moth-like flutter at the periphery of his vision, then becoming clearer, a woman in black gliding between the graves.

Dalton, too, grew aware of a presence. Perhaps panicked, he re-holstered his gun and swung around to face her. The back of his thick neck was sunburned. "Mrs. Porteous. What a surprise. You must be here to visit your . . . your . . ."

"Aunt, Constable Dalton. My Aunt Ginny."

"Ah. Yes. Poor lady. *Lovely* lady. Terrible thing."

By now this Mrs. Porteous was only ten feet away. Her hand was raised in a stiff salute to shade her eyes. She was perhaps ten years older than Quinn. He had only the slightest recollection of her. She was dressed in black and clutched a posy of flowers.

"Indeed she was," she said. "And, yes, it is a terrible thing. One wonders when it will all be over."

"Yes," Dalton agreed. "Indeed. One wonders."

"If at all."

"Yes, if at all."

Mrs. Porteous looked at Quinn. He was by now a frightful sight and was ashamed to have allowed himself to deteriorate so far and in such a manner. He stared down at his broken, dusty boots. At least he had washed the lamb's blood from his clothes. The air hummed and burned.

"This gentleman here was telling me of his time in Gallipoli," Robert said, grabbing Quinn's arm with sudden bonhomie. "Heading to Bathurst, aren't you, mate?"

Mrs. Porteous looked unimpressed, even hostile. "I see."

There followed an uncomfortable silence, into which swelled the buzz of insects. Then the woman asked him something.

"Pardon, ma'am?" Quinn said.

"Where were you, sir? In the war, I mean."

Quinn cleared his throat. "In France. Gallipoli, too, for a time."

"Those bloody Turks," Robert exclaimed. "Excuse my French, Mrs. Porteous, but it really riles me."

Mrs. Porteous nodded. "My husband was there. In the Infantry. 13th Battalion."

Quinn had little enthusiasm for this sort of conversation but managed a thin smile. He recalled what Mrs. Cranshaw had told him of the hatred sometimes harboured by those who had lost loved ones in the war for those who had survived. "What was his name? I might know him." This was, after all, the convention; one had to engage in such enquiries these days. It was as if the war had generated a kinship among men that attendance at a famous social occasion or school might.

"He was at Bullecourt. He died there."

"Oh. I'm sorry."

She waved his condolence away. Perhaps Mrs. Cranshaw was right; the war widows grew sick of sympathy, of good wishes, of the chatter about bravery and honour. They needed something more substantial from their dead men. "It's not your fault," she added in a rather more conciliatory tone.

Robert looked uncomfortable at the swerve in conversation. He released Quinn's arm and began carrying on about the shame of that damn war and how he would have loved to get into the thick of it all but for his duties here as an officer of the law . . .

Quinn grew concerned by the manner in which Mrs. Porteous was watching him.

"You are a little familiar, sir. Are you from the district?"

He blushed. "No, ma'am. Just passing through. Never been here before."

Now Robert peered at him with renewed interest, as if the lady had spotted something he had missed. "Yes," he said, brandishing his notebook. "That's right. Papers. I was this minute asking Mr.— Wakefield, wasn't it?—for his papers to prove he is not infected with the influenza. Just a formality, of course."

Quinn steadied himself against a stone angel. Pale green lichen had gathered in the prayerful hands of the creature. He was doomed and looked around in vain for Sadie, foolishly imagining she might rescue him somehow, as she had done that first day.

But Mrs. Porteous swung around to address Robert Dalton. "Lucky you were around the other night, wasn't it, Constable?" Some women were undone by grief but others, like this Mrs. Porteous, were given authority by its everlasting company.

His uncle faced her and dropped his notebook. "Eh? What's that?"

"At Mrs. Higgins' place? The other night. *Evelyn* Higgins?"

Robert winced. "Ah. Yes."

She turned to Quinn with eyebrows arched in mock amazement. "Mr. Dalton—*Constable* Dalton, I should say—happened to be passing by the house of a certain widow a few nights ago when the poor lady spied the ghost of her late husband who was killed in Europe. Quite late. *In the house.* The lady had quite a chat with him, before Mr. Dalton managed to shoo him away."

Robert ducked his chin and said something under his breath.

"Well, Evelyn was sure it was Dick. Said it was just like him, in uniform and everything. Do you believe in these things, Mr. Wakefield? Ghosts and such?"

"I'm not sure, ma'am."

Robert attempted to reassert his authority. "There was no man there. People sometimes see what they wish to see. It was that orphaned Fox girl I've been trying to find. I saw her run across the lawn as clear as anything. Right across the lawn. Even found a divot taken out of the grass. I daresay no ghost could do *that*. Took Dick's revolver, too. Girl's armed now, believe it or not. She must have been wearing an army tunic, though; we found it by the fence, which is why poor Evelyn must have been confused."

"What on earth would a girl want with a gun?" Mrs. Porteous asked.

"Who knows. She's a wily one, though. Damned if I can catch her. Almost got her a couple of weeks back. Nearly got bitten by a snake, too." He held up his bandaged wrist. "I'm not much good at tracking, but Jim Gracie is back tomorrow morning from Bathurst and he can track anyone over anything for a few bob. Especially now we've got the jacket she was wearing. He caught that Wynne chap who shot his wife. We'll grab the girl by tomorrow afternoon, no question. We'll take care of her."

Quinn started. *By tomorrow afternoon.*

"Take care of her?" Mrs. Porteous asked.

Robert coughed. "She has no family here. I'll take her to an orphanage."

"Yes, I am quite sure you will take care of her."

His uncle's brow furrowed. "And what is that supposed to mean?"

Mrs. Porteous and the constable stared at each other for a second before she turned away and indicated the surrounding countryside. "Lucky you were here, sir, to look after the poor widows and orphans of Flint. Who knows what we might have done these past few years without you. We might have been lost."

Robert paused before hazarding a response. "Yes, well, I was telling Mr. Wakefield here before you arrived—"

"It doesn't matter," she snapped, and picked her way over to Quinn. The widow's suspicions of him seemed to have been miraculously dispelled.

Robert had picked up his notebook and waited to proceed.

"Maybe you did know him?" Mrs. Porteous asked Quinn. "Sergeant Porteous. Reg, they called him. Reginald Porteous. He was quite tall, as tall as you. Blond, blue eyes. Broad in the shoulder. 13th Battalion, 4th Brigade. He was at Gallipoli. Egypt, then Gallipoli. The Army sent me a letter about it. A Captain something-or-other sent me a letter. Captain Murray, perhaps. We have two daughters that have survived. He was shot, this captain said, and is buried there. At Bullecourt. One day we shall visit, of course. I shall take the girls. Soon. One day we will go. You know, I had never even heard of the place before. *Bullecourt,*" she added with distaste.

"Already they are building a monument in the town," she went on, as if now unable to keep up with the torrent of her own emotions. "A column with the names of all the dead. Already it's a memory. The dead men are already a memory. But there are, of course, many others who didn't return. The fallen are many. We widows as well, naturally. And orphans. Not that that is any consolation, or not to me."

Mrs. Porteous looked steadily into Quinn's eyes. "Reginald Porteous," she was saying. "Do you remember anyone by that name, Mr. Wakefield? P-O-R-T-E-O-U-S. Porteous."

Quinn vaguely remembered Mr. Porteous from his boyhood, but had not encountered him in the war. The 13th had fought alongside his 17th at Pozières, but the other men were little more than bobbing shapes in the darkness, voiceless, awaiting their deaths. But Mrs. Porteous stared up at him with the stem of her posy wrung ragged in her gloved hands. For some reason she was sympathetic to him, and for that he felt he owed her. Besides, she had saved his life by her very presence here in the cemetery. He was dismayed to note a penny-sized stain on the brim of her blue hat, a presage, without doubt, of the poverty she would now endure.

Another silence as they all waited for the echo of the widow's words to fade. At any moment Robert would start up again and demand Quinn's papers and he would be undone.

"Yes," Quinn said. "I do remember him now. A blond fellow. I met him in Egypt."

The widow's relief was palpable. She stifled a cry. "Really? In Egypt?"

"In training there. He was an excellent shot, a good rifleman, as I recall."

"Oh, he was a marvellous man."

"He was," Quinn agreed. "Quite the joker. I remember he tried to ride a camel in Cairo but the damn thing refused to stand up with him on board. He tried and tried, but the creature refused. Gippos had a good laugh at his expense, the devils."

"Yes, that sounds like him. He made me laugh so much. I would give anything to have him back again. I have all his letters, you know. He was always so cheerful because he didn't want me to worry, but it sounded awful, so awful."

Robert Dalton had by this time regained some of his composure and moved to interpose himself between Quinn and the widow. "A terrible thing, but it might be better not to talk of it. Now, Mr. Wakefield, your papers . . ."

But Mrs. Porteous angled past the constable and drew so close to Quinn that he got a whiff of the rosewater she had dabbed on her neck. It was the scent of widowhood. "Did Reg speak of me? I know it is vain, but I can't help but think of it. At night I wonder about it. All night, sometimes. When you knew him in Egypt? Did he talk of me or the girls?"

Quinn hesitated. He had lied himself into a trap. At war, men spoke of all sorts of matters, trivial or otherwise: of girls and their homes; of food they yearned to eat; of pets and their football teams; of the time their old man gave them a hiding for nicking apples. As he lay bleeding to death from a shrapnel wound to his stomach, a fellow called Greedy Thompson had rambled almost incoherently of a sandy flathead he had caught once near Bermagui, saying over and over how all the town's fishermen said it was the biggest flathead they had ever seen. Quinn thought of Fletcher Wakefield and of what he regretted not telling his fiancée before she died. Fletcher was killed before the war ended, and now Quinn supposed he could tell Doris himself without the intercession of mediums and their ilk. He thought, too, of the vicious query Mrs. Cranshaw had hissed at him that night at the séance. *What would you say to a woman like that?*

"Yes, ma'am," Quinn told Mrs. Porteous. "Now that I think about it, he did talk about you. He said you were without doubt the most beautiful woman he had ever seen. Without doubt. He always said you were too good for him. That's exactly what he said. Far too good for him."

Mrs. Porteous sagged with relief. "Can you stay with me a minute, please, Constable?" she murmured.

"Of course, but I need to check this fellow's papers, it's my job—"

"Don't worry about this gentleman. Can't you see he was wounded, for goodness sake? Look at him. Leave him be. Goodbye, Mr. Wakefield. Good luck to you. And thank you so much. Come on, Constable. Take me over to Ginny's grave. It's over there by that bush. See there?"

Robert Dalton huffed but took Mrs. Porteous' arm and they tottered away between the graves. Quinn pocketed the shell that he had been clenching in his palm and hurried away. The tracker Gracie would be back tomorrow morning. They had to leave at once.

Part Four

THE ANGEL OF DEATH

24

Sadie was sitting on a tree stump outside the shack eating an apple when Quinn arrived back from the cemetery. He told her what Dalton had said about the tracker's return.

"Are you sure?"

"I'm sure."

She became thoughtful. *"Sometimes things speak in a voice not their own."*

"What?"

"Something my mother told me. What about Thomas? He'll be here any day now. I know he will."

Quinn sighed. He would have to tell her Thomas was almost certainly dead. He kneeled in front of her. "Sadie," he began, but couldn't summon the courage to say anything more. After all, the girl actually had faith in something, which was more than most people had in these dark times. It was wrong to destroy it.

"You promised to wait with me until he came back, remember?" she said, as if reading his thoughts.

"I know, but—"

"But what?"

"The tracker will find you. Dalton, too. You know what he wants with you. He'll kill you. We have to leave. I have thirty pounds from my mother. It's enough to go anywhere. We have to leave now. Tonight."

She stared at the roll of money he had wrenched from his pocket, but shook her head. "There's not enough time. Not if he's back in the morning. He has dogs."

The girl was right. Already the light was thickening. There was no way they could make their way through the bush at night and they would be seen if they travelled by road.

Quinn paced again. He had an idea. "Do you know where the tracker lives?"

"Of course I do."

"Does he have a wife, children?"

"Just dogs."

"Then I'll go to his place tonight and wait for him to arrive in the morning. I'll tell him that I'm Thomas, that I'm your brother and there is no need to search for you. Have they ever met?"

"Yes, but years ago."

"I'll give him money *not* to look for you, if needs be. But we have to leave as soon as we can afterwards. No more waiting."

"What about Thomas?"

"I'll come back for him later, in a few weeks. When they've stopped looking."

"Do you promise?"

He ignored her question. He felt desperate. "Is it a bargain, girl?"

With her front teeth, Sadie nibbled at her apple. She spat out a seed. She nodded. "But what if Jim Gracie won't do what you ask him?"

Quinn paused. "Then I'll kill him."

She wiped her mouth and gazed around at the trees for a moment, as if consulting them on his idea. "Then you need to take the gun this time."

⁓⁊⁓

Quinn stood—shirtless, arms akimbo—while Sadie wrapped lengths of blue wool around his waist with the concentration of a tailor measuring him for a suit. To one of the strands she had fastened a leather pouch the size of a child's fist. The pouch contained items she deemed crucial to the success of his mission: snail shells, a stone wrapped in red twine, whiskers she had trimmed from his beard, his broken tooth, an earring.

"The dogs won't smell you if you wear these," she assured him as she issued him with directions. "So he won't know you are there when he gets back. Follow the cart track past Willow Creek. Mr. Gracie's place is a stone cottage on the rise above the old Chinese Village. You can't miss it. I'll wait for you here."

"Will you be alright?"

She severed a piece of wool with her teeth. "Of course."

"Hide under the floorboards."

"I still have my knife."

"Hide under the floor. In case Robert comes up here."

"He'll never find me by himself."

He grabbed her arm. "Please."

She shrugged him off. "Alright. I will."

"Cross your heart?"

"Cross my heart."

Quinn had come to love her seriousness, which seemed pilfered from someone much older. "I remember when you were born," he said. "You were so small that you were like . . . an insect wrapped in blankets. Eyes closed. There was blood on the floor and on the bed, of course. The sour smell of birth. Mother had a hard time in labour. You know we had a brother who died before? Before even I was born. But on the night you came, William and I were outside on the veranda listening to her scream like an animal. We weren't allowed inside. Father pacing up and down. Afterwards, the doctor left in his sulky and you cried louder than you would think a baby could. All night you screamed. Mother tried everything, but in the morning I took you up off the bed and you stopped straight away. In my arms. And you opened your eyes and looked at me as if I had saved you from something. Most people can't remember things that happened when they were four, but I can. I'll always remember that."

Sadie had finished wrapping the wool around his tattered body. She stared up at him, as if about to respond, then changed her mind. She tucked an apostrophe of hair back from her eyes. She scrabbled in her box of treasures and, still kneeling, took Quinn's hand in her own. Onto one of his fingers she slid a large ring. "This will help, too. Gold is the best thing. The gold for this was probably mined right here in these hills. Now go. Soon it will be dark."

With both hands, she swept up the remnants of her secret things—her charms and baubles, her trinkets and wool—and crammed them back into her tobacco tin.

Quinn held up his hand to admire the ring. *Gold were the Gods*, he thought, *their radiant garments gold, and gold their armour*. "Where did you get this?"

But she had slipped away. From next door he heard the hollow *clunkety-clunk* as she angled the broken floorboards into place over her crawlspace. He checked his revolver and set off.

⸭

By the time he was in sight of Jim Gracie's cottage, a hot wind had sprung up. He stood at the bottom of a shallow rise that led to the house, in wheat grass that was golden in the dusk light. It was as high as his hips and swayed like a silken congregation in the breeze. He raised his hat to wipe his brow. He felt sick and was possessed by the feeling that, with a slight effort of will, he could allow himself to be borne away, featherlike, on the late northerly. Would that it were so.

After several minutes he became aware of a shuddering, as if the earth were atremble, but soon realised the sensation was, in fact, in his own body, all along his intestines and deep in his knees. His hand began to shake, then his entire arm. Fear, then. Just human fear. It was a sensation he recognised from his years at war, as familiar as the boom of the sixty-pounders and the stench of mud.

He was aware of the lengths of wool beneath his grubby shirt, and of the leather phylactery that bumped against his ribs. He did feel somewhat protected by these girlish charms; after all, there was no doubt Sadie knew strange things of the world.

Emboldened, he walked up the hill, slipped between the wooden fence rungs and crossed Gracie's dirt yard with its chickens pecking at blackened corn roots. The man wouldn't even be home yet. The cottage was stone, with a bark roof. Empty tins and jars were scattered in the yard beneath a large gum tree that offered a piecemeal shade. He mounted the few steps to the veranda, opened the door and stood in the doorway, waiting for his eyes to adjust to the gloom.

Even with the door open the interior of the cottage was dark. The only window was covered by a tattered lace curtain. The air was muggy with dog sweat and dried meat. Something shifted. A thin figure materialised blinking from the darkness. It was a man.

"Who the hell are you?" the man said.

25

T here was the frenzied scratch of canine toenails on floorboards. The floor whirlpooled around Quinn's feet as dogs nuzzled and sniffed at his calves.

"Are you Mr. Gracie?" he asked in a weak voice.

"I am," came the suspicious reply.

Jim Gracie was sitting on a low bunk by the wall. He was a raggedy man, with forearms like twists of rope. Quinn was rooted to the spot with fear and indecision. For a moment, he thought he recognised Gracie; he was sure the fellow would know he was not Thomas Fox. The idea was idiotic. His revolver was jammed in the waistband of his trousers, but he was unable to move and feared that his breath would fail. The sensation passed. No. The man was as strange to Quinn as, hopefully, he was to Gracie.

The tracker leaned in and inspected him with murky eyes before turning his attention to his dogs. He aimed a vicious kick at one that sent it slinking into a corner. He turned back to Quinn. "Who are you?"

Quinn wiped his dry mouth.

"You're a bloody quiet fella." Jim Gracie's hand butterflied in the air, displaying a palm dark with grime. "The dogs always tell me when someone is coming, not that that happens much. Must have flown here like a bird . . . or an angel. Are you lost?"

He shook his head.

"Then where you going, mate? Nearest town is a mile that way. The town of Flint. Don't want you here that's for sure."

The fellow was agitated, perhaps even afraid. Quinn found it difficult to understand his somewhat clotted manner of speech. One of the hounds reappeared and sniffed about their feet. Quinn was seized by a coughing attack. His chest felt thick with burning coals.

"Do you have any water, sir?" he asked when he could speak again. "Please."

Gracie hesitated but, complaining to himself, got off his bunk and poured some water into a battered tin cup. Quinn straightened to drink.

The tracker stepped back and shielded his nose and mouth with one hand. "You don't got that disease, do you, mate?"

"No. I don't have influenza, if that's what you mean."

"Bloody Bolsheviks."

Quinn gulped again. "What?"

"People that started this whole thing. Put frogs and spiders in the water up in Sydney, dead people, you name it. Bastards."

"I was gassed in the war."

"Oh, yeah. Heard about that. They reckon the world's ending. The fella at church—Mr. Smail—said so. Locusts as big as horses, with girls' long hair. Dragons, a lamb. He told me God was waiting for us in the clouds. Our Father. Blood from the sky and all that. War." He said something further and crossed himself. "What you reckon?"

Quinn shrugged. He was still standing in the doorway and had again begun to doubt the wisdom of this visit. Gracie was mad. Although it was almost dark, he saw the cottage was neat aside from the clutter of poverty. There was a roughly hewn bench opposite the low bed. The walls were plastered here and there with sheets of yellowing newspaper. On the table in the middle of the room was the enamel jug from which Gracie had poured his water. The two stinking dogs blinked in the gloom, their forms almost invisible against the earthen floor.

Gracie asked him something.

"What?"

"What you reckon happens to all them dead fellas in the war and that?"

Quinn made a helpless gesture with his hands. This wasn't the moment for a theosophical discussion.

"That Smail says they in heaven but I don't reckon heaven can be *that* big."

The man had a point. So many dead. What with the war and the epidemic, the recently dead must outnumber those still living. No doubt they move among us, Quinn thought.

Gracie snatched his mug away and put it back on the table, clearly wishing to draw their little conversation to a close. He lit a pair of candles, their light meagre. "You want to be careful walking about in them hills. There are old mine shafts. It's risky. Fall down one of them and you're done for." With that he turned away to fiddle in the gloom.

Quinn remained in the doorway. "I need to talk to you about a girl."

The tracker stopped what he was doing, murmured and swung around. Quinn now saw it was a rifle he had been tinkering with, a battered Lee-Enfield, by the look of it. Gracie shuffled back to Quinn on his bare feet. His eyes glittered. "A girl, you say. What sort of girl?"

"My sister. She's been living up in the hills."

Gracie stared at him as if he had uttered something preposterous. "Your *sister*?"

"Yes. She's been up there since our mother died from the influenza."

"I been told about her."

"What have you heard?"

The fellow ducked his head, muttered.

"What was that?"

"I know the constable is worried about her. Said she needs saving. I thought you was him. I thought he'd come around as soon as he could. He wants me to . . . to help him find her. To take care of her, mind."

Quinn slapped at a mosquito feasting on his neck. "No. There is no need anymore. I am her brother, Thomas. I'll look after her now. This is why I came here, to tell you this."

"You're Thomas? You're different than I recall."

"I was injured in the war."

Gracie considered him. "You need to tell Mr. Dalton, not me, he's the one who decides. He makes me help him. Anyway, her brother is dead in the war. That's what Mr. Dalton told me ages ago, even before I went to Bathurst. We'll find her. The dogs'll sniff her out." He raised the tips of his fingers to his nose. "Girls that age have a particular smell about them. My boys can find anyone, anywhere."

Quinn had begun to feel unsteady. The room blurred. Gracie was peering at him and speaking in a language he could no longer understand. The flickering candles bathed the room in an unearthly light.

The tracker pressed the tin cup again into Quinn's hand and wrapped his fingers around it. Quinn drank. Something hot and bitter seared his throat. Alcohol. The liquid prompted him to cough. He gagged but drank more. Gracie dragged a chair across and sat Quinn on it.

It was several minutes before he could focus or make sense of anything. The empty cup was in his hand, and Gracie was sitting on an upturned metal bucket, staring up at him. Quinn placed the cup on the table. The alcohol had stopped burning quite so fiercely and instead a benign warmth seeped through his innards. "What do you call that stuff?" he asked.

Gracie's face lit up in a smile. "No name. Just grog. Bloke out near Gray's Creek cooks it up. Good, isn't it? Now, you sure about your sister?"

"Of course."

"She's a young thing, maybe twelve or thirteen years old?"

Quinn adjusted himself on the wooden chair. "Sadie? Yes."

"She's the one, alright." He became thoughtful. "Sadie, eh? Poor girl. That Mr. Smail at church says the disease is our own doing. The Lord smite people with a great plague until we all be destroyed. We been bad and we're going to pay. He's probably right." He clicked his tongue. "So, you're going to look after her? Good."

"Yes."

"Where you taking her?"

He said the first destination that entered his head. "London."

"Ah, good. Long way from here. That where your missus is at?"

"I'm not married."

Gracie held up his left hand and waggled his fingers. "What about your ring?"

Quinn had forgotten the ring. It gleamed dully. It occurred to him that he was already drunk from the little amount of grog he'd imbibed. "Yes," he said. "I mean yes. I am married. But she died a long time ago."

Gracie nodded and made a sympathetic noise in his throat.

"She was murdered."

The tracker's eyes widened. He sat up straighter and wiped his hands on his belly. The two dogs lurched into activity and were circling about Quinn's calves, faster and faster, like the tigers in that story that whirled themselves into butter.

"She was very beautiful," Quinn said above the noise. "Everyone thought so, not only me. Like an angel, they used to say. She loved to play games. You know that game where you have to get rid of all your cards before the other person? Once we played it for six hours. She wouldn't let me go even though I had things to do for my father and he gave me a hiding when he found out."

Gracie shook his head. Of course he had no idea what Quinn was talking about.

It was stuffy in the cottage and the myriad cuts over Quinn's body had begun to itch and burn. He removed his jacket and scratched at them. "Two men," he continued, "took her away one day and . . . raped and killed her."

Gracie looked terrified. One of the dogs whined. "By God. What happened to them fellas that did that?"

Quinn thought of what his mother had said about the murderer and replied, "God will have his vengeance."

"You really think that? You think God is watching us, taking notice of what we do?"

Quinn stared into his empty cup and belched stickily. "Of course."

"Is that what you pray for then? This vengeance?"

"I suppose so. Among other things."

They sat in silence for several minutes before Quinn managed to speak again. "Could I perhaps have something more to drink, Mr. Gracie? Some more grog?"

Gracie poured him another cupful and squatted on the floor, arse low, elbows on his bony knees. He was nodding. "You're not Thomas, but I *know* who you are."

From deep within his melancholy reverie, Quinn registered a faint pulse of fear but he pressed on nonetheless. He fumbled around in his trouser pocket until he located the thick roll of money. He pulled it out, along with the shell he had picked up at Sarah's grave and the red button from her dress that he'd taken from Sadie. The tracker stared at the items in Quinn's dirty palm.

Quinn gulped more alcohol. "This is for you," he went on, indicating the money. "A token for you. In order that you *don't* find Sadie and me. Will you do that, sir? Please? We need to get away. We only need a few days."

"Yes! Don't worry. I'll lead Dalton astray. He don't know a thing about the bush. But he's a suspicious bastard. After a few days, he'll question me."

The fellow's enthusiasm was puzzling, even taking into account the sum of money on offer for his cooperation. "But can I trust you, sir? Constable Dalton is a terrible man—"

"I know that! He's made me do things. He tempts me, the bastard. Like the *Devil*." He gestured around at his hovel. "I got nothing. I been waiting for you, you know. I know who you are. Mr. Smail says we all get judged sometimes for the bad things we done. Our sins will seek us out. I been praying a lot, you know, because I helped Mr. Dalton do things . . ."

Not really listening, Quinn nodded and drank again from the tin cup. He waited for the revulsion to pass and for the more agreeable chemical warmth to settle in him. When he spoke again it was only with much concentration and he was pleased to notice a clumsiness in his voice. "But who is it, who is it you think I am, Mr. Gracie?"

Jim Gracie pursed his lips and shrugged as if what he prepared to say was apparent to anyone. "You're the Angel of Death."

They stared at each other in the flickering light. A moth blundered into the candle's flame. Quinn was drunk and overwhelmed by an absurd desire to sleep. He felt as if all parts of his body were suffused with an irresistible exhaustion.

He drank the rest of his grog. Some of it sloshed down his chin. With difficulty, and only after several fumbling attempts, he placed the money on the table, along with the button and the shell. Against his better instincts, he closed his eyes. He heard Gracie talking on and on in his rusty voice.

Quinn dreamed he was walking in a monstrous field of black, button-sized flowers that covered his boots as he trudged. The flowers had a strange perfume, like old rags. The field enlarged as he went on, but when it seemed he had reached its middle, the flowers took wing and revealed themselves to be, in fact, thousands of tiny crows that flapped about his face, obscuring the horizon. It was at that moment, moored in his silent nightmare, that Quinn realised where he had seen Jim Gracie before: he'd held Sarah down all those years ago.

26

When Quinn came to, he was sprawled on a filthy wooden floor. His head felt filled with something heavy and pulsating. It was dark, but he could hear birds calling outside. Chickens clucked and fussed in the yard. Where was he? After a minute he remembered. Jim Gracie's cabin. He cursed and sat up, which only made the pain lodged in the back of his head worse.

Judging by the cool breeze, the door was open. He fumbled about and located his revolver and jacket on the floor beside him. There was no sign of Gracie, but on the table were the items Quinn had placed there the night before—the roll of money, the shell and the button. He pocketed them all. From outside came a dog's long, low moan.

He slipped into his jacket and, clutching his revolver, stepped onto the veranda. The top of the distant Blue Mountains was edged with a smouldering hem of light as the sun rose beyond them. He called out Gracie's name, but the only response was a slight increase in the pitch and urgency of the dogs' whining. He couldn't make them out in the near-dark, but sensed their angry, shining gaze.

A breeze drifted over the hill. The gum tree creaked. He shouted again, but Gracie must have fled. Perhaps he would return with Robert Dalton? At least the dogs were still here, which meant he wasn't out searching for Sadie yet. What could he tell Sadie? He thought of her face drenched in terror as she realised what was about to happen; the way she managed a breathless *No* before a hand was clamped over her mouth; the way she fought and bit, fought and bit; the scrape of her shoe, his uncle's wheezing laughter.

The night started to give way to the brittle chill of morning. Quinn stepped into the yard and walked around the cottage. Its bulk was by now visible against the blueing sky. His breath came in shallow clumps. His tongue was so thick and clumsy it might have been made of wool. Soon he was able to make out smaller shapes in the darkness. The line of a fence, a tin bucket. He tripped over a length of wood.

By the time he reached the gum tree, he saw that one of the dogs had assumed a spiky crouch, head low, teeth bared, eyes aglow. The beast growled a deep warning. The other dog followed suit and they prepared to attack. Quinn raised his revolver in a shaking hand. He stepped back until the gum-tree limbs glowed stark against the sky, as if the tree were a fork of milky lightning caught fast in the earth.

Then he saw him: Jim Gracie, hovering in the air with his toes high above the ground, his bare chest glistening, eyes bulging. His head lolled, tongue swollen and empurpled. His trousers were slack on his boyish hips and there was a dark stain down one leg. The rich stink of human shit. The rope creaked as it swung lazily with its human cargo. Quinn stumbled backwards, unable to tear his eyes from the hanged man. He watched him for some time. He felt relieved, rather than avenged, not at all as if he had gained anything.

Finally, he turned and fled. He scrambled over the fence, panicked at the thought of those hounds pursuing him. He listened for their slobbering snap at his heels but heard only the saw of his own breath and the pummelling of his heart.

Several minutes later, he was overcome by a coughing fit and slumped to his knees. He vomited onto the ground. Birds whistled and whooped around him. The ground under his knees was moist with dew and carpeted with bark. It was satisfying to dig his hands into the surface to the damp loam beneath.

He was startled by a voice.

"That was a right *bastard*, wasn't it?"

About ten feet away, lying on his side, was a soldier around Quinn's age. His boots and puttees were blotched with mud and he was nodding, as if desperate for Quinn's agreement.

Quinn scrambled to his feet. "Who are you?"

The soldier motioned for him to sit down. "Careful, mate. What are you, barmy?"

Quinn did as he was told.

The soldier stared at him. His exhalations were visible in the cold morning air. "Are you alright?"

Quinn nodded, and indicated with a jerk of his thumb the way he had come.

"Terrible, wasn't it?" the soldier said.

"You saw that?"

"I was there, alright. But we survived another one, eh?" A bird trilled a brief, elegant song in the trees overhead. "You sure you're alright, though? Your arm is shaking pretty bad there."

Only now did Quinn realise that his left arm was twitching as if attempting to detach itself from his shoulder. He clamped it between his thighs. "Not injured. Nerves, that's all. The shells, you know, it's the shells."

The fellow nodded. As the day lightened, Quinn realised they were surrounded by men lying on the ground smoking and sleeping. Some had heads or legs bandaged; some cradled their arms in makeshift slings; they stared about dumbstruck and picked at their skin. The air was ripe with the smells of mud and gas, and the mildewy odour of bloodied bandages. In the distance he made out a tumbrel cart piled high with bodies, scraps of uniform, pieces of men. A horse pawed at the earth as if displeased at its inability to dig itself a grave. There was a grumble of artillery. Someone nearby was weeping. A heartbreaking sound, a man weeping. There was a crackle of rifle fire. Quinn wiped his hands on his shirt. He needed to keep moving, to get away from here.

"You don't know a bloke called Shawcross, do you?" the soldier called out. "Keith Shawcross?"

Quinn ignored him. His arm, at least, had stopped shaking. He stood and picked his way through the dead and sleeping men. The ground was lumpen, greasy with blood.

The soldier worried at a fingernail. "Thought not. He was a mate. I was wondering if he made it, that's all. You never know, do you? But I think he'll be alright. Lucky, too."

"Lucky?"

"Lucky to be alive, like us. Be careful, mate. It's still dangerous out there."

⚜

It was light by the time Quinn managed to half run, half stumble back to the shack. He imagined Sadie's grim satisfaction at the news of Gracie's suicide. He called out to her as soon as he glimpsed their shack between the trees, but she must have been still hidden beneath the floorboards. She was a good girl, really. He stumbled through the stinking kitchen but was shocked to find the boards that covered her hiding place dislodged, her knife lying discarded on the floor. Panic started to take shape in him. He yelled out again, to reassure her.

He crouched on hands and knees to peer beneath the floor. "Sadie?" In the gauzy light he made out desiccated fruit peel, grubby blankets, and dozens of rocks and broken bricks, some of which were wrapped in strands of coloured wool. There was a disordered pile of shells, a hollow worn into the dirt by her sleeping form. But no Sadie.

Panicked now, Quinn returned outside and shouted, louder this time. Nothing. No sign of her. No sign of anyone. There was the wreckage of the fire over which they had cooked the remains of that lamb. Some of its bones were strewn about in the dirt. Crows cackled in the surrounding trees. A willy-wagtail hopped about on a branch. The birds alone might have seen what had happened, where Sadie had gone, with whom. Again he screamed her name and listened. Then he spied her tobacco tin at his feet. It was open and scattered among the leaves were a playing card, several marbles and some of the knuckles. He picked up the tin: all that remained inside was a cigarette card with a colour reproduction of an elegant woman posting a letter into a London pillar box. Sweat poured down Quinn's face. Where was she? Then he realised: Robert Dalton had managed to track her down. He had taken her to the cabin at Wilson's Point.

He began running before he'd even considered the best way to go. It didn't matter; his legs, acting independently of his mind or the rest of his body, took him down hills and across gullies he didn't recall seeing before. He wished now he'd taken Jim Gracie's rifle, but his revolver would have to suffice.

Dotted here and there were the rusted carcasses of mining equipment and the collapsed, mud-packed walls of ponds or houses. Lizards flickered underfoot, and a haughty mob of grey kangaroos bounded away as he passed. He spoke to Sadie under his breath as he ran, assuring her. *Will soon be there. Not to worry. Don't worry.* He imagined the words streaming from his lips and settling in his wake like petals that would enable them to find their way back once he had saved her. A smile split his face under his beard. He felt alive in a way he had not felt since he was a boy, and the world around him was suffused with a reciprocal energy. *Soon. I'll be there soon. Just hang on.* The trees crackled with excitement. They urged him onwards, their leaves vibrating. The bush opened before him and he surrendered to its current.

He arrived at Wilson's Point fifteen minutes later. The level of the kidney-shaped reservoir was low. The cabin was three hundred yards from where he emerged from the dense bush. He checked his revolver before wading through the muddy shallows, careful to remain unseen. He was determined not to halt again, despite the heaving of his flayed lungs. *Nearly there.* He felt exhilarated at the prospect of capturing his uncle and of saving Sadie from his clutches. The future materialised before him clearer than anything from his past. *Don't worry.* He would push his way through the reeds by the shore and clamber over the boulders. He would burn with courage. *Almost there.* He would approach the cabin as he should have done all those years ago. He would kick open the door that sagged from its hinge. He would take aim with his revolver.

All of which he did.

27

As the door swung wide, Quinn could see in an instant that the cabin was empty. Grief and confusion jolted through him. Not a soul. Indeed, the place looked as though it had not been visited since that dreadful afternoon all those years ago. A pair of cockatoos flapped from their perch, squawked in the half-light and flew through a gaping hole in the roof. There was a pile of rotten wood in one corner. A fern shouldered through the floor. He stood there breathing hard, the revolver in one shaking hand. Unspent adrenaline pulsed through him. The place stank of mouldy wood, spider webs, animal droppings; of rape and murder. If only the darkness would speak.

Embarrassed and exhausted, he sank to his haunches to draw breath. The cuffs of his trousers were heavy with water and drying mud. After a moment, he slumped to the crumbling floor. This, then, was how it would end; as it had begun: at Wilson's Point, wishing he had never been born. First exile, then war. Everything was in ruins. Everything. He lay down and sobbed.

How long he'd been lying there with his eyes closed he didn't know, but after some time he became aware of a distant chorus of voices. The people of Flint were coming for him. He imagined them tramping across the banks of the reservoir, slipping here and there in the mud. His father and uncle would be at their head; then Jack Sully with his rickety gait; Mrs. Porteous in her widow's weeds; old Mrs. Crink with her gauzy eyes, tap-tapping along with a stick; Bluey and McLaverty; the Harvey Brothers; Evelyn Higgins. He opened his eyes as if that might assist his hearing, but he soon lost track of the voices in the wind. No matter. Soon enough they would burst in on him and take him away. They would beat him and fill his pockets with rocks before throwing him into the reservoir, as the miners had done with outlaws in days gone by. And that would be that. He shouldn't have been surprised at the outcome: in any endeavour, the possibilities for failure were almost limitless while happy endings offered but one result. The scabs and scars on his skin stung with sweaty irritation.

On the floor, hundreds of ants scurried about carrying shards of leaf in their pincers. So many of them, and all so inconsequential. As a boy, he had been fascinated by insects and spiders, and spent many happy hours inspecting redback spiders, centipedes and cicadas. Like humans, they inhabited their own universe of beauty and terror, the borders of which they thought they knew. He wondered if this might be the way God saw the human race as it went about its daily business. It must be simple to allow war and pestilence to flourish when the suffering of individuals was so distant, easy to permit them to murder and defile one another. The affairs of men were inconsequential.

He became aware again of voices calling out with some urgency but didn't move. They would find him soon enough. One ant was beneath his nose and stood on its hind legs like a dog. The creature was gesticulating with its tiny pincers. It fell onto all six legs, scurried forward and stood again. He became aware of someone speaking. *She's not here*, the voice was saying. He wiggled a finger in his ear to clear his damned hearing. He stared at the ant, who was by now just an inch from him. The insect was talking in a husky voice, repeating the same phrase over and over. *He took her to the lock-up. To the lock-up.* The ant tossed its head the way a horse might its mane, dropped down and trotted away. He heard the scratch of its claws on the boards and it was only then he understood that the voices were not those of people, but of the ants that swarmed over the cabin's rotten floorboards.

Quinn picked up his revolver and lurched to his feet. His ears crowded with the urging not only of the ants but of the entire bush. As if a great engine were coming to life, the air throbbed with conversation, with currents of insistence and lament. It occurred to Quinn he might be able, should he try, to discern the shy whisper of nearby blades of grass. *He took her to the lock-up, to the lock-up.* Perhaps it was not too late, after all? He burst from the cabin and set off again through the bush, this time towards the police station on the other side of Flint.

Quinn passed the small dam and the perimeter of Sparrowhawk Mine at Flint's eastern edge. After ten minutes he staggered from the bush like a crazed saint. He had lost his jacket somewhere, and scattered all over his filthy white shirt were the bloodied imprints of the crosses and other hieroglyphs scratched into his body. He crossed the river and skirted the Flats, where he paused under the shade of a lone birch tree. From the Anglican church came the swelling and falling tide of voices in hymn. It must be Sunday. He could see the police station fifty yards away over Gully Road.

A grey horse was tethered to the wooden fence and a sheep grazed in the deep shade of the garden's elm tree. The police bicycle leaned against the station's sandstone wall. Quinn's heart was swollen with fear, but there was no room for hesitation. He crossed the road and entered the cool, dark station. This time. This time he would have his way.

28

His uncle was snoozing in his chair when Quinn entered. He roused himself, but Quinn was able to stride across the room and stick the revolver in his uncle's face before the constable realised what was happening. Quinn considered shooting his uncle straight away but hesitated. He wanted Dalton to know why he was to be killed; that was the very essence of justice.

Dalton uttered something—*Whoa* or *No*—shielded his face with both hands and slid down in his wooden chair. His left hand was still bandaged.

"Where is she?" Quinn demanded.

"You again!"

"Where is the girl?"

"What are you talking about? Put the gun down at once. I'm the constable here. Don't *threaten* me, man, or I'll—"

Quinn gestured with the revolver. "Tell me where she is or I'll shoot you."

Dalton had managed to get to his feet, but he cowered anew at Quinn's threat. The desk was a mess of papers and books, a tin plate with the glutinous carcass of a roast chicken. The station smelled queerly of smoky stone, like a church. "No," he said weakly.

Quinn paused. "You still don't recognise me, do you?"

"What? Yes, you're that fellow from the graveyard the other da—Wackfield? Wakefield? I should have taken you in right then and there."

"Try again. Closer. Stand up straight and look at my face, Robert."

Dalton did as he was told. Then his gaze fell to take in the bloody patterns across Quinn's shirt.

"Well?" Quinn asked.

Sweat glistened on Dalton's pink forehead and there was a fresh scratch on his neck below his ear. His trousers were undone and his generous belly swooned over his belt. He motioned with his hands. "Put that revolver down, sir."

"You really don't recognise me?"

"Well, I don't know. Tell me, then, if it's so bloody important."

"I'm your nephew."

Dalton stepped back. His mouth curled into a sneer and then he craned forward like a pale, dumbstruck turtle. "William? Not little Quinn? It can't be. They said you were dead. I saw the telegram myself."

"The one that said I had been killed in the war?"

His uncle was taken aback. He inspected him again. "Don't be ridiculous. You don't look anything like him."

"A lot has happened."

"Indeed it has." Dalton ran a hand across his brow. "Prove to me who you are, then."

"I have no papers."

"Then why should I believe you?"

Quinn thought for a moment. "I was born in 1893. I was named after my mother's father, Quinn Dalton—your father, too —who died when a ship sank between Shanghai and Hong Kong. Sarah was born in '97. You came here from London in"—he pondered for a few seconds—"1894, I believe. Or maybe '95. Some said you had been forced to leave England."

Whether Dalton believed Quinn or not, revealing his identity now felt like a miscalculation; his uncle looked less afraid, not more. Dalton hitched his trousers and straightened his disordered jacket. His eyes darted around, perhaps seeking his own revolver. "You are a lunatic, man. Anyone can learn dates. Leave now and I won't take you in. Go on, clear off."

But Quinn waved Dalton back against one of the stone walls and located the police revolver among the papers on the desk. He jammed it into his trouser pocket. "Where is Sadie Fox?"

Dalton examined him. It seemed he prepared to answer, then thought better of it. He belched.

"Well?"

The constable wiped his brow again and ventured a dry laugh. "You're disgusting. Why did you come back here, eh? You animal. You know you *destroyed* your mother by what you did. You're lucky you got away."

"No such thing as luck."

"Well, they would have hanged you, no worries. I would have hanged you from a tree myself if I got my hands on you. That poor girl. I saw you, Quinn. I saw you with that knife in your hand. You can't fool me. Your father saw you, as well. Everyone knows you are guilty. They used to laugh about you and your sister. You know what they used to call you around here, eh? Do you know?"

"And I saw what you did to her. You and that fellow Gracie. Through a hole in the wall. I heard what you said that day, after you'd . . . finished with her." Quinn gagged, hardly able to repeat those words yet again. "You said, *Good day's hunting, after all.* I saw everything. I saw what you did to my sister. How you bickered with Jim Gracie afterwards. You're the animal, not me."

Dalton shifted from one bare foot to the other. His gaze flickered about the room. "You don't know what you're on about, you should be ashamed of yourself."

"Oh, I am. Now. Where's the girl?"

"There's no one here but you and me." Dalton eyed Quinn's revolver. "Is that really you? Quinn? You've changed a lot. Why don't we sit and have a drink, eh? Let's relax a minute. You look dog-tired, you know that?"

Quinn allowed Dalton to move to the desk and dig out a bottle of liquor from a drawer. His uncle sat in the chair behind his desk and poured two glasses. He pushed one across to him. Quinn shook his head. "Where is Sadie Fox? I know you've been searching for her."

Dalton sipped his drink. "Yes, that's right. I have been keeping an eye out for little Sadie. Her mother died in the epidemic, you know, just a few weeks ago. Poor girl has no one left. Her brother went to war, her father vanished years ago. I have arranged for her to be taken into care, in an orphanage in Bathurst. That is part of what I do here in Flint, part of my job. She can't possibly live up in the hills all by herself, can she? Sit down, Quinn, for God's sake, you're making me nervous."

"You might think you got away with it, but you didn't, you know that? I saw you that day. Jim Gracie is dead. I visited him yesterday. He's strung up from the gum tree beside his house. He's no use to you now."

Dalton sat forward with something like triumph in his eyes. "Hah! There you go. Gracie was in Bathurst yesterday, you lying little shit. He's back today."

"No. He came back last night. He told me everything. Told me about the other girls. The Gunn girl."

"Gracie is dead?"

"Yes."

"And you killed him?"

Quinn thought about his response. "Yes."

This news appeared to throw Dalton off balance, but he soon regained his composure. "And what do you want with this girl, eh?"

"I'll look after her."

Dalton snorted and emptied his glass. He leaned forward with his elbows on the desk. "No. Tell me. What do you *really* want with her?"

"I should just shoot you."

"You'll not get away with it. They'll find you."

"Like they found you?"

Dalton considered him with his amphibious gaze and rapped the desk gently with his knuckles. "I had a feeling you would return," he said. "A bad feeling, mind. Mary has been talking about you a lot of late. About you and Sarah. Nathaniel noticed it, too. The poor woman is delirious, of course, but still . . . I've been keeping an eye out for you. For years I thought you would come back, but as time passed it seemed less and less likely. I have to admit, this is quite a surprise."

"I bet it is."

"If you are who you say you are, that is. What the hell did you think you would achieve in coming back here, anyway? Your poor sister is still dead. Everyone knows you did it."

Quinn thought of the note in the match-safe in his pocket. Its fragile words. *Don't forget me. Come back and save me. Please.* "I came to protect Sadie Fox," he said. "And to get justice for my sister."

His uncle gestured vaguely towards the distant sound of hymns coming from the church several streets away, then poured himself another drink. "They'd love to get their hands on you. All that talk of love and so on, but what they *really* like to do is tear some wrongdoer limb from limb. Make them feel like their God gives a damn, which doubtless he does not." He emptied his glass in a single gulp and grimaced. "Is that all the evidence you have—that you *say* you saw me?"

"I saw you stab her."

"But no one was with you, were they? Eh? You were alone? It isn't as if you had any other friends."

"I know what I saw." Quinn's voice was thin and reedy. Dalton had somehow managed to wrestle the initiative from him, even though Quinn had both revolvers.

"*I know what I saw,*" Dalton mimicked. "You're bloody pathetic, you know that?" He wiped the back of his hand under his glistening nose. "Tell you what. Put the revolver down. Leave now and I won't bother coming after you. Even considering Gracie. Get away from here and never come back. Let's forget this ever happened. You're not the kind of man who'd shoot an officer of the law, are you? I mean—"

From somewhere there came a high-pitched squeak. Dalton glanced at a door to his left that led to the adjacent cell.

Quinn jerked his head. "Is she in there?"

"I told you. There is no one here. That was just a mouse or something. This country is crawling with bloody vermin." Dalton rubbed his cheek, then fingered the fresh scratch on his neck. "Why don't you go in there and take a peek for yourself, if you're so sure? Go on. It's open. Look for yourself, Quinn. Go on."

Quinn stared at Dalton. All these years his uncle had been dwelling like an imp in the back of his mind, and now he was here in front of him.

Robert took advantage of Quinn's momentary disorientation. "Who the hell are you?" he demanded. "Everyone knows little Quinn is dead. You don't even look like him. You're just some crazy bastard. You know, after we left you that day in the cemetery, Mrs. Porteous commented on how strange you were. *Highly disturbed*, she said to me. Who the hell are you?"

Quinn had shuffled across to the cell door. A curious calm had entered him. He placed one hand on the heavy iron handle and paused. He faced his uncle and raised the revolver. "I'm the Angel of Death," he said, and pulled the trigger. A shot, loud and hard.

Dalton grunted and fell back in his chair. His pudgy hands clasped at his chest. Blood oozed between his fingers. "Shit! You *shot* me, you crazy bastard." He staggered wheezing to his feet. He fumbled for balance against the edge of the desk. "What are you doing? What are you doing? Help me." Papers slid off the desk. The bottle smashed to the floor and the office was at once infused with the acrid smell of liquor. Dalton sprawled across the desk, and then slapped fishily to the floor where he groaned for several seconds before he was silent.

Shocked, Quinn stared at him and coughed. His hands shook. The Sword of Justice, he thought. After all these years. From the nearby church he heard hymns again. *There's a land that is fairer than day, and by faith we can see it afar* . . . He crouched beside his uncle and listened for his breathing, but there was nothing. Blood seeped from beneath Dalton's body and spread out over the floor. Quinn stepped over him and yanked open the heavy cell door. He started at an orange cat that blurred between his legs and bolted outside. "Sadie?" he whispered into the darkness. "It's me."

Quinn was terrified of what he might find, of what he might fail to find. When there was no answer, he stepped into the unlit cell. At first just dimness and the farmyard whiff of shit and hay. No one there. Again he whispered Sadie's name. Gradually, his eyes adjusted and, sure enough, the girl materialised from the gloom, sitting on a lumpy mattress on the floor. She was gagged. Her eyes bulged at his entrance. There was straw in her hair and a fresh bruise on one cheek. Again that brief, unbearable squeak. Her hands were secured behind her back with a pair of cuffs, so he dashed to Dalton and rolled over his uncle's heavy corpse to detach the ring of keys from his belt.

He loosened Sadie's gag and unlocked the cuffs with trembling, bloodstained fingers. She was dishevelled and shaking. As soon as she was able, she ripped the gag off and threw it down before cowering against the wall. She spat on the floor and wiped her swollen mouth with the back of one hand.

"Are you alright?" he asked.

She threw him a quick and bitter glance. "Did you shoot him? I heard a shot."

He nodded and raised the revolver, as if to prove it to her.

"Is he dead?"

"Yes."

"Are you sure?"

"Yes."

"He won't come back again?"

"No. He's dead."

She sat back on the edge of the mattress with her hands on her knees, staring at the floor as if deep in thought. Then she looked up and prepared to stand. "What about Mr. Gracie? We have to go now or they'll send him out to track—"

"No. He's dead as well."

Sadie slumped back again. "Thank God. Did you kill him, too?"

Quinn made a helpless gesture. He leaned down and put a hand on her shoulder, thinking to comfort her, but she shrugged him away with a grunt of annoyance. She retrieved her filthy cardigan from the floor before tucking her legs up beneath her, primly, as if awaiting inspection. She seemed to have forgotten his presence, almost like one of those shell-shocked people he had seen during the war.

Quinn sat beside her. In silence they stared at a shard of light that crept over the cold stones with the passage of the morning sun, illuminating as it did so the various marks and words scratched into the wall. He was surprised no one had arrived to investigate the revolver shot, but perhaps it had gone unheard. He stared up through the tiny window set high into the wall, out of reach of even the tallest man. The sky was blue, unchanging. He knew it was possible to feel this bad and still not die because he had felt this way before. Small, hard tears of despair rolled down his cheek, one by one. He wondered if his heart might fail for no reason better than pure grief, the way his voice-box did all those years ago.

"I kept hearing angels," Sadie said after a long time, and tapped her ear, as if she might dislodge the magical creatures lounging there. "All morning I heard angels singing and I thought they were coming for me." She wiped her eyes with the heel of her hand. "I thought I would die. I thought I was going to die from it."

"I'm sorry. I'm sorry I was too late. I didn't know where he had taken you. I'm so sorry."

She sighed and turned to him. Her eyes were blurry with tears. "It's not your fault." She dusted dirt from her knee. "At least he didn't kill me," she said without conviction. "At least I didn't die."

Quinn stared down at the revolver in his lap. He supposed this was something. He thought of the Military Medal tumbling drowsily across

the ocean floor, wedging here and there in coral, accumulating grime
about the engraved image of King George.

She sighed again. "What do we do now?"

"I'm not sure. We should get away from here, though."

The patch of sunlight had meandered across the floor and glowed
on the dull bluestones at their feet. Sadie waggled her grubby toes in its
warmth. "Quinn? I've been thinking. I don't think my brother is coming
home. I think he would be here by now."

Quinn coughed. "There are stories, you know, about soldiers
coming back to visit people. I heard about that a lot of times in France.
In hospital I met a fellow who had been in a battle when the men around
him lying in . . . lying dead in the trench for days got up and began
fighting. Dozens of them. The battalion had been outnumbered but they
managed to fight off hundreds of Germans. And this man had seen it
with his own eyes. He was there. Incredible things happen in war, you
know. It's not a normal time, everything is different."

Although she had cocked her head to listen to his little story, Sadie
didn't respond. A spider scuttled across the floor and darted into the
shadows. She cleared her throat. "But the war is over now, isn't it? It
ended ages ago."

Quinn fingered the revolver. "Well, yes."

"How long ago did it finish?"

He calculated. "November last year. A few months ago."

She pondered this. "But we won, didn't we?"

"Yes."

Again she faced him, and he noted how her smile had been made
crooked, as if one of the hinges of her mouth were now broken. "But
you're like a brother, aren't you?"

The dark coal of Quinn's heart glowed hot and hard. He choked
back a sob. He nodded.

"Perhaps we should go to Kensington Gardens? In England.
Remember we talked about that once before?"

He shrugged. It was as good an idea as any. At least there it would
be green and fresh. There would be water and mist. He could probably
get some kind of work quite easily in London; after all, able-bodied

men were in short supply. He and Sadie would find somewhere to live. Perhaps he could build them a house? From outside came the sound of the grey's iron shoes clopping on the flagstones. He heard the wavering, watery drift of a choir—the singing of angels.

"That's it," Sadie went on, excited now. "The Gardens are full of trees. There are tricky fairies dressed in flowers. They are everywhere, even though you can't see them. They live under tree roots. We could live on that island in the lake. There are birds that turn into real boys and girls. *Swans*, a raven called Solomon, they have parties at night where all the fairies come and dance and there is a queen fairy and she grants wishes. It will be marvellous."

It sounded an extravagant plan, but Quinn was reluctant to dampen the girl's sudden enthusiasm after all that had happened. Besides, he was quite taken by the idea himself. "Yes. Why not, eh?"

"How would we get there?"

"We would have to go on a boat."

"Over the sea?"

"Of course."

"How long would it take?"

"Well, we would have to go to Sydney first. It might take a few weeks."

"Goodness, that's a long time, but it might be worth it. I have nearly four pounds I took from people. Mr. Harman keeps money in a sock. I know it's wrong but . . ."

"It doesn't matter," Quinn said and fingered the barrel of the revolver. "God is not watching us. I think perhaps we are on our own now. Nothing matters."

She grunted in assent, stood and patted down her dress. "Yes. He finished with us a long time ago, I think. He has forsaken us."

Quinn was exhausted. Beneath his feet he detected the grinding of the earth as it revolved in space, a lone machine tracing its eternal orbit. He squatted a minute longer on the filthy mattress. Then he stood, and they both stepped over Dalton and shuffled from the station into the quivering sunlight. He untethered the grey and led it and Sadie south along Gully Road, past Smith's orchard. Strangely, he felt no urgency, and the girl was content to amble beside him. It was an ordinary Sunday morning in the dying days of summer. Most people were in church or going about their business at the upper end of town. A breeze stirred the trees. There was no one about; indeed, if not for the sound of hymns that once again floated over the treetops as they crossed into the bushland beyond, he might have presumed the town abandoned.

EPILOGUE

Mary Walker did not live long enough to hear what had happened to her beloved brother, Robert. The weather of her dreams had become dark and turbulent in her final days. One afternoon in March 1919, several hours after Robert was found dead from a single bullet wound to the chest, Nathaniel leaned in at her window, as usual, but did not speak. He knew, at once, that she had passed away and did not wish to confirm it any quicker than necessary by asking a question that would go forever unanswered.

In her last weeks, Mary was tormented and, it must be said, comforted by visions of her lost children, Quinn and Sarah, who she claimed gathered around her bed to bathe her burning forehead and sprinkle gifts of lavender. She said all was forgiven. She said everyone was fine. As soon as the death certificate was signed, she was taken out and buried immediately, in accordance with the regulations of those terrible months.

Afterwards, Nathaniel Walker stalked the dusty yard alone for days, staring into the distance, smoking his pipe, muttering prayers and curses to himself. Plates of food and bunches of flowers from neighbours piled up around him until the sagging veranda resembled the scene of a melancholy feast.

Several months later, he sold the property and moved to Queensland to be with William and his wife Jane. He became withdrawn and lost interest in the world and its possibilities. His hair turned silver. In 1924 he fell from a horse, was rendered insensible, and died two weeks later, never having regained consciousness.

Of the girl, Sadie Fox, nothing definite was heard again. There were rumours she had been seen in Newcastle; that she was travelling with her brother, who had returned from the war much changed; that she wore a necklace beaded with snail shells, gave birth to a rabbit, stowed away on a cargo ship bound for Ireland; that she perished in the epidemic.

Robert Dalton's brutal death shocked the tiny town. There was nothing stolen except for his service revolver and horse, and no evidence as to whom the killer might be, aside from a pair of bloody footprints that wandered out of the station, along Gully Road and faded away. Young George Carver was despatched that afternoon to tracker Jim Gracie's place, but the poor boy stumbled on a scene that disturbed his dreams for years to come. Gracie's starving dogs—seizing their chance to take revenge on the man who had for many years treated them so poorly—were leaping high into the air and fastening their great jaws around the tracker's bare feet. The Carver boy fled and told his tale, but by the time another man arrived at Gracie's place the dogs had vanished, leaving the tracker hanging like a man in a gibbet, his feet resembling a pair of butchered chops.

The two murders were assumed to have been committed by the vagrant Fletcher Wakefield, whom Kimberley Porteous recounted talking with that day in the graveyard, although a search of records soon revealed that Wakefield had perished in the last days of the war. It was yet another mystery, deepened by Edward Fitch's yarn about his encounter with the ghost of Quinn Walker up in the hills, whereupon the sharp gaze of accusation again fell on the man known for so long in Flint as the Murderer. *Of course*, they said. *Of course.*

By this time the epidemic had secured its grip on the nation. Hospitals were filled to the brim with coughing patients. Schools closed. Many died each and every day. Mary Walker was only one of a dozen in Flint to pass away as a direct result of influenza. By the end of 1919, when the epidemic had run its course, thousands lay dead in its wake.

With those connected to the Walker family dead or gone from the district, the stories associated with them grew, like untrimmed bougainvillea, in strange and untended directions. So too did Edward Fitch's account of his time with the Murderer, wherein Quinn—hunchbacked, his face a sunken pudding, odd as a prophet or grizzled saint, now bearing a sack of bones—uttered cryptic slogans that clarified his past and foretold the future. Fitch was known to be unreliable, but the suspicion surrounding his meeting with the damaged man in the hills only served in the eyes of some to give his tale the shimmer of truth.

In the years that followed, a miner or rabbiter would sometimes spy a lone man lurching among the abandoned mines, whereupon the town biddies and those gossips at the bar of The Mail Hotel would be atwitter with renewed speculation as to what really happened in 1909 and again in 1919. Quinn's dark, rumoured presence became a warning to children not to stray too far of an evening, and there developed around the schoolyard a skipping rhyme that waxed and waned in popularity:

Quinn Walker had a sister, a sister, a sister
One night he kissed her, he kissed her, he kissed her
She tried to run away, run away, run away
But he said: You have to stay! Stay! Stay!

ACKNOWLEDGMENTS

Bereft received nourishment from many quarters. For both inspiration and information, I am indebted to: *Phantasmagoria* by Marina Warner; *The Great War* by Les Carlyon; *Sites of Memory, Sites of Mourning* by Jay Winter; and *Faces of the Living Dead* by Martyn Jolly. In addition, I would like to thank Lyn Tranter, Kirsten Tranter, Ian See, and Roslyn Oades for their invaluable encouragement and advice over countless drafts. But, most of all, thanks to my editor Aviva Tuffield, who worked tirelessly (or so it seemed), and without whom this novel would have been twice as long and half as good.

ABOUT THE AUTHOR

Chris Womersley's debut novel, *The Low Road*, won the Ned Kelly Award for Best First Book in 2008. His fiction and reviews have appeared in numerous journals and anthologies, including *Granta New Writing 14*, *Best Australian Stories 2006*, *Best Australian Stories 2010*, *The Monthly*, and *The Age*. In 2007 one of his short stories won the Josephine Ulrick Literature Prize. Visit him at www.chriswomersley.com.